BOMB

Other titles by Sarah Mussi

Riot
Siege
Door of No Return
The Last of the Warrior Kings

BOMB

SARAH MUSSI

Hodder
Children's
Books

A division of Hachette Children's Group

Hodder Children's Books

First published in Great Britain in 2015
by Hodder Children's Books

A Catalogue record for this book is available from the British Library

ISBN: 978 1 444 91786 4

Typeset Berkele Oldstyle by Avon DataSet Ltd, Bidford-on-Avon, Warwickshire

Printed and bound in Great Britain by Clays Ltd, St Ives plc

The paper and board used in this book are from wood from responsible sources.

Hodder Children's Books
An imprint of Hachette Children's Group
Part of Hodder & Stoughton
Carmelite House
50 Victoria Embankment
London EC4Y 0DZ

An Hachette UK Company
www.hachette.co.uk

To the Sisterhood
'Fair is foul, and foul is fair'
Macbeth, Act 1 Scene 1

'Here, we are in danger of focusing only on Isis, when it is quite likely that another group, perhaps a splinter group even more ferocious, might spawn from this current spate of violence . . .

'There is something else about Isis that has emerged as different from other extremist groups and that is their treatment of women and girls. Male violence against women is nothing new and unfortunately knows neither racial nor cultural boundaries.'

From 'Isis: a contrived ideology justifying
barbarism and sexual control'

Mona Siddique – *The Observer*, 24 August 2014

THE PURPOSE
OF LIFE
IS TO GIVE LIFE
PURPOSE

LAST NIGHT

They held the girl face down. The man knelt on her legs. The teenage boy sat on her back.

'Pass the straps under her chest,' said the man.

The boy lifted her limp form, passed the webbed belts beneath her breasts.

'Careful. Don't use the clip.' The man's voice, sharp.

The boy hesitated.

'Pack the explosives over the ribcage. Adjust the clasps on the corset. Hold them in place.'

A bead of sweat trickled down the boy's face. He pulled both straps tight.

The man fixed the tracker over her heart. Then he stood up. 'Roll her over.'

The boy stood up as well. Together they eased her on to her back.

'Now pack the cylinders over her stomach.'

The girl's face shone pale, unearthly. Beautiful.

'I'll do it,' said the man. Voice tense. Annoyed. 'Bring the wiring and the tape.'

The boy obeyed. He stood and watched the man deftly tape the wiring to the explosives, connect the detonator.

Another bead of sweat trickled down the boy's face.

The man got out his mobile, and keyed in a code on the small electronic device now wired securely around the girl. 'Now her ear,' he ordered. He put the phone back in his pocket.

The boy knelt down beside her. Gently he fastened her blouse back over her breasts. He zipped the jacket over the explosives. He touched the girl's head, lifted it. He smoothed away the damp hair. Such beautiful hair. Carefully he turned her face to the side, laid her cheek on the cold cement.

He saw how a stray curl fell across her mouth, how her slightly parted lips were ashen, bloodless.

The man poured superglue first over the zip and the bottom of the vest where it covered the belt, spreading it liberally around, then over the earpiece. He jammed the thing hard into her ear, pressed down, held it in place.

The boy turned his head away.

'Let's get out,' said the man.

The boy stood up. Then bent down again and brushed the curl away from her lips, pinned it back with her hair clip.

'Don't waste time,' ordered the man.

They left the girl lying on the floor.

The last glimpse the boy had was of her cheek, turned sideways, the curve of her face, twisted away from him.

Then he turned out the light.

THE PURPOSE OF **LIFE** IS TO GIVE **LIFE** PURPOSE

THIS MORNING
THE LIFE LIST

(Twenty Things To Do Before I Die)

1

Go On a Blind Date

THERE'S SOMETHING WHISTLING right in my ear.

And it's loud.

My head's ringing. And I'm cold, lying here on my back. And stiff. I can't seem to sit up. And something's dripping, like I'm in a cavern. There's a sour taste in my mouth.

I raise my head and open my eyes. A blinding flash slices, like white fire, through the edge of my vision.

Where am I?

'Hello? Anyone there?'

Has there been an accident? *It's so dark.* An earthquake?

My head pounds. My ear hurts.

I close my eyes and put my head back down. Wait till the flashes go, and lie very still.

There's some kind of smell around here. Almonds? And it's so cold I'm shivering. My armpits are sticky and my back's damp. I raise myself up, try opening my eyes again. Slowly.

Searing flashes, jagged silver, purple, some random pulse pounding behind my eyes. My head totally hurts. I feel like vomming. My ribs feel strapped together, and I can't breathe out. Flipping hell, where am I?

This must be a dream. Or a total nightmare. How come I'm here, lying in the dark? I try to remember. I flex my fingers to get a bit of blood flowing through them. What time is it, even?

Something must've happened. Where was I last night? A thought begins to struggle into my mind. Just an idea. Like a butterfly flickering coloured wings. I catch sight of myself as if through steam and see . . . my fingers. I'm painting my nails. Last night.

'*HELLO?*' I try to shout this time.

My voice echoes weirdly. The walls must be bare, but I can't see *anything*. Am I in a cave? Some kind of underground place? A cellar, maybe? My ears feel totally blocked.

My ears.

I was wearing my lucky silver earrings. I feel for them. NOT THERE. Though something else is. Did I have earphones in last night? One of them's stuck. Maybe that's why it sounds like I'm in a cellar.

A shiver jolts through me. *Locked in a cellar like those girls you read about.* Twenty years underground, waiting to be brought food by the pervert who locked you up.

OK, don't panic. Call someone.

I look for my phone. It's got to be here somewhere.

I check my clothes, I pat at pockets. Nothing. Just a travel pass. I'm in some kind of sleeveless body-warmer vest that I can't unzip. There's something strapped underneath it. *Try to stay calm. Breathe properly.* I prod around, then try again. The zip's well and truly stuck. I try to get my hand under the body-warmer thing but everything feels glued together. NO PHONE. ANYWHERE.

My phone's gone.

OK, breathe. Now figure out what you've got on.

I edge my fingers under the body warmer again and find the edge of my blouse. Plus something that feels like an upper-body chastity belt, a corset with steel ribs. *A chastity belt?* Like the Brightness make their girlfriends wear? Why on earth am I wearing one of those?

Sudden Scary Thought (8/10 on the Richter Scale of Scariness): Have I been brought here and used?

I don't feel used.

I'm pretty sure: not used.

But how the hell *did* I get here? Images like postage stamps drift in my mind. *Me, sitting in a bar? Hotel? Café?*

9

Holding a glass. My beautiful nails. Looking at a boy. I am on a date. Missing Naz. My top is ironed. I can smell how fresh the cotton is. The pictures fade out.

I try to sit up but the vest/belt thing is bulky. It won't bend. I have to roll over on to my stomach and push myself up on all fours.

Very unsteadily, I crawl forward. My head pounds. I raise my hand to my face, press my eyelids, feel my ear. Whatever's stuck in there is well and truly jammed in. *Breathe out, don't puke.* The place smells like old musty churches. And that really chemical, almond smell.

I don't trust myself to stand.

I bump into something. I run my hand along it and feel slightly crumbly mortar. Loose bricks? Powdery joints under my fingertips.

Last night I went out. *I wore my short glitzy skirt, my beautiful shoes, my handbag, my lipstick. I met someone. Then blank.*

I shuffle. I work my way round the wall. There's something woodish. Old furniture? Maybe crates? Not sure. Something sharp drives up under the quick of my nail but I can't see to pull it out.

Keep crawling. Keep opening your eyes. Fight the flashes. Press your eyeballs. Suck your fingertip. Try to remember. I explore under my nail with my tongue. A splinter? It feels huge. I manage to pull it out with my teeth, then taste blood. *Keep going.* This vest/belt thing feels like something's packed into my stomach. I find the wall again and carry on working round that.

Keep going. I feel pipes. Wet. Something slimy clings to my fingers. Something wet drips on me.

It's raining. I am going to a café. I know the place. It's nice. I'm carrying an umbrella. The street lights are on.

Suddenly I'm really, really scared. I scrabble at the wall. Frantically, I sweep my hands from side to side. I fumble my way to the right. *Help me, someone. I don't know where the hell I am and I don't know what's happened and I don't know why I'm wearing this stupid vest thing and I don't know why I have an earphone stuck in my ear when I don't have my phone.*

I hit an obstacle. It's large. I struggle to my feet; with one hand on the wall, I push myself up. I feel as if somehow I've put on kilos overnight. My knees are weak, shaky. Nausea. I want to sit back down again. *Don't stop. Get out.* I kick at the obstacle. It's hollow. *Kick it out the way. Keep going.* I try to work out if there's a space behind it, as if by some lucky chance it might conceal a magic door – if I could shove it aside and squeeze through, I could somehow get back to yesterday.

Yesterday. I walk down a street. I'm meeting someone.

11

I can't remember who. I'm excited. Scared. My skirt is too short. I pull at it. What will he think of me? I'm meeting a boy and it's not Naz.

There's a space behind the obstacle, but the thing's fixed against the wall, and it's too large. I bash at it.

We eat inside. I'm eating a pancake with ice cream. I don't fancy this guy at all. I'm missing Naz and I want to call him.

Naz. If I could call Naz he'd come and get me, wouldn't he?

There's no secret door behind this thing. *Calm down. Work round it.* I try to steady myself.

He wasn't even interesting. And I didn't like him.

I meet the crumbling surface of the wall again and grope at it. *Help me, someone.*

Then I feel something. *I've found the door!* Hardly daring to breathe, I search my way over the panels. Grime. Flaking paint. I hunt until I find the edge of the door. A crack? I dig my nails in to make sure and then stop. I scrabble my hands down the door to find the handle.

Oh God, don't let it be locked.

I find the handle, press it and push. It doesn't open. I bang on the panels. My blood pounds. My head aches. The door's locked. *The door's totally locked.*

I push with all my strength. The door shakes. *I'm locked in a cellar.*

12

I turn the handle and pull. I nearly fall over as the door opens into me. I lurch back, heart hammering, struggling with myself, trying to clear my head. *Stupid. You had to pull it, you idiot.* NOT LOCKED IN.

Beyond the door is a bit of light. I can just make out some kind of corridor.

Another Sudden Scary Thought (7/10): There could be someone on guard. *To stop me from escaping.* I creep very carefully, brushing my fingers against the walls to keep balance. What if there is someone?

Someone waiting to get me.

I pause. I listen, willing my head to clear. The flashes begin to subside. My knees straighten. Then I tiptoe – very slowly. I keep a sharp ear out. Except that my hearing isn't sharp. This stupid stuck-into-it earpiece blocks everything. It feels like one of those Bluetooth ear things. I don't even own a Bluetooth thing.

I try to remember. Did I borrow one?

I met someone on HeartBeat. I was working on my life list. Number One: Go On a Blind Date. Holly said it would help, said it would cheer me up. Holly told me I have to try to live again, since Naz stopped seeing me. Naz and I were supposed to Have A Talk. But it didn't happen.

I was wearing my black leather jacket. My nails were turquoise. I wasn't wearing this stiff vest girdle thing.

13

I hear cars in the distance. *Must focus on listening.* This whatever in my ear is making me half deaf. I raise my hand to see if I can remove it. I run my finger around it. It's a pretty big earphone. I dig my finger in as far as I can and try to pick it out.

Instant pain. White. Unbearable. I stumble. I scream. Ice races around my skull. *A piercing, high-pitched whistle.*

My head rings.

And a weird electronic voice says: '*Do not attempt to remove the instruction connector. You will need it for the job you've been selected for.*'

Another shrill blast short circuits into my brain.

I collapse, hit the wall, hit the floor.

2

Swim With Sharks

MY HEARTBEAT ROCKETS. *Who said that?* I squeeze my eyes tight.

When I open my eyes, let me be somewhere else.

I open my eyes.

I'm not somewhere else.

I'm still in the corridor with the dull light at the end and I don't know where the hell I am.

I straighten up, rock my head, nurse my ear. An earphone. I've got some random earphone jammed in my ear. And I'm hearing voices. Sinister horrible Dalek voices. This can't be happening. I won't touch it again. I won't touch anything. It's all going to get sorted when I'm out.

I lurch forward, stagger against the walls. I use the palms of my hands to keep myself upright. Get to the end of the corridor. A flight of stairs, another door at the top, with a crack underneath it, a silver line of light slicing in.

I hesitate. The steps are covered in grey dust. Pale marks on old boards where a stair carpet once ran. A creepy thought: *what if I'm in some totally horrific experiment, and I'm being monitored? To see if I'm going to fight or flight or freak out?*

I'll fight. I'll fight all of them. I need a weapon. I glance down. Old stair rods? I prise a loose rod from its bracket. I test its weight in my palm. Pretty rubbish. Better than nothing.

I inch up the steps. My heart races as I think about what could be on the other side of the door. I feel for the handle. There is none. Only a deadlock latch. I twist it carefully. It opens inwards. I step back. Slam it open. I raise the stair rod.

And blink.

Daylight.

Sunshine.

Brightness hammering into my brain.

I stumble on to a doorstep, on to a pavement. A slaked concrete pavement in the dazzling dawn. Tall houses opposite. Iron railings. Shops. People.

I'm on a street I've never seen before in my entire life.

And I just stand there for a moment, breathing in the smell of the city. *It did rain last night.* I was right. Traffic ploughs through pooled water. Spraying rainbows. Tears suddenly start to my eyes. I'm back in a world that was lost to me. Out of the cellar. I can get this earphone thing removed. I can get out of this stupid vest. I can go to the hospital. I can go to the police.

I can go home.

Aunty Gill will be wondering where I am. I hardly ever stay out all night. Not without calling.

I think of home. My room with its patchy green paint. The wooden floor laid over with cheap laminate. Posters held on with Blu-tack. The big bed. The photo of Naz and me in Gloucestershire. Me and Naz on his dad's boat, speeding up the Severn Estuary. I can call Holly and tell her I'm NEVER NEVER NEVER going on a blind date EVER again.

I take one deep breath, my chest tight, and before I know it, I'm crying and repeating, *Thank you. Oh thank you, God.* Adding, *And I'm so sorry, God* (because it's not fair to only turn to God when you're in trouble).

And the weird, metallic Voice inside my ear says, 'Take the tourist bus towards the city centre.'

My knees nearly give way. I shake my head. I raise the iron rod, then drop my arm. A rubbish iron stair rod is no use against a creepy electronic voice.

'Find the travel card.'

There must be some mistake. Because I'm going home. I'm not going on any tourist bus.

17

'It's an all-day, all-transport pass. In the right side, zip pocket of the vest.'

The vest? The body warmer? I fumble wildly, find the zip pocket. Then I stop. I clench my jaw so hard, my teeth hurt. *Why am I wearing this vest?*

'No,' I say.

I don't obey random voices.

I'm going home.

I'm not going on any bus.

'Do as instructed and you will not be harmed,' the Voice booms out.

You will not be harmed? Are they going to harm me?

Run. Run and scream and find help.

But I don't. They'll blast that foghorn whistle thing through my head again. And I don't know where I am. And I haven't got a phone.

Rip the thing out of your ear, before they blast you.

But I just stand there, too afraid to touch it. 'Indicate that you've heard us and are ready to obey.' The Voice rings through my head, and I feel like puking all over again.

'I heard you,' I say.

'And you will follow instructions?'

'I'm going home,' I say.

There's no reply. My voice grows a little stronger.

18

'I don't care who you are. I'm going home.'

No need to run and scream. Just go. Get this thing out of your ear. Sort the vest item out – it's so stiff and tight – and change. Then stop by old Mrs Hallet from next door and pop down the shop for her, like you promised. Then call Aunty Gill and fix some lunch, so when she gets in, you can tell her everything. Then spend the afternoon on your overdue sociology coursework. Full stop.

I may not remember exactly what happened last night, but I can remember all the important things: I'm Genesis Wainwright. I'm a sixth form student. I come from Somerset. My mum works at Hinkley Point and is the best mum in the world. And I love her. And I'm staying with my aunt, because I'm going to college in London. My best friend is Holly. And I love her. I play the guitar (badly). I'm searching for answers to the meaning of life. I believe in true love. I believe I have a soul mate. AND I'M IN LOVE WITH NAZ. I want to be a performance poet. I *am* a poet. (I wrote a whole heap of crappy poems about Naz. And a few other ones about LIFE.) And I love motorbikes.

I can remember everything.

Except last night.

Yes, I'm Genesis Wainwright, and I don't need to stand here waiting for some random voice to issue stupid orders. So I add, angry, determined, 'And I'm going to call the police.'

I think of old Mrs Hallet on the next floor. She'll be out of milk and wanting her cup of tea. She'll be waiting for me Right Now. I look up the street trying to figure out which way to go.

The whistle SHRIEKS.

Like an electric shock.

Straight into my brain.

My eyes water. And in the shrieking, aching, numbness left behind, the sinister, electronic Voice says, 'Please indicate you will do everything we say.'

I cup my hand to my head. My palm comes away sticky.

I'm bleeding. They've frigging ruptured my bloody eardrum.

I stand there, dizzy. I can't stop myself from suddenly opening my mouth and retching. Dry heaves. A drizzle of yellow bile. I gag and wipe my mouth against my sleeve.

'Unless you indicate you will obey, we will continue,' threatens the Voice.

What if they do? What if they keep on until my brain haemorrhages? *Just agree. Do whatever it takes. Get on any stupid bus.* I take in a few sips of air. *Just for now. Then go home. Find a way.* I try to relax. My heart pounds.

I try to w

and say, 'W

as I can.

There's a s

rerouted throug

See London To

instruction. After th

Contemptuous.

'Whatever,' I say. I c

Their response is dire   ...s right
into the back of my neck,   ...ny skull, circles
it in blinding jabs, behind n ...es, through my poor ear,
and like a vice tightening around my head settles in every
nerve of my teeth. I lean dizzily back against the wall.

The whistling stops.

I suck in air. Then the Voice adds, 'And don't forget,
we're watching every move you make.'

3

Go on a Road Trip With No Destination

I GET TO THE CORNER OF THE STREET. The flashing light behind my eyes is back, the disorientation, the ringing in my ears. I miss my footing. I stumble, trip on a slab and smack down on to the footpath. I feel the bulk of the vest, forcing something hard like a canister against my ribs. My head hits the pavement. Just a ringing noise. And the sky tumbling.

I remember.

I was in a cavern with these three women, except there weren't exactly three of them there all the time – just the one – and she was telling me something. Something really important.

I roll over and sit up, slightly winded. I pause and wait to get my breath back. *And there was a bracelet, or some kind of thread.* Was that real? Or just a dream?

I'm not wearing any bracelet now. A car slows down, pulls near to the kerb and unwinds a window. A voice calls out. 'You OK, love?'

I look up, open my mouth.

'Tell the car to go away.' The raised note of this instruction hurts my ear all over again.

'I'm fine,' I say. I stare into the dark interior of the car, willing the driver to understand: *I'm not OK. I need help*. His radio blares out: 'WORLD TABLE TENNIS CHAMPION CONVERTS TO THE BRIGHTNESS. STAY TUNED FOR EXCLUSIVE INTERVIEW.'

He laughs. 'Hear that?' He jerks his head. 'Everybody's going Lumin these days.'

'Tell him to go.' The evil Dalek Voice screeches at me.

The Brightness's jingle rings out from the car radio.

Their slogan flashes through my mind: *We radicalize your sons. We sacrifice your daughters. You cannot stop us. Until you convert and embrace the true faith we are at war. You are the enemy.*

The guy says, 'You don't look fine.'

Are the Brightness behind this?

'I'm fine,' I repeat. I turn away. I hear the window wind back up. The car drives off.

'Good,' the Voice says. 'You will not talk to strangers. You will not address anyone. You will not ask for help.

You will not contact the police. You will not speak unless we tell you what to say.'

'Anything else?'

'And you will speak to us with respect,' says the Voice, raised, irritated.

And despite the sickening ringing in my ears, I think: *You're touchy. You don't like being challenged. You've given something away.* Though I'm not sure what.

'Understand?' The Voice bounces through space again and does that weird echoey thing.

And you're trying to hide your location by bouncing your stupid signal off some satellite or other. Because you don't want to be found.

Which means you can be found.

I'm reminded of something. Something about hidden command centres. Cells across Britain. Each with their own territory. Small but effective. Militant extremists. Date-rape drugs. Hostage taking. Images fed into internet streams. The Brightness slogan: *We radicalize your sons. We sacrifice your daughters.*

What if it is the Brightness?

I get up. The vest is heavy. I bend forward. It presses uncomfortably into my stomach. And another Sudden Scary Thought hits (10/10). A cold chill ripples through me. *Why am I wearing this girdle vest thing? I'm sure I wasn't wearing it yesterday.* Immediately I feel for the zip.

But the zip doesn't budge.

Then there's a noise in my inner ear, like a fire alarm.

'Don't touch the vest.' The Voice is shrill, almost panicky.

I drop my hand, my heart bangs violently against my ribcage. Dimly I see an aeroplane above me shearing off into the morning. A white vapour trail in its wake. Traffic on the road sluices past. And I'm on my feet. Knees shaking. In terror I touch the vest again.

Taken hostage. Dumped in a cellar. Controlled. Ordered to commit some terrorist act. Filmed. Blown up. Posted on YouTube.

The Voice says, 'Walk to the corner on your right.'

I scan the pavements. They saw the car. They saw me touch the vest.

This is not happening. Not to me.

'At the corner, take your first left. Stay on this side of the street. There is a See London Tours stop two hundred metres up. When the bus comes, get on it. Sit at the front on the lower deck of the bus. If there is no seat at the front, choose the next one by the roadside window: right hand side.'

'What's in the vest?' I say.

An unthinkable reality is dawning.

I don't know what to do.

The fear of the whistle is overshadowed. I forget everything. I stumble down the street, turn the corner. *What were the instructions? What am I supposed to do now?* My mind's numb. I see the buildings rising above me. *What's in the fricking vest?* My heart thumps like a drum. I can't think. Can't hear. I see the bus stop. The advert on the bus stop. **SEE LONDON AND DIE**.

'Who are you?' I say.

Silence.

'What have you done to me?'

Silence.

'*Speak to me?*'

'You have been chosen.'

'What?'

'You have been chosen for an assignment.'

4

Send a Message in a Bottle

I GET INSIDE THE COVER OF THE BUS STOP. There's a group of Japanese tourists. One of the women is very beautiful. One of the kids eyes me suspiciously. I hover by the red plastic bench along with the adverts: Madam Tussaud's, Windsor Castle and a big picture of the sun with the Brightness slogan: THE END TIME IS HERE. HAVE YOU CONVERTED YET?

The Brightness Brotherhood, more violent than any extremist group ever spawned. A blood cult of Bright warriors in a war against anything that opposes them.

I know it's them. They selected me. They drugged me. Now they're going to . . . I stop. They said they'll let me go, if I complete the bus tour. I won't think any further. I won't. I can't. Instead I bite down on my knuckles, hard.

I look up at the tour timetable:

Hop On, Hop Off: From every transport hub, every 20 minutes to Westminster Abbey, Big Ben, the Houses of Parliament and plenty more.

The Houses of Parliament.

Guy Fawkes.

I don't understand. I didn't volunteer. I'm not a member of the Brightness. I'm not a Lumin. I'm not part of any mission.

But what about those other teenagers? That collar-bomb girlfriend forced to go to that World Cup final? That girl from Scotland? That pizza delivery student? Those videos were all over YouTube.

That girl from Scotland.

My heartbeat rockets. My palms go clammy. I can't think. *How will Mrs Hallet get her cup of tea?* I look down my front at the vest. Examine the zip. It's glued fast. I turn up the front edge of the material, but it won't bend very far. It's a regular kind of body warmer thing. V-neck, dark blue, two zip pockets. Slippery material. Underneath is my blouse, then the corset belt thing, packed with something hard. The vest is kind of glued on to all of it.

That means they took off my blouse to put the belt thing on.

They touched me. *They touched me. I must wash. I must get out of this thing and scrub myself.*

What happened to me?

The boy I met last night?

My mind whirls. *What happened last night? What's under the vest?*

Who was he?

And then I remember him.

A Lumin. One of the Brightness. Dyed yellow hair, that ring of fire tattoo thing on his wrist, shooting flames up his arm. Like the one Naz had done.

I remember him, and I can replay everything.

'So your name's Genesis,' he says.

Instantly I want to leave.

'That's a cool name,' he continues, 'the start of things.'

'It's the first book of the Bible,' I say.

He smiles and says, 'I'm not a big fan.'

I know he's not. He's one of the Sons of the Sun, the Brightness Brotherhood. They hate every other religion, even ones that believe in the same God as them. They go around prophesying the End Time: 'The sun will be darkened and all the unbelievers will die.' And they're violent.

Maybe I'm being unfair. Maybe he's OK. Maybe he's like Naz – not really violent. Just doing the Lumin-cool look.

But the conversation is going to be awkward.

'You're religious, though?' I say, indicating his dyed yellow hair.

'Very,' he says.

'Oh,' I say. 'My last boyfriend was too.' I didn't mean to say that. Why does every thought I have lead back to Naz? I don't want to think about Naz. I just want to go home.

He just smiles.

'One of the Brightness, like you,' I say, making it even worse.

'Oh,' he says.

I shouldn't have said that. Girls aren't supposed to Play The Field in their book. I shouldn't have come on this date. Let me finish my pancake and just go. This guy is NOT The One. I don't even want to talk to him any more.

I start to fidget. Where are all the nice guys? What's so wrong with being an honest-to-goodness regular bloke? Why must they all get tattooed and join extremist sects?

WHY?

It's all about 'eternal rewards'. That's what Naz said, anyway.

He said, 'You get valued in the eyes of God and in heaven you're blessed.'

(How can you be blessed for dying your hair a stupid colour?)

But it wasn't the truth. Well, not about Naz. I remember talking it over with Holly. I remember the shock in her voice after I told her he'd converted.

'Why?' she said.

'I don't know,' I said.

'Didn't you ask him?'

'He just said he wanted to be one of them.'

'But doesn't he know they're violent? They're fighting some kind of extremist war, for God's sake. Dave says they're sadistic and brutal. I don't see Naz as a killer, I'm sorry.'

Dave is Holly's brother. He's in the army. Dave and I had a thing once. Long story. Awkward ending. Not going there.

Not with Holly.

She was really upset it didn't work out. And it was my fault. Naz happened. So she's very biased against Naz in lots of ways. Not that I blame her or anything.

But I try to explain. 'I think Naz just finds life pointless. Think he wants to commit to something bigger, more meaningful and more powerful.' God knows I don't want to defend him. I'm searching for meaning too.

'But didn't you notice it happening?'

I lift one shoulder and let it fall. Where do I start? There's no easy place. It's like asking, when did you start noticing his online life was more real to him than you were? It wasn't when he hijacked my 'LIFE IS' one-line poem idea, and was tweeting out those weird unfunny tweets to let the world know what a dumb place it was, was it? LIFE IS A TOASTER: YOU NEVER KNOW WHAT WILL POP UP NEXT. He was just being smart, courting followers, and only doing it because others did. Pretty corny really. Punchline: AND IT ALWAYS BROWNS YOU OFF.

Or LIFE IS A TOASTER: PRETTY CRUMBY UNDERNEATH.

We laughed about that kind of stuff. He didn't lock himself in his bedroom – or do anything weird then. Even when his tweets got a bit darker, I didn't think anything much of it.

I didn't even get alarmed when I found that picture of him posing with a sandwich crust in the shape of a gun. DEATH IS OUR BREAD AND BUTTER. Or the one with him holding a jellybaby with its head bitten off. BEHEADINGS HAPPEN. GET OVER IT.

No, I just woke up one morning and felt uncomfortable, so I blocked him and all his Facebook posts and tweets. I never asked why or how he'd got so freakish. I just blocked him, to teach him a lesson. He said sorry. I unblocked him again. He said he'd been asked to post them by some online friends. That was all. Just a joke. I never thought he was serious about becoming a Lumin.

But I suppose, after that, it changed.

'I dunno why he converted,' I said.

'Aren't you interested?'

'How do you mean?'

'Like why do guys join radical extremist groups like the Brightness, and get into killing people?'

Holly's so earnest sometimes. I guess when you have a brother who has to fly off to foreign parts to fight extremists all the time, you get kind of earnest. It's allowed.

But we all know the reasons for wanting to be part of the Brightness. All the Ps.

1. Parent problems.
2. Poor performance.
3. Progressive pointlessness.
4. Peer pressure.
5. Power.
6. Promised paradise.

So we don't really have to keep going on about it, do we? I think that just makes matters worse. Guys like Naz get supersensitive (paranoid even) if you keep asking them stuff. Plus I think guys become Lumins because they like to. Because nobody says NO, and the worst that happens is the Government threatens to impound their passports and restrict their travel cards. Oooow. SCARY.

Maybe because their girlfriends block them on Facebook. Maybe they decide that if they aren't wanted, they'll go somewhere where they are.

For Naz it was about him feeling special and significant. And that was kind of sad. Because I did want him and he was special to me. But I didn't count.

He felt he was marginalized by his mum, and usurped by his stepdad (his words). And the Brightness were a group of people he could shine with. Literally.

And we were all doing it. I mean, all us students. Buying the Lumin-cool gear.

Those black tees with SONS OF THE SUN – DEATH IS A DUTY; VICTORY OR MARTYRDOM; LIFE IS A STRUGGLE, DEATH A RELEASE screened across them. The black durags, the camouflage trousers. Those crazy crazy crazy boots. Dark glasses. Sexy smiles. We weren't thinking about cult messages and killing. We just wanted to look cool.

Plus the authorities at school made it worse. Trying to ban dyed hair. They should know better. Ban anything and you double its value.

But it was pathetic too, in a scary way. At last a chance to be The Man. Oh, look at me (all you other insignificant mortals), I'm hard. Don't mess with me or I'll *really* convert and do things with a blunt knife. And guess what,

I don't die, like you. When I'm a full cult member I'll become exempt from 'normal' reality.

I'll get rewarded in heaven for murder.

The Brightness: a cult of violence, just for boys. One that gives them the identity they've always longed for. And an excuse to escape from their boring predictable little lives.

Anyway that's what I think.

And if I'd known this guy was one of them, I'd have run a mile.

Instead I try to smile. 'No place for a girl called Genesis then!' I say, trying to hint that I Am So Out of Here.

He doesn't smile back. 'Poor you,' he says. And I see a glint of something predatory in his eyes.

'Should've been called Zoe,' I say. 'You know, zed, last letter of the alphabet, instead of first book of the Bible?' I'm really floundering. He's not just one of those who dye their hair to be cool, is he? This guy's really mean.

'Zoe means life,' he says, 'in Greek.' Then he adds, 'You should have been called Nemesis, not Genesis.'

I laugh. I don't get it. Though I love the Greek reference. (Love Greek myths.)

I so do get it now.

He must've been the one who did this to me.

Bastard.

The little Japanese kid stares at me. I stand very patiently, thoughts racing in my head, nursing my ear, until the bus comes: a blue and red open-topped double decker. SEE LONDON BUS TOURS.

I get on the bus with the others. Show my travel card. There're no seats anywhere near the front downstairs. I follow my instructions and sit at the first available one on the right by the window. *Why here?* The Voice says nothing. Can they see me on the bus? Maybe they've downloaded every known kind of CCTV on to their computers. Or they're following me. They *could* be on the bus. It could be *him* or *her*. It could be that nosy little Japanese kid who's still staring at me.

I've got to do something. Try and message someone. Without speaking obviously. I check the pockets of the jacket. NO PEN. No scrap of paper; absolutely nothing. I look up and down the bus. On the seat beside me is a newspaper, a London freebee. I snatch it up.

OK – got paper. But no pen. I look at the headline. POLICE CALLED TO HELP OUT WITH ECLIPSE TRAFFIC AS MOTORISTS QUEUE TO GO WEST.

I tear out the words POLICE and HELP. I rip CALLED in half so that I have the crude message: HELP CALL POLICE.

Nothing happens. No blast in my ears. They can't be watching me that well, then.

I glance at the rest of the article to see if I can expand my message.

At Oldbury Naite today the most spectacular total solar eclipse is expected. An eclipse like this only happens once every 300 to 400 years in the UK. The moon's umbra or Line of Totality (a path outlined on the earth by the moon's shadow during a total solar eclipse) will travel from New Mexico across America to New York, and from there across the Atlantic to reach Europe by afternoon. Its first port of call after New York will be the UK, where it will hit Bristol and travel thirteen miles up the Severn Estuary, ending at Oldbury. Totality is expected at 4.44 p.m. precisely. It will be visible for two hours and forty minutes, with a spectacular total eclipse lasting exactly seven minutes at Bristol and seven minutes and two seconds at Oldbury.

I scan the words, and the map of the Line of Totality. There's nothing obvious I can use. Plus the text is too small. But it gives me an idea. I could communicate by pointing to words. Maybe. Once I have someone's attention.

I read the next page to see if there's any phrase there I could use.

LONDON ON HIGH ALERT AS HEAD OF
M.O.D. DECLARES CRITICAL CODE RED

In response to intelligence gained over the last few days, the Ministry of Defence has taken immediate steps to increase defence measures in the capital, authorising heightened security precautions for the next twenty-four hours. In addition the Government has raised the nation's threat level to Critical, or Red. The adjustment to Critical represents the highest alert level to be implemented in the United Kingdom since active cells affiliated to the radical group the Brightness and their extremist wing the Luminaries declared their End Time terror campaign . . .

A chill shivers down my spine . . . *the radical group the Brightness and their extremist wing the Luminaries declared their End Time terror campaign* . . . What if I'm part of the campaign? The Voice said '*You have been chosen.*' Maybe he was One of Them.

And what *is* in the vest?

Get help.

The paper's too thick to shove all of it in my pocket.

I rip off the front page and keep it. I put the words CALL and POLICE on the seat beside me. I pick up HELP. I take a deep breath. I grip my hand around the chrome bar of the seat in front. I squeeze it, hoping. I get ready to turn my good ear. Then I tap the person in front on the shoulder.

It's a man. He looks up. Not friendly. Plus he's listening to headphones. He turns his head, sees me and is annoyed. 'Eh?' he says, in one of those cross voices, which means Don't Talk To Me. I Have Nothing To Say To You. If You Want Anything, Go Away.

I sit up in my seat, clutching the word HELP. I show it to him.

He pulls a headphone out of his ear and says, 'Wot?'

I make a face, lay my finger across my lips. *Please don't speak. Don't give me away.* Then I hold up CALL and POLICE.

He shrugs, makes a tight unhelpful smile. 'No speaking English,' he says. He picks up his earphone, plugs himself back into it and moves seats.

I sit there and think. *So what do I do now? What the hell do I do now?* And I can't work it out. My sociology teacher once said: 'Break things down step by step until you see the pattern.'

I try.

39

What happened yesterday? The Voice said I'd been 'selected'; so that means the blind date wasn't random and that guy must've slipped something into my drink. I try to remember what I drank. I think it was a Coke.

I force myself to remember.

We sat in a café. He drank tea. He made me try some of his through a straw. Bubble tea. The tea was cold and sweet (with lumpy bits). Really weird. I didn't notice anything else. Usually I notice things. But I was on my phone. Someone was messaging me.

My phone?

I pat the pockets of the vest in the vain hope of finding my phone. Pointless. *I need a phone so badly.* Maybe I could ask somebody. *Excuse me, would you mind, could you lend me your phone?* Someone will, won't they? Just to text. They can't hear me if I'm texting. I bite my lip. Stay on task. One step at a time. Look for the pattern.

Last night.

Long dark streets. I don't remember the car. But there was a car. I heard it revving up, screeching its tyres on tarmac. Flashes. The voices of people, directing, sharp, strained. Somebody turning me over.

And that weird vision thing.

* * *

I was in a cavern. And she came in a dream dressed in a cloth of gauze, her light playing over the flowing walls. Like arctic nights where the aurora borealis plays colours out against the swallowing deep. Water dripping, in that deep cave, intoning the hours of the earth.

Why am I remembering that? It's not even my kind of language. What the heck does *intoning the hours of the earth* mean? And I've never been to the Arctic.

Allow yourself to remember, I tell myself, *whatever your subconscious throws up.*

Find the pattern.

Anything, everything, may be important.

Find the meaning.

She stood in the stone chamber by a black lake, and I was uneasy. I wasn't sick, but I felt my spirit gone away from me.

And she was spinning a thread from her distaff on to a spindle, and her hair was wound about with shells. And her skin was as pale as coral. And she said: 'All hail Genesis. You are a seeker and we are the Moirai.

> *We are the three.*
> *We spin the thread.*
> *We water the tree.*

Your birth. Your life. Your death to be.
We are the Moirai. We the three. Life and death
and destiny.

And I did not understand. Except that I felt a weight lift off
my shoulders. And it felt beautiful.
And she said:

I am Clotho, first of the wayward three.
I spin the thread of life to be.
And you must answer the riddle single-handedly.

She seemed to grow bigger somehow and she held out her
hand and on her wrist was a bracelet.
She loosened the catch and the bracelet slipped off. She
fastened it about my wrist.
And I tried to understand the riddle. What riddle?
And then I said, 'Behold, I am your handmaiden.' I don't
know where the words came from or what I meant.
And then the lights around her faded, until I was left in
darkness by the shores of that ancient, subterranean lake.

Why remember that dream?

But for some reason I check my wrist to see if the
bracelet's still there again. And of course it's not.

Obviously. Though I can see it on my wrist very clearly
– in my memory – all shimmering in the rainbow colours
of the northern lights, and somehow fiery.

Fiery.

And then my phone rang. *I can remember!*

No. Not the phone.

The whistle.

LIFE IS A WHISTLE: YOU MUST ANSWER ITS CALL.

Why did I think of that? My poetic one-liners: LIFE IS
A . . . You have ten seconds to come up with a pseudo
truism. Find the right metaphor. Be the poet. Develop the
idea. Make it count.

LIFE IS A RIDDLE: AND RIGHT NOW I NEED
A CLUE.

Yes, that's it: the riddle. LIFE is the riddle. And I must
understand it, single-handedly.

I bite my lip.

Stay on task. One step at a time. Look for the pattern.
But just thinking of the poem game gives me a clue in an
unexpected kind of way.

Life is a whistle and I must answer its call. And
right now its call says: Get a phone. Get help. Get to a
hospital. Get them to take this thing out of your ear. And
get the police.

And remove this vest.

I run my hand over it *again*. Try the zip for the twenty zillionth time. Tug at the shoulders, feel the round hard cylinders against my diaphragm. *Please get me out of this vest.*

OK. First step: Get a phone.

But this is London, only a total nutter's going to let me use their phone. My heart sinks. Get off the bus then? But what if they blast my eardrum until my brain haemorrhages?

So get that phone, beg, borrow or steal it, and call for help. Because whatever is going on, it isn't nice.

I remember that jerk's line. *'You should have been called Nemesis, not Genesis.'*

Nemesis was the spirit of divine retribution, the inescapable, the remorseless goddess of revenge.

Nemesis was chosen to destroy the world.

5

Make a Prank 999 Call

Two GIRLS GET ON THE BUS. They take the empty seat in front of me. They're laughing. I watch them, jealous. One of them is taking a selfie, the other is trying to squeeze her head into the picture. She pokes the girl beside her, and says, 'C'mon Sophie, with me in it.'

They tilt their heads together, hold up the phone, catch sight of me and giggle. They angle, pout, toss their hair back and forth. Not a care in the world. I bite my lip. LIFE IS A SELFIE: YOU CAN NEVER FORGET WHO THE MAIN PROTAGONIST IS. They review the pictures, beautify them, change the filters.

'Awesome,' says one. She takes hold of her friend's phone and balances it up at arm's length. She puts her own phone down on the seat next to her.

She puts her phone down.

Just within my reach.

Am I thinking what I am thinking?

Slowly I inch forwards. This is it. I hold my breath. I edge my hand out. The bus slows. We're somewhere in South London. Up ahead there must be a tour stop.

Heart thumping, I slide my fingers round the side of the seat. I press my lips tight, grit my teeth. My neck goes all sweaty. I dart a quick look sideways. Nobody's noticing. I wait a split second till that nosy kid shifts her eyes. Nearly lose my chance. Then I close my hand over the phone. The girl in front of me doesn't clock it. LIFE IS A SELFIE: YOU NEVER KNOW WHAT IS GOING ON OUTSIDE THE FRAME. I lift the phone swiftly round the side of the seat; snatch it towards me.

I stand up and move two rows back. Find a new seat.

What crazy madness good luck.

The bus stops. 'All those for the Imperial War Museum,' says the bus intercom. One guy gets off. Someone gets on. I swipe the phone, so it doesn't lock itself down. I slip low in my seat, watch the girl, take a small breath. She still hasn't noticed. All scrunched down, fingers trembling, I call the police. I let it ring. I hear a woman pick up and say: 'Fire, ambulance, police?' and ask me my name.

I daren't answer. I try to cup my hand around my mouth and whisper, 'Police,' but it won't come out. My throat goes all weird and closes up. No sound comes out at all. 'Do you want fire, ambulance or police?' she repeats, her voice indistinct, though I'm holding her to my good ear.

For a split second I imagine telling her everything. Then I think of the receiver in my other ear.

And the vest.

There: I've thought the unthinkable.

I hang up. There must be some other way. *Text* the police? But you can't text the police. So text someone else then, so you won't have to speak. I could text Mum, but I don't know her mobile off by heart. And anyway, what could she do, miles away in Somerset, except panic? I don't want her to panic. I don't know Aunty Gill's number either.

I know who I'll text. I find the message app on the phone. I tap in: U got to help me. I don't know what's happening. I think I was given some kind of drug. There's this thing in my ear. It's telling me to do stuff. Please find me. I'm on a See London Tours bus. We're near Elephant and Castle. Check the route. Call the police. I'm not being dramatic. I'm really scared. Genesis.

I tap fast, fingers hovering over the screen: terrified I'll be caught, terrified the phone will shut down. I key in the only number I know by heart. I press send. And pray. *Please let him get it. Please let him help me.*

I don't let myself think of all the reasons why he won't. Instead I think of all the times I used to message him, all those before times, when we were so close. Before he just randomly blanked me out. Surely he'll know I'm not just trying to get attention?

Suddenly I'm seized by doubt. I text again. **Call an ambulance – get this receiver thing out my ear. It's unbearable. I swear I'll die if you don't. We're heading towards South Bank, I think. Come quick. This isn't me just being hyper. It's really, really serious.** And then I add **xxx**. Three kisses are too many. It's like we're still together. Or maybe too much pressure. I delete two. And add: **I think it's a Brightness thing. I think they've taken me hostage. I'm terrified. You know them. You must help me.**

I send.

I erase the two sent messages. I erase the contact. I press my lips together. Yes, Naz was the best person to text. He *does* know them. Maybe he'll find a way to let the right cell know they took someone of interest to him. He still does have an interest in me, doesn't he?

The bus starts up. Suddenly there's a wail from the girl. 'WOAH!' she screams. 'STOP THE BUS.' She points wildly at the guy disappearing down the street. 'HE'S GOT MY PHONE!' The bus stops. The driver opens the doors. I bite my lip.

And it's all going in a different direction. Because it wasn't that man who took her phone, was it? And if she calls the police?

- They'll board the bus.
- They'll trace the phone. (It'll have some kind of locator app, bound to.)
- They'll arrest me.

I've just nicked a phone. I start to sweat. I don't want to be arrested. If they arrest me and the Voice overhears? *And there's something in the vest? What will they do?*

There, I've done it again. Thought what I am refusing to think.

What will they do?

A bead of sweat trickles down the side of my face.

What's in the vest?

It's all too much. Naz will come soon. He'll help me. I swing out of my seat towards the girl. I hold the phone out. I pretend I just found it.

Her face twists up. 'OH MY GOD,' she shouts. She snatches the phone from me. 'OH MY MOBS! MY BABY – BABY! I GOT YOU BACK.' She goes pretty mental.

There's a crackle in my ear. The girl looks at me. A puzzled expression distorts her face. I must look strange. If I could speak, it'd help. But I can't, so I back away.

'You are not to communicate with anyone,' the Voice

49

commands. Metallic. Acid. Deadly.

The girl turns to her friend. 'OH MY GOD.' Then her friend gives me the weirdest look ever too. That little Japanese kid on the seat opposite crowds forward and starts staring again.

The girl who lost her phone starts kissing it. Then she pulls on her friend's arm. 'WE'RE GOING BACK TO THE HOTEL.'

'But,' says her friend, 'we gotta see London.'

'I'M TOO STRESSED.' The girl stares at me. She's such a drama queen.

'Make up your mind,' says the driver.

'HOLD THE DOORS,' the girl says, her voice high, squeaky. She stands up, almost dragging her friend. Total OTT.

And then they're off. I watch them walk arm in arm along the street towards the back of the bus. They stop to cross the road. I'm waiting to see if the girl reaches for her phone, answers a call. Looks at me again.

Will Naz call them? Will he come and rescue me?

I should have phoned the police. *I should have.*

The two girls step out to cross the street. The bus pulls off. Two guys on a scooter suddenly race out of nowhere. They shoot past the inside lane, swerve and do a sharp turn towards the back of the bus. They cut inwards. They pass right by the girls standing there. As quick as a flash the guy riding pillion grabs one of the girls' bags. *The one whose phone I stole.* There's a quick tussle. The girl is dragged screaming a few metres along the bus lane. Then the shoulder strap snaps. The scooter screeches away. As it disappears, I notice its number plate is obscured by something flapping from the trunk.

I sit there, frozen.

The Voice speaks. 'You have broken the rules.'

My breath sticks in my chest. *Those girls and that phone?*

'You tried to communicate.'

I shake my head.

'From now on you will do exactly as you're told.'

A crowd gathers around the girls. One passenger on the bus screams. The driver stops the engine. Gets off.

'If you try to double cross us again,' the Voice threatens through cyberspace. Cold. Menacing.

My throat dries up. A siren sounds through the morning.

'If you do not follow our instructions.' The Voice pauses to let the threat sink in.

There's so much noise. A crowd is forming. I cup my hand over the earpiece. It chafes slightly. Irritates the skin. My hearing goes muffled.

'You should know two things. Firstly, we can find and

51

destroy every member of your family. Your mother in Bridgewater, for instance.'

People crowd to the back of the bus to see what's happening outside.

'Secondly, the vest you're wearing is packed with high explosives.'

My chest. My throat. *My mother?*

'And with one mobile call we can detonate it.'

I gulp air.

Detonate it?

I swallow.

'We will simply terminate you and the project you've been selected for.'

6

Learn to Meditate

I DON'T KNOW WHAT TO THINK.

The unthinkable.

I sit there. The air around me throbs and presses down. *What am I going to do?* WHAT THE HELL AM I GOING TO DO? I'm trying to believe what's happening, but trying to believe it is making me freak out. This can't be happening. *This doesn't happen.*

A high explosive vest.

How has it come to this? My heart's pounding so hard, it's going to burst through my chest and explode into a million bloody pieces. *My mother.*

I must think.

I was on a date. I was just on a stupid date. I was needy, far from home, rooming with my aunt. Holly thought it'd help me forget Naz. He'd been EVERYTHING to me. I'd given up so much for him. Given up Dave for a start.

Nearly destroyed my friendship with Holly. Broke Dave's heart. That nearly broke Mum's heart. I went out on a total limb for Naz.

A total limb.

And he dumped me.

I just wanted someone to like me again, tell me I was special. Tell me I wasn't a freak. I'd been feeling like a freak ever since Naz'd deleted me on every social media site going, spammed me. Unfollowed me. Refused to talk to me. Changed the classes we took together in school.

Was going on a date so terrible?

Did I deserve a suicide vest?

I whimper. Let out a moan. I swallow it. I press my knuckles into my mouth and bite down on them.

I'm strapped to a bomb.

The bus driver gets back in the bus. The bus starts up. Every shake terrifies me. Does a bomb detonate if it's bumped? If I move too quickly? I want to beg for help. I want to scream. But what good will that do? I clamp my jaw tight, grind my teeth. I look around. Everybody's getting on with their lives: taking pics out the window, listening to their headphones, reading their guide books. *How can they?* Except that nosy Japanese kid. *Nobody can help me.* They'll detonate the vest. Everyone will die. We'll all be splattered into a million bloody pieces. I look at the little kid. She can't stop staring at me. They'll blow her to pieces too.

How did they know I used that girl's phone?

They must be watching.

All the time.

Unless it was just a coincidence.

Naz will think of something. Course he will. Even though he's dumped me, he won't let this happen. And they won't turn on him. And he'll do it without calling the police. He's probably sorting it all out right now. *It'll be OK,* I tell myself. IT WILL BE OK. Course it will.

Course it won't.

They're not going to let me live. Naz doesn't know about the bomb. I didn't put that in the text. There's no way to tell him now.

I stare out of the window. We're somewhere really boring: some backwater in South London near Borough.

They didn't go to all this trouble to blow me up here, did they? That's why they warned me not to touch the vest. Remember that girl they sent into the football stadium with that collar bomb? They didn't blow her up until the final penalty kick.

Maximum impact. Maximum terror.

If they want to blow me up, they're going to do it in the middle of Oxford Street or outside Westminster Abbey.

Somewhere like that. Or the Houses of Parliament. I'm on a tourist bus. It's all falling into place. The London Eye. Trafalgar square. Piccadilly Circus.

Could be any of them. That's what they do. *Strike at the heart. Petrify the nation. Show us how weak and defenceless we are.* That's how they've risen so quickly. That's their appeal. If you're one of them, you're safe. I remember hearing something like that on the news.

'. . . *The meteoric rise of the violent extremist group calling itself the Brightness has taken the West completely by surprise. The radicalization of British teenagers in our schools, on our street and over the internet has reached epidemic proportions. If the Government cannot find early ways to roll out its planned scheme to protect people at risk of radicalization, we will see many more home-grown bombers like the cell responsible for last month's attack on the Channel Tunnel. One of the parents we interviewed today said, "We don't know what to do. Our children are saying that joining the Brightness is the only sure way to stay safe . . ."*'

And now this new tactic. Hostage taking. *Your daughter could be next. We can reach right into your homes, take your beloved children and turn them into weapons to destroy you . . .*

The Houses of Parliament, St Paul's Cathedral, Waterloo, Kings Cross. This bus goes to every major transport hub, every iconic landmark in London. *And I'm on it.* I'm their walking weapon. I'm one of those daughters, snatched from her home, strapped to a bomb, sent to show everyone how weak they are.

But I won't be weak.

I must answer the riddle single-handedly.

I understand now. This is the riddle. How to stay alive. It's not death that matters. We all die. It's life. It's how we stay alive.

It's how we face the struggle. That's what counts. (I read that somewhere and I SO need to believe it, right now.)

Plus, knowledge is power.

Quickly, I re-examine the vest. How does it work? Everything has a weak point. I check the front, the pockets. It's really tight against me. I try to reach round to the back. I slip my hands inside and realize it's right up against my skin. Apart from my bra, underneath the vest and the corset, I'm naked.

My hands are shaking. I have no idea how to get it off. What will happen if I try?

I'm going to have to be a walking weapon, then?

But weapons, like knowledge, are powerful too.

So though I may not be able to remove it, right now it goes where I go. And that kind of makes me powerful.

And if I have any power at all, I'm going to use it.

I stand up and move seats. Just because I can. At any minute I expect a blast in my ear, but I'm beyond that. Being deaf is no longer the worst thing that can happen. The blast on my eardrum doesn't come anyway.

But a Sudden Scary Thought does (110/10): That newspaper article about London being on Critical Alert. The Brightness are going to strike today. *Maybe there are more hostages out there?* Sitting, like me, on other tourist buses?

Like a cold finger running down my spine, a shiver goes through me. I've got to figure out what's going on. Figure out exactly where they're taking me and how long I've got. Are they going to send their hostages to different places? *Oh Naz, please get through to them and save me.*

HELP YOURSELF.

First: figure out what they can and can't see.

- They can track me.
- But how can they know – minute by minute – what I'm doing?
- Why did they want me to sit in a certain place?
- They're not magicians. They must be using known technology.

The little nosy Japanese kid suddenly gets out of her seat and walks up to mine. 'What's in that?' She speaks slowly and frowns as she gets the words out. Then she prods my vest.

I shrink away from her. 'Don't touch it, stupid,' I say.

'But what's in it?' She wrinkles up her nose and sticks her face near mine.

'Go and sit back down.' How can I think with a pesky kid around? She might frigging set it off if she pokes me again!

'私は, 探偵' she says. She shoves an electronic translator in my face. *I'M A DETECTIVE*, it reads.

She leans in even closer. I move back against the window.

The Voice booms out. 'You are instructed not to talk to anyone.' Its sinister electronic tones grate. They reverberate in my damaged inner ear.

I flinch. I flap my hand at the kid, shoo her off. I grit my teeth, expecting a whistle.

How do they blast my ear? Have they put something like a phone or a receiver somewhere inside the vest? Are they remotely operating it?

Does that mean the line is open all the time? *Are they listening to every breath I take?*

If they are, it means they can track me too.

OK. Just rip the earpiece out of your ear then. Rip the skin with it. That will stop the whistling. I hesitate – what

59

if they've poured superglue into my ear and fixed the ear piece right to my eardrum? Rip that out too?

Wait, I tell myself. None of that will defuse the bomb. Keep working out what they can and can't do. They can't hear everything that well, anyway, or they'd have heard what the Japanese kid actually said. Wouldn't they?

Plus, how do they see me?

'あなたのパーカーに爆弾を持っています' types in the kid. *YOU GOTTA BOMB IN PARKA, LADY?* reads the translator.

'Look.' She holds it up.

I whirl round and glare at her.

'What?' says the Voice in my ear. They heard something that time.

And suddenly I'm terrified. *They'll get the kid.* They'll grab her, splatter her. I have to work out if they can see me – see her – fast.

What could they do? They could access every CCTV system along the route they've planned. They could remotely access the bus's security cameras. I look up at the camera. It flicks from vista to vista. It's very patchy. So they couldn't possibly have seen me texting that way? I was slumped down in the seat, all crouched over.

There must be someone on the bus.

I screw my head round and scan the passengers. They all look like tourists. But they would wouldn't they? If

60

they saw me texting, then there *has* to be someone on the bus. I turn back to the kid. I make as if to itch my nose. I tap it quickly. Mind Your Own Bloody Business.

She sees. She grins. She's got dreadful braces.

Suddenly I know what to do. I push her out the way. I get out of my seat. The idea of climbing up to the top deck is immensely exciting – and terrifying. It sets the blood in my veins hammering. Will they think I'm disobeying them? What if I'm wrong about them not wanting to explode the bomb here?

But I don't stop. They're going to blow me up anyway. Aren't they? It's only a matter of time. No miracle's going to save me. Is it? And I need to get away from this kid, see if anyone follows me. Because I need to know who it is.

I move back down the bus till I reach the stairs. If someone on the bus *is* watching, they'll have to do something. And that sets me thinking something else. Are they going to detonate a bomb with one of their own sitting next to it? They like taking other folk's kids hostage and blowing them up – and once in a while they'll send some suicide bomber to do something, which often backfires. He chickens out, or he's so dumb everyone guesses. They like sticking how great they are on YouTube, but I have a huge wild hunch they won't want to blow themselves up. Not here and not now and not in Central London.

I just sooo hope I'm right.

I climb up the stairs to the open deck. The fresh air chills the sweat on my neck, and I shiver. Ahead the river is laid out like a long silver-blue snake, winding its way through the city down to an eventual sea. LIFE IS AN ESTUARY: YOU HAVE TO TAKE YOUR CHANCES ON THE TIDE. (Or maybe LIFE IS A SNAKE: PERIOD.) The London skyline is lit up. Sunshine glints off mirrored towers. There's the Gherkin. The Shard. Canary Wharf. Blue sky. Fresh breeze. And the sun blazing from a thousand windows. I glance down at the street. Cars. People. A road sweeper busy sweeping.

I must answer the riddle single-handedly.

One thing is for sure: LIFE IS A BUS LANE: YOU HAVE TO TRAVEL ALONG IT ALONE.

I pick a seat at the back. If anyone follows me, they'll be forced to sit in front, and they'll have to keep turning around to watch me. Then I'll know.

But no one does follow me upstairs. I sit waiting, heart pounding and very puzzled.

What if they're using cars, then? They could be following the bus. They could be in front of the bus. They did that in some film I saw. They followed the bus from the front. They knew its route, so it was easy. I start clocking cars up ahead and from behind: Hondas. Fords. Mitsubishis. Reg numbers. Colours. Makes. Logging all of it in my memory.

Then the pesky kid appears. Before she can ask another of her dumb questions, I lay my finger over my mouth. She nods, wide eyed. She points to the vest and makes a boom gesture – puffing out her cheeks and throwing open her arms.

I nod.

Her eyes – already wide – get wider.

I point to my headset and roll my eyes. She dives into her pocket and gets out her Japanese to English electronic translator again.

ARE YOU AN AUTOBUS BOMBER? she types.

SORT OF, I type.

ARE YOU DANGEROUS SPY? I AM HIGH-QUALITY AT KARATE.

YOU ARE IN DANGER. PLEASE GET OFF THE BUS.

I AM RESPLENDENT DETECTIVE AND I AM A YOUNG ONE. ARE YOU GOING TO BLOW BUS UP. BOOM?

PLEASE CALL THE POLICE WHEN YOU ARE WELL AWAY FROM THIS BUS AND TELL THEM I AM WEARING A BOMB.

The kid giggles. Her face lights up like this is the

funniest thing that's happened to her since she woke up.

I AM GOING TO RIDE THE LONDON ICE WHEN I GET OFF BUS AT NEXT STOP. SORRY. She giggles again.

THE LONDON EYE, NOT ICE.

This is hopeless. I want her to go away.

CAN I DO PHOTO?

OK. Anything to get her to go.

WITH ME?

JUST SHOW THIS TO YOUR MUM AND GET HER TO CALL THE POLICE.

OK. BINGO. NOW PHOTO PICTURE.

The kid gets out her phone. I try and straighten my hair a bit, readjust my hair clip. Then I think: *Do I really want my face out there in a suicide vest?* What if she posts it online with a ME AND AN AUTOBUS BOMBER caption? So I puff my cheeks out in a mad way and suck my lower lip back in and bulge my eyes till I look really stupid (and hopefully not like me). Then the kid snaps a selfie of us. A cloud rolls across the blue above. I exhale all the puff from my cheeks. I'm so desperate; I want to grab the phone off her.

'Mitsuki,' calls a voice.

THAT IS MOTHER. THANK YOU FOR FRIENDSHIP, AUTOBUS BOMBER. I GIVE YOU FRIENDSHIP BRACELET SO YOU REMEMBER MITSUKI.

The kid pulls a multicoloured loom band off her wrist and stretches it wide, so that I can put it on.

And I get goosepimples.

I remember the dream I had in that cavern last night. The dream of the Moirai.

And Clotho seemed to grow bigger somehow and she held out her hand and on her wrist was a bracelet. And she loosened the catch and the bracelet slipped off. And she fastened it about my wrist.

And I tried to understand the riddle.

And then I said, 'I am your handmaiden.'

And then the lights around her faded, until I was left in darkness by the shores of that ancient, subterranean lake.

Like déjà vu.

Like it's all somehow connected.

I shiver. It's stupid. But as I slip my hand through the band, and it closes about my wrist, I get this feeling, like I remember it there. The way it caught on the tiny hairs of my arm and stung, like embers on bare skin. Ring of fire. I look at it. All twisted, multi-coloured, bright like a rainbow.

Fiery.

Mitsuki stands up and runs downstairs. I hear her

talking in rapid Japanese. I hear her mum fussing. *Just let her phone the police*. It's funny that the only person who's actually spotted I'm in trouble is a kid. Somebody should study that. Somebody should write a paper on why kids see things others don't. Maybe I'll write a poem about it. If I ever get out of this mess. LIFE IS A CHILD: THE MORE YOU KNOW, THE LESS YOU SEE. THE MORE YOU GROW, THE LESS YOU'RE FREE.

Nobody climbs up the stairs. Nobody seated on the top deck turns round. So they don't know I've changed seats? They don't know I communicated with the Japanese kid? That tells me there's nobody currently on the bus.

But they knew I tried to communicate before. So there must have been someone on the bus then? Maybe it was that guy who got off when I gave the phone back. Did he clock which girl it was? Did he get them mugged on purpose? Did they snatch the phone to figure out who I'd texted? Or was it just a random street mugging? Happens every day in London. But if it wasn't, and if they're not on the bus now, does that mean they're preparing to blow me up? Or are they just happy to follow?

I don't know. *I just don't know.*

SO CARRY ON LOOKING TILL YOU DO. Clock everyone getting on. Clock everyone getting off. Sink low in your seat, turn and peer out over the back rail and

66

redouble your search of cars on the street below.

There's a goldish BMW, maybe it's more champagne colour. It trails the bus at an exact distance. It seems to get snagged in behind us, when it should go past.

I decide it has to be that gold car, and I memorize the number plate: EC21 PSE

But it still doesn't make sense, because if it *was* the guy who got off the bus he got off before the girls did, so how did he know they would get off too?

My head starts to ache again.

Think, Genesis, think – there must be something you can do to save yourself.

7

Say Yes to Everything
for a Whole Day

THE HOUSES OF PARLIAMENT will be on this route. Somewhere. Either on the outgoing or return loop. And thinking about how long I've got left before we get to them gives me an idea.

Though I may not be able to stop them killing me, I have the power to stop them blowing up Parliament, if that's their plan. And that's their weakness. It has to be. I don't have to wait to be killed. I can force them to do it earlier.

It's a crazy kind of a power. And I can't immediately think of any advantage to getting blown up quicker, but I don't give up. Instead, I ask myself if I was Dr Who and in this jam and I could only go forward in time to make something happen more quickly, where would I go?

I reckon Dr Who would go straight to the point where

they detonate the bomb. Obviously, he can't go past that point, unless there's some kind of afterlife for Time Lords, but if he went straight there, he'd be able to figure out why and when and where and how – and Save The Day. Obviously.

So that's what I've got to do. And even though I still can't figure out any advantage to me in getting blown up earlier, I have a definite feeling that it may be a big disadvantage to them.

And I'm going to test that out.

After all, they must've gone to a lot of trouble to set all this up – so they'll want it to work out the way they planned, won't they?

And the fact that they didn't do anything about me going up to the top deck inspires me. Now I'm going to get off the bus. Yes, right here, in this boring backwater, and slow their programme down to a standstill.

Or speed up mine.

My heartbeat accelerates at the idea. It goes so fast I feel dizzy.

Am I really sure about this? Won't they just detonate? My nerve weakens. I tell myself, Stop pushing your luck. While there's life there's hope. Take no chances. Play along. Pray for a miracle.

I try to remember other cases of Brightness hostages.

That famous one of that poor teenage girl from Scotland, sent from Inverness to Falmouth, through every major transport hub across the UK. How they filmed her journey. And after she was blown up in Cornwall, they posted the footage of her all over the internet, with the chilling message: *We Can Get You. Anywhere. Anytime. Anyplace.*

What would they have done if she'd got off her bus in Borough, South London?

And I have to conclude: nothing. They wouldn't have blown her up. They'd have tried to force her to continue. Because the whole point was to get her *through* every hub and *show* that they could. They didn't want to give out the message *We Can't Get You. Anywhere. Anytime. But We Can Get You In A Boring Backstreet In Borough*, did they? What terror value would that have? Apart from if you lived in Borough, of course.

I gaze down at the street, at the morning traffic, at the cyclists and the commuters. Trying to steel myself for action. I take in the coffee shop, the off-licence, the fast-food store. *I'm going to get off the bus. I'm going to fight back. And I'm going to outthink them, or I'm going to die trying.*

And then I remember something. It comes to me like that prayed-for miracle.

We're near Holly's workplace.

Holly, my total bestie.

What if I get off the bus and find Holly?

A trembling starts in my gut, my heart starts pounding. Holly, the twin I never had. We don't actually look that much alike, except from a distance, though we're so totally alike in other ways that Dave calls us soul sisters. He reckons we have this telepathic wavelength thing going on. Like if I wear a cool new outfit in, say, mad pink, Holly will as well. Same day. Same stuff. Like we'd totally planned it.

What if I go and find Holly?

A surge of hope courses through me. *I'm not going to do what they say. I'm going to push them to act.* I'm going to try and find Holly. *Oh God, let her be there.* And if she's there, I'm going to beg her to call Dave.

Call Dave. My cheeks! My cheeks! Total blushing! I can't believe I just thought that! I squeeze my eyes tight. THIS IS AN EMERGENCY. IN AN EMERGENCY YOU CAN DO WHAT YOU LIKE.

But call Dave?

After the way I dumped him?

OH CHRIST.

TOTAL CRINGE.

But you need his help.

I remember the last time I saw him – his face. The two of us standing there on that street in Streatham. And the way he said, 'I don't understand, Gen. Make me understand.' How he traced me out, waited for me on my way home from college. Confronted me. Forced me to tell him.

But it wasn't you, Dave. There was nothing wrong with you. You were the nicest guy ever. And I thought I loved you, until I met Naz. And I adored you (as a kid). And you were fit and big and toned and tough. And hot too. But I met Naz. And he was different.

Oh, how can I explain?

Naz taught me to ride a motorbike, fast down country lanes. Without a helmet on.

You wanted to teach me to swim in the local kiddies' pool. With arm-bands.

Naz took me for rides on a speedboat when the wind was high and the tide racing.

You took me for walks in a park.

Naz planned holidays – just the two of us – travelling the world on jet planes.

You planned holidays with my mum and yours and Holly and probably the dogs and push bikes and what fun is that?

When I loved speed.

And then you joined the army.

And I hardly saw you.

And I know I said I'd wait, but I didn't.

BUT THIS IS AN EMERCENCY. AND IN AN EMERGENCY I CAN ASK HOLLY TO CALL YOU. (Though, obviously you might not even be in the country, let alone on leave.)

But if Holly calls Dave – and if he still cares? Then he might help. He always used to help. He used to say: 'Dave rhymes with Save,' every time he rescued Holly and me from some scrape: like missing the last bus home (he'd borrow his mum's car), or getting in some fix at school with playground bullies (he'd show up and wag his finger at them and say: DON'T DO THAT. And they'd actually stop).

'Dave. That's my name. Save. That's my game.' His words.

If it's still his game, maybe then, together, we might swing the odds in my favour?

I realize that's a lot of 'If's.

I cross my fingers. PLEASE BE THERE FOR ME, DAVE.

That's pretty sad, crossing your fingers when you're strapped to a bomb.

8

Go on a Self-help Course and Free Your Inner Soul

To ACT, OR NOT TO ACT: THAT IS THE QUESTION.

I lecture myself. I imagine the bullet points. I let myself have it.

- You must refuse to be directed here and there, like a lamb to the slaughter.
- This is your chance to defy them.
- Maybe the only chance you'll get.
- Because they aren't going to let you go. Are they?
- Get real. THEY ARE NOT GOING TO LET YOU GO. GET THAT IN YOUR HEAD.
- But they'll try to fool you, they will, if you comply.
- But they're liars.
- They'll promise and threaten, but they'll still blow you up, when you complete their mission.

- Obviously.

I squeeze my eyes tight. I go cold all over. My breathing goes mental, all gasping in and not coming out, and I'm shuddering inside. *And I'm going to die.* And unless I can get a grip on myself there's no hope for me, and I feel so tiny inside. Despite all my lecturing, I want my mum and I'm fighting not to cry.

- And they'll use you to KILL as many other people as they can.
- So are you up for that too?
- Are you going to let them?

I bite my cheek hard. I force myself to breathe normally. Because I know the answer. So I'm going to have to choose to act. How strange that feels. *To choose.* To move through the streets like a pestilence or a monster, carrying death with me. Horrible, stalkerish and spooky. *Shall I sit down by you? Or you?*

Will it be in your company that I make my Last Stand?

And with a shudder I realize I have a hideously new and deadly power: at some level I can decide who lives, who dies.

At some level I can CHOOSE to be the suicide bomber.

So while I still feel that appalling thrill, I put my plan into action. I lean back in my seat and I act.

'Please don't kill me,' I say. I make my voice as soft and

submissive and small as I can. 'I'll do whatever you say,' I sob. (I don't have to pretend.) 'I'm so sorry. I won't try to contact anyone, ever again.'

There's a pause, an echoing. I get the feeling someone is conferring with someone else. *How many of them are there?* Maybe it's just the quality of the echo, the suggestion of half-smothered voices. *There can't be that many. Can there?* Naz told me these Brightness Action Cells can be really small. *'They're sometimes only one-man operations,' he said. 'You just have to show your Love of God by taking action in Our Bright War, even if it's only something you do on your own. It can be as small as posting slogans online. That's what I did. Or as big as taking a hostage. As long as it is for the Glory of God . . .'*

There's a sharp click in my ear. 'We are pleased you have decided to work with us,' says the electronic Voice. Then someone else takes the phone. A smooth, suave, chocolatey tone purrs down the air waves at me. 'We can *promise* you, that if you do *exactly* as we say, we *will* let you go *free*! You *must* TRUST us about this.'

Pukesville. I totally preferred the Dalek voice.

'But only once you have *completed* the task we've chosen you for, *naturally*, of course!' The chocolate Voice makes a supernatural effort to sound reassuring.

And despite all its fakery, I *am* reassured. My heart

leaps wildly. *They might be telling the truth. Maybe they will let me go.* 'Oh thank you. Thank you,' I choke out, in genuine relief.

Bastards.

They strap me to a bomb, then pretend to be on my side.

Total bastards.

I look down again at the street and try to figure out exactly where Holly's place is. If this bus stops at London Bridge I'll get off. I know she works near there. I bite my lip and steel myself. I look up at the sky. The summer day is unfolding. Huge sun. Beautiful, fluffy white clouds. Streaming sunshine. It reminds me of other blue sky days.

At home, on my mother's lawn, me five years old and wondering about life. Asking her unanswerable questions.

Why am I me? Why am I alive? What does it all mean?

Mum, dangling a tea bag into her cup. 'The meaning of life, Gen? Don't ask me. I work in a place which generates electricity, gives power to the nation. Keeps those heart monitors monitoring.'

She smiles proudly. 'You know, like when we play hospitals – my job keeps people alive.'

I look at her, pull a Yes, Yes, Yes face and wait for the answer to my question.

'But one wrong move and it could light up the sky, destroy everything.'

I don't understand. How can something that keeps you alive make you die?

'The meaning of life? Keep looking for the answer to that riddle, hon. Tell me when you find it.'

Oh Mum, I wish you were here now. I get an insane urge to call her. I imagine the mobile in my hand. I imagine saying, 'I found out, Mum. I found out what life is all about.'

'Yes?'

'Just stay alive.'

And I'm going to try as hard as I can to do just that. So screw these jokers.

I put my next plan-point into operation.

Find out what part of Our Bright War they've lined up for you.

'You mentioned a task,' I say to the Voice: 'What task?'

But in answer, all I get is a shrill blast on the high-pitched whistle.

9

Complete a 1000-piece
Jigsaw Puzzle on My Own

As soon as the tour bus gets near London
Bridge, I take a deep breath, and get off. I'm going to
find out exactly how they're tracking me now, that's for
sure. One up for Dr Who.

I look around. If that gold car is still there it can't see
me, because this bus stop has a covered-over waiting
place and a huge advert is blocking it from the road. So I
can see them (theoretically) but they can't see me. Two up
for Dr Who. I wait behind the advert till the bus pulls off.
There goes the gold car, and a stream of traffic. Right.
Anyone trailing me has definitely gone past now.

With my heart doing some kind of weird, fluttery,
irregular thing, I head for Holly's workplace. Every second
I expect the whistle. I hold my breath as a dad with a

buggy pushes past. I reach the entrance to Holly's beauty salon, before the electronic Voice says, 'Why are you not travelling towards your planned destination?'

Bingo. Good voice. Bad voice.

And I'm right. They can't see me. They're just charting me on a grid.

'Because,' I say – I've thought up an answer to this already – 'because, I really have to pee.' Whimper. Two can play at the manipulative game, can't they?

There's a pause. I'm lying. But will they be able to tell? And what will they do? Blow me up Not-Very-Near London Bridge? Was that in their plan? Plus, people need to pee, you know. Even those strapped to high explosive vests.

The silence continues. They're thinking. Good. The Voice says, 'Wait. Do not move until further instructed.'

'But I'm bursting,' I cry.

There is no whistle. I hear shuffling. I can almost hear what kind of room they're in. It's as if someone has their hand over a microphone. This definitely wasn't in their plan. I smile. (More like twist my lips.) Three up to Dr Who. Their plan was that I would do as I was told, all the time, to the bitter end. Total domination. Go here. Do this. Use the toilet at this point. We are in control. When we say pee, you pee. And then they'd blow me up.

They'd banked on that. They thought being strapped to a bomb made me their toy.

Good.

Suddenly the craziness of what I'm doing makes me break out in a cold sweat. *For God's sake, what am I trying to do? Just get back on the bus. They said they'd let you go.* But I don't waver. Every nerve in my body tells me not to. Defy them, one step at a time. Find ways. Excuses. Reasons not to do what they want. Confuse them. Make them think twice.

And then they may make a mistake.

So very carefully I feed them my first daring lie. 'There's a One-Stop Express Grocery Store up ahead that I've used before,' I say. 'It has toilets.'

Before the Voice can answer, I rush out: 'And I'm so sorry. *Please don't blow me up. Please don't.* I wanted to ask you if I could stop to pee, but I didn't want to get overheard on the bus, talking about a BOMB. *Please – I'm trying so hard to do the right thing.*' I say it in my best, most confused, most pleading voice. And I *am* pleading. *Please let them see that.*

Then I hold my breath.

Assholes. Bastards. Didn't expect that, did you?

Before my dad died, he was a teacher. He used to say, 'You can have everything planned out for a perfect lesson

81

– but if you forget you're dealing with human beings, it'll all go pear-shaped.' *Oh God, I miss you now, Dad.* But he was right, and I can almost hear it all going pear-shaped in their secret little cyber control-room. Almost hear them saying, 'Shush,' as I say, '**BOMB**.'

So I know it's round four to the Doctor, as well.

'OK. Talk to no one. Use the toilet. Wait for the next tour bus.'

You see!

Another pause.

'One will be along in twenty minutes.'

Twenty minutes! I cheer. My eyes involuntarily fill up. *I've just gained one third of a precious hour.* Long enough to find Holly. Long enough to communicate everything to her. Long enough to come up with another Death Defying Strategy.

Hopefully.

And maybe even long enough for Dave to find us.

And as I walk up the street, I think of Holly.

Dear, sweet Holly.

Oh Holly, I breathe, *just be there*. Just bloody be there.

10

Spend a Day
Without Speaking

UP AHEAD, I see Holly's salon alongside the Express Store. They won't know exactly which shop I go into, will they? The blue dot on a digital map is so large; they can't possibly. The map may not even have shops on it. Unless they've got some state-of-the-art precision satellite positioning equipment thing. Which I doubt.

If Naz was right, and Brightness terrorists work in small cells, then that means they're going to have limited funds too, doesn't it? The teenage girl from Inverness thing was, apparently, only the work of a five-man outfit. Plus they didn't figure on me deviating from their plan. At least not like this. So why would they have prepared for it?

I take a deep breath. I tell myself: Believe. *Twenty*

minutes. Think how you can tell Holly everything. Without talking.

What I need is a pen and paper. But I don't have any money to buy them. I fish the words out of my pocket: HELP. CALL. POLICE. I pull out the newspaper sheet. SOLAR ECLIPSE ATTRACTS THOUSANDS. How the hell am I going to point out words and get her to understand using that?

Forget the newspaper. I'm going to have to think of something else. I turn towards the salon. I try to imagine what THEY can see. Just a movement on their map? One little dot, scarcely budging? I'm pretty certain they've lost me at street level here. I wish I'd been more on it when I got out of the cellar. Maybe they had that gold car waiting then, following me all the time, but if they did, it's gone now. This street is a red line no-stopping zone. They won't want to attract attention to themselves by stopping here. Will they? I've probably got a few minutes before they do a U-turn or something, or get another car or a pedestrian to the place.

A few minutes to get Holly out of the salon and into the grocery store.

I move quickly forward. I make it across the gap of the pavement and into the entrance of the salon. Nothing happens. I check the street. All clear. I push the salon door open. A bell rings. *Shit. What if they hear the bell?* Grocery Stores don't have bells. I clap my hand over the ear piece to muffle anything else. Tell myself: *Stay calm. Carry on.*

Three ladies are sitting having hair extensions done. Girls bend over them. No Holly. I stand there with my hand over my ear. One of the girls looks up and says, 'Can I help you?'

I shake my head. I mouth out, 'Holly?'

She crosses over to the back of the beauty salon and presses another bell behind the counter. It rings long and loud. I silently groan.

The girl comes out from behind the counter again, comes up to me and says, 'Please wait, someone will come.' Then she returns to her client.

A woman bustles out of the back room. 'Yes?' she says.

The Bad Voice in my ear says, 'What's going on?'

I thank my stars they didn't clock the bells.

'Can I help?' asks the woman.

I try to think fast: some reply to let the woman standing in front of me know I want Holly, and at the same time, be some sort of an answer to the Voice.

So I say, 'I am,' so only the Voice will hear, and 'HOLLY' louder, so the woman will hear too. And then I finish up mumbling to the Voice again, 'in need of the toilet.'

It's a pretty weird sentence: 'I am, Holly,' (*wholly*?) 'in need of the toilet.' I cross my fingers. It was the best I could do on the spur of the moment.

The woman looks at me as if I'm a mental goldfish. She moves off towards the back room again.

'Speak to no one else,' the Bad Voice says, with an even more ominous Dalek staccato, as if someone has just turned up the *Sound As Menacing As Possible* knob.

Oh God. Where are you, Holly?

Wildly I look around for something to write with. That's what I need. If I could even leave her a note? The Voice continues, 'Do not draw attention to yourself. Use the bathroom and get back out to the bus stop.'

Where you can see me, I think. *Now you've put someone on the street. Or parked your flipping gold car where you can scope everything through your field glasses or something.* Whichever. I can't hang around anyway.

Where the hell is Holly? What's that woman gone to do now?

In desperation I back up towards the door. I'm terrified someone else will come in; the bell will ring again, and this'll be The Place Where She Died. Maybe the woman's calling the police. The door's going to ring as I go out too. *For pity's sake don't let the Voice understand I've gone for help.*

86

Holly appears from the end of the shop.

Holly.

Thank heavens.

She comes hurrying towards me. She throws out her arms and sprints into a bit of a run. And I know beyond a doubt that she is going to scream out 'OH MY GOD! GENESIS!'. I put out my hand. Frantically, I stop-signal her away. I put my finger over my lips. I flap my hand wildly. Shake my head. She looks puzzled, screams, 'WHAAAT?'

Hysterically, I zigzag both hands at her, wagging my finger, doing a little PLEASE SHUT THE HELL UP dance.

Holy Mary Mother of God, Please Be Quiet!

She does the puzzled eyebrow raising thing. I jump up and down with my finger fixed across my pursed lips. Everyone in the whole place is looking at me. They must think I'm totally barmy. But Holly nods. She knows me. She understands.

I hope to heaven she understands.

I run to her, still doing the frenzied, non-verbal, BE QUIET face. I link my arm in hers, and steer her towards the door.

Her supervisor gives us A Very Funny Look. Holly breaks free from my arm, quickly trots back and says,

'She's doing a sponsored silence.' Clever Holly. 'In aid of Save the Children.'

Everyone nods and someone says, 'Oh, good for her.' Then they all get back to work, like it's totally normal to have bonkers friends randomly showing up, doing sponsored whatevers. I heave a sigh. Thank heavens Holly's smart.

Now I've got to be smart too. I've got to think up a way to tell Holly everything. And I've only got ten minutes left. I think of the words in my pocket. HELP. CALL. POLICE. But I realize I don't want the police to come within a million miles of me.

Of course not.

Sudden Very Very Scary Thought: (1000/10). If my captors see the police, they'll detonate me here and now.

And cut their losses.

11

Learn a New Language

By THE DOOR THERE'S A MIRROR. Hot, wet air has formed a sheen of condensation on it. Quickly, I sidestep there.

I write in the steam: *Help. Don't speak*. Then I draw a sad face at the end to show her it's not a joke ☹.

Holly looks at me. I wipe everything off the mirror. Holly nods. I motion her to follow. I clap my hand back over my ear and, squeezing my face up tight – *Please, don't let them hear the bell* – I step back outside the shop. The bell rings. My heart jumps. I move quickly away, round towards the grocery store. Holly runs back inside.

Hol-leee! I can't wait here!

I see her say something to the woman. Must be her boss. *What's the matter now?* My heart is bashing so hard against my stomach, a pain shoots up under my left shoulder blade.

Through the glass I see Holly remove her salon coat. I scarcely register she's got on the same colour clothes as me. She runs to the counter. She grabs a beautiful tie-dye scarf, her rucksack and something else. I watch her. I watch the street. *Holy crap.* Then she's outside in a flash. Bell ringing. But fainter from outside. And at last, she's here.

In her hand she's got a pad and pencil. *I should have trusted her.* Quickly, I steer her into the grocery store. *Not too many people.* I walk past the fruit, past the bread, down towards the meat counter. Holly follows. Right by the bacon we stop. There's some stupid sign over it saying YOU HAD ME AT BACON. Holly stands beside me. She doesn't make a sound. She writes on the pad, *What's wrong? You look terrible?*

I take the pen. I write: *I'm in trouble. Just do as I say. I'm strapped to a bomb. They can hear everything. Don't call the police yet. Call Dave.* I point at my ear.

Her eyes grow wide. She looks at me and bites her lip. She shakes her head. She mouths out: 'OMG.' She looks at the vest. She lifts up the hair covering my ear. She sees the earpiece. She mouths out 'OH MY GOD' properly. She fans herself with her hand. Then goes very pale. I wait. I don't write anything more. I cross my fingers. *Please help.*

Holly gets out her mobile; her hands are shaking.

She moves aside and stabs at buttons.

I move away, let the sounds of a trolley being pushed, a kid complaining, block out her call. The trolley and kid disappear down the Home Baking aisle. I wait. Every tiny noise grates. That stupid background music. Why do they do that? I've never even noticed it before. Stupid piped music, playing 'Jingle Bells', of all things. It's not even Christmas! And it's so cold by the meat counter. I shiver. A woman with a shopping trolley barges past.

Noises? They'll know I haven't used the loo! Frantically I signal to Holly, then rush into the shop toilets. I slam the door, bang the lock. Let it echo. Flush the cistern. Run the tap. Then I rush out.

Holly is still on the phone. She finishes and rejoins me. How long have I got left? I seize the pad and write: *We haven't got long. Only mins.*

She takes my hand and squeezes it. '*Be OK*,' she mouths. And for the first time since this morning started, my heart contracts and suddenly I'm sobbing. My body is shaking in huge, great, soundless sobs. Tears are rolling down my cheeks and I can't seem to stop them. And I'm bending over the cold meat section and my tears are dropping down on to the bacon packs, and I'm biting my lips and no sound is coming out.

Holly puts her arm round me. Taps into her phone.

Takes up the pad. *Dave's not picking up* she writes.

Oh Christ. I try not to sniff. I wipe my nose with my sleeve. *I have to get on a See London Tour bus* I write. *They're directing me.* I point to my ear again.

OK she replies. *I'm gonna come too.*

I shake my head. I point at my chest. My eyes fill up again. The back of my throat aches. *She mustn't come with me.*

NOT LEAVING YOU she jabs down on the pad in capitals. She underlines it. Then texts Dave again. I wait. My face twisted, my chin crumpling.

I've left him a message to get back to me, but will keep trying she writes. She holds up her hand to indicate that she's going to buy tickets online for the bus tour. I pat my pocket, check my travel pass, wait while she taps again into her phone.

Then she writes on the pad, *We need to contact police. Tell them everything – like not to speak to you.* She points to my ear, writes: *Don't worry. luv u. We will think of sumting.* She takes my hair clip out, styles my curls over my ear, pushes the clip back into her own hair, gives me a little smile and a tissue. *You look a bit better now* she writes. Then she starts biting her nails and goes as pale as a ghost.

And I can't do anything except nod my head and try

not to sniff and swallow the lump that is growing so fast in my throat, it feels like it'll choke me.

It's gonna be OK writes Holly, as tears trickle down her face.

I only know I must get back outside. So I flick my hand forward and beckon her. Then I start walking out of the shop and back to the bus stop. Holly follows. Only just in time too. Because the next tour bus is stuck behind a big white van, which has stopped at a loading bay. I step into the bus shelter, behind the massive advert and a huge tourist guy, where I take the pad off her. *That bus* I write.

The Voice (still the tinny, bad one) crackles in my ear. 'Get on the next tour bus,' it says.

Quickly I add: *they'll b watching. No more notes.* I show her. Then push the pad into her rucksack.

Holly squeezes my elbow then steps back. The bus arrives. I queue up with about four or five tourists. Holly drops to the back of the line. I show my pass. I glance behind. Holly holds up her phone to show her e-ticket. We climb up the stairs. I sit at the back of the bus. Holly sits on the seat in front. She gets out the pad. I cross my fingers, hold my breath. The Voice doesn't tell me to move. Perhaps they're not on this bus either? *How many people do they have?*

I'm beginning to think, *Not That Many.*

Or perhaps they're staying off it because they've decided to blow me up at the next bus stop. What *is* the next bus stop?

It can't be the Houses of Parliament yet?

I bite my lip. And pray to God and Dr Who.

12

Learn to Play a Strategy Game

WE PASS A BRIDGE. WE STAY ON THE SOUTH BANK. Not going to the Houses of Parliament. I break out in sweat. More time? Westminster must be on the return loop. I look around for a map of routes, but there's nothing. Everyone else seems to have one on their phones.

I lean over the seat in front, tug at Holly's jacket. Holly turns her head just enough to see me. I mouth: Map? Map?

Holly doesn't do anything obvious. She just flips over her phone and puts it where I can see. There's London with the bus route marked on her e-ticket. It's so small I can hardly figure it out though. Looks like we're going over Tower Bridge and towards Canary Wharf.

I allow myself a small sigh of relief. On a scale of ten of London terrorist targets I think the Tower of London ranks about five and Canary Wharf maybe six.

I don't think it will be them. I still may have some time.

One stop passes. London Bridge. And then we hit traffic. We slow down. No Voice – Good or Bad. Holly seems deep in thought. I hardly dare breathe. Another stop. The Globe. Nobody seems to be looking at us.

Over the back rail I watch cars. The goldish-coloured BMW is back. Holly lays out the note pad where I can see. *I'm just gonna try call Dave again* she writes. *Be back*. She picks up everything and goes downstairs. I hear her talking. I wonder if she'll just leave, just get off the bus. If she's thinking: *My God, I love Genesis to bits, but now she's turned up strapped to a bomb, and we both might end up in bits. Lol. NOT FUNNY. I so don't fancy being blown up today. I have my own life – I'm going back to it! I'm going to leave Genesis to get on with hers. Bye. Girl gone.*

I wouldn't blame her.

I catch my breath. I press my lips tight and swallow, thinking, *Don't leave me, Holly. I don't know who to trust any more.* I lift up my chin to stop the tears welling up in my eyes from rolling down my face. Up in the front of the bus a couple are smooching. They look so happy. So in love.

I thought I could trust Naz.

We were the most in-love couple any in-love couple could've been. We did everything together. We laid out rugs on grass

96

and gazed into each other's eyes. We held hands as we walked down the street. Our hearts danced high above the street lights, zooming up to the stars. When I looked at Naz, I wouldn't have changed places with anyone in the world.

I was so happy. I didn't care what happened.

I trusted you with everything, Naz. What happened? Why can't you tell me? Why don't you want to see me any more?

The bus pulls up at the next stop. St Paul's. With a sinking heart I realize Naz won't know I've changed buses. Holly comes back up the stairs. I should have had more faith in her. After all, we swore a pact when we turned thirteen. And I said, 'We are now officially teenagers and will have to face DATING!' And Holly said, 'Though Boys May Come And Boys May Go, Friends Go On Forever. Innit?'

Holly looks very troubled. She sits down beside me and gets out the pen. Spoke 2 Dave, started 2 explain, but got cut off. Called x 100 - but no luck - so left Vmail. Told him 2 join us be4 he tells anyone - just in case

I look over at the dome of St Paul's. *Please, St Paul, send Dave to us. Please let him forgive me for dumping him so cruelly. I'll do everything I can to make it up to him.* The security camera on the bus catches my eye. A small group of tourists are moving around downstairs. One

97

is wearing a hoody and two of them are women.

Instantly I'm worried. Are they on the bus to monitor me? They speak to a few passengers, as if they're asking for seats. The passengers look a little bemused.

The bus sets off, but we scarcely get a little more than two streets away before it pulls over again. An unscheduled stop near Tower Bridge. The drivers announces: 'Due to new EE regulations we're changing the driver here. We apologise for any inconvenience and will be back on route as soon as possible. The bus parked in front is leaving in five minutes if you'd rather not wait.'

The Voice says, 'What's that? What's happening?' (Evil Voice.)

'They're changing the driver,' I say. 'What shall I do?'

There's no reply.

'Some people are changing to another bus too,' I add, 'should I?'

'You talk too much,' says the Voice. 'Stay where you are.'

The driver gets off the bus. One of the tourists comes upstairs. He sits down two seats ahead, right beside a young mother with two kids. The guy leans over to her and says something, I can't hear what. I hear her reply though.

'Oh no,' she says.

Holly writes on the pad, holds it up. *Do u think he is making moves? And should we?*

I shake my head.

The man says something else to the woman and she gets up. 'I'm going,' she says. She turns to her two children. 'C'mon.' She grabs one of them. She picks up her bag, slings it across her shoulder and grabs hold of her other kid.

LIFE IS A BUS JOURNEY: PEOPLE GET ON. PEOPLE GET OFF. YOU CONTINUE TO YOUR FINAL DESTINATION.

Holly rolls her eyes at me. I'm too anxious to respond.

The Voice (Good one this time) suddenly takes me by surprise and says, all smarmy, 'You will stay on this bus until it reaches London City Airport. Where we *may* be able to *release* you!'

London City Airport! I start to panic. *They're going to get me to blow up the airport. Along with zillions of travellers.*

Holly sees the horror on my face. She raises her eyebrows. Surreptitiously passes me the note pad.

Hastily I scribble: *They're telling me 2 go 2 London City Airport. What shall I do? What if they want 2 blow it there? I gotta get off the bus.*

Holly grabs the pad, seems to take it in at a glance, writes: *Wait – we will think of sumting. Dave WILL*

99

<u>DEFINITELY</u> come. He's probably on his way RIGHT now.

But why hasn't he called back? I write.

She pulls an I-don't-know face. *Maybe not easy. Maybe on his bike? He'll get here quicker that way.* She rotates her fists up and down, like she's riding a fast motorbike.

Oh God, I wish I were riding a fast bike, doing a ton down a motorway, getting as far away as possible.

Another tourist decides to get off. The bus waits, doors open again. I lean against the side and look over the top. At least ten passengers have left the bus, maybe more. Looks like just about everyone's going for the earlier bus. I should be glad. I *am* glad. If they do detonate the bomb, ten fewer people will die. But I feel strangely alarmed too – just me and Holly left, and the man who tried to chat up that young mum.

I watch as the last straggle of tourists get on the other bus. The old driver stands by a parked van with a puzzled look on his face. Two men, dressed in grey track suits, carrying backpacks, board our bus at the last minute. Weird. Why not get on the quicker one? I suppose they might not care. I wish I could tell them what a bad choice they're making.

And I start to panic. Maybe Dave won't come. Maybe he'll

get on the wrong bus. Are we even going to stop again after Tower Bridge? What would Dave be able to do anyway? I should try to do something myself. What can I do?

One of the new tourists decides to sit on the seat farthest away from me. I'm glad of that at least. As the security camera flicks through its vistas, I see the other one has taken up a position right at the back, downstairs. Almost as if they knew. Actually, what *is* the range of a suicide bomb blast?

I should try to learn more about the vest.

I take the pad and write: *Look up explosive vests on phone – see what u can find out. Like how much explosive is in 1 – how do they detonate? How do I get it off? How fragile are they? What's their range? Anything.*

Holly gets out her phone, starts typing. The bus goes very quiet. Nobody says a word. It's terrifyingly silent, actually. I shut my eyes. *It's too silent.* I grab the pad. *Check what's going on? The news, anything?* I thrust it at Holly, and dig my nails into the palms of my hands. I try to breathe normally, but it's so unnaturally still that even my breathing seems loud.

The bus in front starts up and pulls off. At last a bit of noise. A new driver gets into ours. The cab door slams. Our engine starts up. And then it's very noisy. The engine throbs so loudly they must be able to hear it in Wales.

'They're starting the bus,' I say to the Voice. *I'm panicking – they did tell me to stay on, didn't they?*

Nothing. No reply.

The bus pulls out. We're on the road. *Try to stay calm. They did tell you to stay on.* Every second, I feel the weight of the vest against me. I feel my heart pound, my hands icy cold, my back breaking out in such sweats that the bomb must be literally sticking to me.

Imagine that. A film of sweat, a few layers of cloth, between me and certain death.

I hold my breath, cross my fingers, pray to everything I believe in. *Please, o ye Fates that govern our lives. Please let Dave come.* Although what magic I think he can work – I don't know.

13

Let Someone Know How Much He/She Means to You

THE BLUE DOT MUST BE MOVING AGAIN on their grid. Holly's face is very pale. She bites her lip. Every now and then she gives me a slight smile, and a thumbs up. I love her so much. I write on the pad. I ♥ U

She writes back: I ♥ U MORE

I make a hugging motion. A tense little smile plays across her lips. She writes: And Dave ♥s U 2.

I give her a feeble grin. I sit and grit my teeth. The bus is pretty empty now. No original passengers. Only those two new guys.

Found this on Wiki she writes and passes me her phone. Sliding it secretively across the seat.

Explosive belts can weigh between 5 to 20 kilograms.

They are loaded with shrapnel: nails, screws, nuts and thick wire. They are designed to cause the maximum amount of damage and the largest number of fatalities when they explode. An explosive belt may be concealed under outer clothing – but is often slim enough to pass unnoticed.

How much does yours weigh? she writes.

About 10K. I indicate using my fingers. I scroll on down her phone page.

The standard suicide vest extends over the chest wall and abdomen and has straps.

I go to roll on further. Holly waves her hand up and down, makes STOP signs. She swiftly leans over and snatches the phone back, but not before I read:

Decapitation is a trademark of suicide bombers wearing vests. Inescapably, the force from the blast finds the weakest link in the body and tears the vertebrae in the bomber's neck away from the jawbone. The head is nearly always blown clean off. This explains the gruesome occurrence of suicide bombers' heads, detached at the moment of explosion, being discovered completely conserved not far from their mangled corpses.

Curiously, the feet and hands often remain intact too. Although sometimes, of course, suicide bombers are completely annihilated by the explosion.

My hands shake. Holly looks mortified, flips to the next page and hands the phone back.

C-4 is a variety of plastic explosive commonly used in suicide vests. It is very stable, smells slightly like marzipan or motor oil and is not susceptible to shock. C-4 can only be detonated by heat (263°C to 290°C) accompanied by a shockwave. It remains entirely reliable when dropped, set alight or exposed to radiation.

We go a few blocks. The bus stops again. St Katherine Docks. One of the backpack men gets off and another guy gets on. The bus pulls off very smartish. There's the roar of the engine, then a pounding of footsteps on the stairs and suddenly, bounding into view, is a flush-faced young man. Good looking, in a regular-bloke sort of way. Broad shouldered. All energy and clean lines.

Holly jumps out of her seat, is about to shriek, claps a

hand over her mouth and looks at me, nodding her head.

'IT'S DAVE!' she mouths.

Dave.

Army Communications specialist. Commando Marine. Served under enemy fire. Soldier techie, Mr Go-to, Can-do, Up-for-it, Faster-than-lightning. Mr Fix-it, Save-the-world, Hard-working, Football-mad, Broken-hearted, Dumped Dave.

I hang my head. My heart pounds. I'm sure I'm blushing.

He stops short. I raise my head. He looks at me. He hides it well. No trace of any feeling. Perhaps there is none left. His eyes widen. '*Gen?*' he mouths.

I nod. Tears well up. '*I'm sorry*,' I mouth back.

I hardly recognize him. Gone is the strain in his face. Gone, that look in his eyes. Gone, the special smile he kept for me.

He's not the Dave I dumped. Boyz-cut hair. Honest face. Square jaw. Square hands. Handsome. Distant. Controlled.

Not mine.

He throws his arms out, goes to hug me. Stops. Holds back. Some memory flickers across his face. The last time we met?

His grip on my arm. The streetlight pooling round our feet. Drizzle. Damp faces. His broken words. 'Don't do it, Gen.'

And mine. 'I have to. I don't want to hurt you, but I have to.'

He looks away. He recovers. He nods – remote, professional.

Holly passes him the pad. The guy in front doesn't even turn round.

SORRY DIDN'T GET HERE SOONER. GOT A PLAN. HAVE CALLED BOMB SQUAD MATES. THEY ADVISE TAKE DOWN COVERAGE – SO NO RADIO FREQUENCY OR MOBILE CAN DETONATE. He points to the vest. THEN ALERT POLICE. WHO WILL ROLL IN THEIR TEAMS – MATES ON STANDBY TOO TO ADVISE MORE.

Oh Dave.

NEED TO LET POLICE KNOW ASAP – OR THEY'LL THINK WE R GENUINE SUICIDE BOMBERS. TRICKY – AS ALSO MUSTN'T ALERT HOSTAGE TAKERS THAT P ARE INVOLVED.

Holly nods. Her face brimming with pride. What to do? she writes.

GUYS FROM MY UNIT WILL WORK ON COVERAGE AND CALL ME. HAVE BROUGHT OWN PIECE OF KIT. CAN SCRAMBLE SIGNALS. He holds up something that looks like a large, brick-shaped mobile, then leans over as if to ruffle my hair. Stops himself. Instead writes, NEED SUM NETWORK DETAILS.

But at that moment, the Voice in my ear says – in the

107

most ultimate, most evillest of tinny tones: 'We have revised your route. When you get to the next stop, you will get off the bus.'

My heart cuts. What if they send me to a different coverage area?

Hastily I scribble it down on the pad. I show Holly and Dave.

I need to respond to the Voice, ask what happens when I get off, continue to plead, try to find out anything, any clues. So I say, 'What will I do then? What about what you said? About letting me go?'

Holly stiffens at the sound of my voice.

'You will get off and await further instructions,' says the Voice (very Bad). 'We have people watching – we are not happy.' Hastily I scan the bus. *So there are people watching? But there's only one person left?* 'If we see you communicate with anyone or if you fail to follow orders, we will detonate.'

A chill goes down my back and into my spine. My stomach squeezes itself into knots. My heart jumps about half a mile up my throat. *They're suspicious. It must be that guy. Did he see Holly and me exchanging notes? Did he see Dave communicating with me?*

I grab the pad from Holly. I write: *I can't speak to anyone. They mustn't see me with u, otherwise they'll blow.*

I'm being watched. They say they have people already watching and I must get off at next stop. I begin to panic.

I'm hyperventilating.

Dave balls his fist. With shaking hands, I continue.

Can yr mates get u the frequency info by next stop?

NOT SURE Dave writes. I sink back in the seat, heart pounding.

14

Unplug for Twenty-four Hours

I SIT AND STARE OUT OF THE BUS, willing myself to be distracted. We're going down some kind of high street. A booze store, corner shop, mobile phone place, chicken and chips. Posters of the sun: *We can get you. Anytime. Anywhere. Anyplace.* Latest movie releases: *Dead Right*, a psychological thriller that will never leave you.

Stay focused on something. Anything.

Like Naz.

When he finds out, will he intervene on my behalf? Surely he will. Although he dumped me for them. I didn't realize he was so deeply involved. I didn't know it was a choice of the Brightness or me. Why didn't I see it coming? All those hours he spent on the internet, when I thought he was doing college work.

Would I still be with him if I'd agreed to convert?

If only I could wind back time. Why does it take something like this to make you understand?

LIFE IS A LOST RELATIONSHIP: BY THE TIME YOU KNOW HOW TO FIX IT, IT'S BROKEN FOREVER.

A blast of chill air seems to whip down the bus. I shiver. I can't stop. I'm shivering and shivering.

Holly notices. She ducks low, so she won't be seen through the back, leans over and grabs my hand. She rubs it between her own. She mouths, '*Shock.*'

I don't know what to say. My teeth are chattering. Holly takes off her lovely rainbow scarf and passes it to me. I loop it around my neck. I push the cloth down, so that it doesn't chafe my poor numbed-out ear.

She rubs at my hands and smiles and smiles, as if somehow, by sheer enthusiasm, they'll warm up. '*Be OK,*' she mouths. '*Be OK. Don't worry.*'

Dave bends his head forward. He checks his cell phone. 'It *is* OK,' Dave suddenly whispers, his voice terrifyingly loud. 'We can talk. Somebody's jammed the air waves. Look, my mobile signal's down. No radio waves. They can't detonate you anymore!'

The phone reads: *No Signal.*

I freeze, terrified. *I can't believe it.* I'm too petrified to speak.

'It really has,' says Dave. He leans forward and hisses right near my ear, 'I am seriously going to mess you up for

111

doing this to Gen, you assholes.'

There's no reaction. No Voice. Bad, Evil or Worse. No muffled background sounds.

I look at him, at Holly. I can't get my head round it.

'Not going to detonate?' I whisper.

'Can't quite work out what's jamming the radio waves,' says Dave, 'but something is.' He checks on his brick-like mobile. 'It doesn't tell me why, but all bandwidths are down.'

'I can take this off?' I clutch wildly at the vest.

'Not yet,' says Dave, keeping his voice low. 'It's the Brightness who're behind this, isn't it? If so, they've probably wired it – so it'll blow if you try. That's their modus op.'

My hands fall limply back on to my lap.

'I think it's them,' I say. 'There was this guy, last night, and . . .' I look at Holly. She was the one who got me out on that date. She encouraged me. 'Let's move out of view of the back,' I finish. I don't want her to feel bad. It wasn't her fault.

I get up and walk downstairs. Position myself where nobody can see me from any car, either in front or behind. I still can hardly believe: NO COVERAGE. It might soon be over. Dave follows, then Holly.

'Can I have a peek?' Dave points at the earpiece.

112

He leans over me. Very close. Doesn't touch. I lift a lock of hair away from my ear. He bends closer. I can feel his breath on my cheek. I freeze. He draws back. A mask of politeness covers his face.

I'm blushing again. I don't know why.

'How long will the signal stay down?' I ask.

'Try not to worry,' soothes Holly. 'Maybe the police already know.' She tucks the scarf over my shoulder.

But if they know, why aren't they here?

The bus picks up speed. Faster and faster, rattling down a suddenly empty dual carriageway. But the connectivity stays off. I can talk. I can shout. I can scream.

I can sob!

Nothing moves on the road ahead. We cross a concrete flyover. Seagulls soar above. A highway roars below. A few miles and the bus loops down to the lower road. Not a car in sight.

'Thank God,' whispers Dave. 'We need to alert the police – now, while it's down. Then get to a safe place.'

'Safe?'

'In case – you know – while they're dismantling it.'

In case the bomb goes off.

I scan the cityscape, wondering if there is a safe place out there. Tall stacks downriver, dim in the heat-haze, the sun climbing up overhead. A dock with boats moored on

113

black water. *The bomb may still explode.*

Dave turns to Holly. 'You're getting off the bus, Holly.' His jaw clenches. A vein stands out on the line of his cheek.

It's not over yet.

'We can't call the police,' I say, 'there's no signal.'

'Shit!' Dave jumps up. 'We've got to get off.' He pauses. 'I'll jog to the nearest phone box. I'll speak to the driver.' He bounds down the aisle towards the driver's cab.

The last tourist left on the bus, seated on the lower deck, stares straight ahead, curiously blank.

We wait. I can see Dave banging on the driver's shield, hissing through the speak-piece.

At last he moves back towards us, looking frustrated. 'Not a very helpful driver,' he says, 'He'll only put us down at Gallion's Point. Told him we'd got a medical emergency. But he said that's the only place he can make an unscheduled stop. He could bloody well see the phones were down. Idiot.'

'Is it far?' asks Holly.

'Luckily not.' Dave wipes sweat from his face.

I glance out of the back of the bus. A few cars are following now. I note them all. The gold BMW is back again.

It really isn't over.

'There were people following the bus,' I whisper. 'And I don't think we've lost them.'

'Well,' says Dave. 'They can follow all they want, but there's F-all they can do.'

I nod.

'Where are we?' I ask.

'Soon be at Gallion's Point,' he says.

'Is it near anywhere?' I ask.

'It's an old wharf on Royal Victoria Dock. Just derelict buildings.' He leans over and peers out. 'But big enough to land a team. That's just about the only good thing in stopping there.'

'Land a team?'

'Explosive Ordnance Specialists.'

'Ordnance?'

'Helicopter bomb-disposal squad.'

'Then you must leave,' I say. 'As soon as we're off the bus, both of you, go. I'll wait for them.'

'No way,' says Holly.

'Yes, you will, Holls. Everybody off,' says Dave. 'You go home. I'll go and call the police. Gen will be OK.'

'I'm staying with Gen until the police come,' says Holly.

I smile my thanks, a tense little gesture.

'Yes,' she says, 'I'm staying. Whatever happens.'

15

Donate Blood

WE VEER SOUTH. A bend in the road, and the bus turns into the old part of Royal Victoria Dock. Rusty gates wide open. Huge exposed space. Tall, neglected buildings. Broken glass. Stone walls.

'Gallion's Point,' says Dave. 'Thank God, the driver's stopping.' He chews his lip, tense.

The gold BMW turns down a street on the near side of the dock and drives parallel to us for a while. I watch it for as long as I can. It heads towards an old mill building on the far wharf.

'What's that place?'

'Over there? Millennium Mill,' Dave says. 'Used in films. Pretty dangerous.'

I look at it. A grid of brick and stone, soaring high. Peeling cement pillars. Wiring exposed. Rotted doorframes lying on its concrete terraces.

We pull into an equally derelict wharf. The bus slows to a halt. Empty windows glower down at us. Brick and grime. Abandoned. Falling into ruin.

A plane overhead starts its descent. London City Airport must be just behind us.

'They could do a controlled explosion, right here, I s'pose,' says Dave.

The bus pulls up on the wharf, its cab just metres from the dockside.

'We get off?' ask Holly. She looks up at Dave.

He nods. She takes the lead. I rise shakily to my feet and follow her, along the aisle to the exit.

'Soon be OK,' says Holly.

The doors swing back. We look out into the morning. Sky. Sun. Dust. Deep, dark water.

The last passenger is somehow ahead of Holly and me; he jumps off the bus before the doors are fully open.

I look out. A huge space stretches around the bus. *No one at all. No tracks. No trash. No sign of life. Hang on*, I think. I know Dave asked the driver to stop, but how come we just drove in so easily? Looks like nobody else ever does. How did the driver know it'd be open today?

I scan the wide wasteland. Little electric shocks jolt across my scalp. The sun beats down. The tarmac heats up. A whirly-whirly dust devil suddenly rises. A silence

117

descends. Seconds tick like in an old Western. Tension in the air. The moment before the Shoot Out at the OK Corral. The vortex in the dust devil spins. Ghost winds. Sand augurs. Evil spirits.

I shiver as if someone has trodden on my grave.

Just get off the bus. Get to safety.

Far away on the other side of Millennium Wharf, I'm sure I see sunshine flashing on the gold car. Out the corner of my eye, I catch glinting on a rooftop.

Holly moves to jump down. Her little rucksack on her back.

I freeze. 'Wait,' I call, unable to say why. No time to understand. Something isn't right. I start forward to stop her. Dave spins even quicker. Holly jumps. I scream after her.

'*No!*'

Too late.

Flickering light from far rooftops. *I'm wearing Holly's rainbow scarf. She's wearing my hair clip.*

We're dressed the same.

Holly just stands there. She seems confused. She turns as if to get back on the bus. *She's the one without the scarf. She's the one wearing the hair clip.*

She's the one carrying the bomb.

'*Holly!*'

118

A rattle of gunfire.

Holly staggers.

Spurts of scarlet. An echoing of bullets. A jet of blood spatters the cracked cement. Blood and bone and pink. For a moment, she sways. Then she just crumples, drops, and is down. A dark pool spreading. Sunshine and the dust devil whirling on blood splatter.

Dull thuds crunch into her.

'GIVE YOURSELVES UP,' demands a sudden loudspeaker.

'HOLLY!'

A round of gunfire rips into the bus.

The driver jumps down, dashes across the apron in front of the wharf, hurls himself behind low, dark blocks.

He knows just where to go.

He's in on it.

An army van arrives from around the far side of the building, screeches to a halt.

I don't get it. Where did that come from?

What's happening?

Holly?

The police?

Why did they shoot Holly? Why didn't they wait? They're the police. They're supposed to help us.

They're going to shoot Dave and me too.

If we get off, they'll shoot.

If we stay on, they'll shoot.

They took the mobile coverage down. They brought the bus here. They cleared the area. They set up the marksmen.

They think we're all suicide bombers.

16

Be Tossed in a Pool
With Your Clothes on

THROUGH THE SHOCK and confusion, I hear: '*Hit the deck.*'

Dave.

He's on the floor of the bus, crawling towards the driver's cab.

'*Hit the deck,*' he hisses again.

'What?'

'*They're going to kill us.*' Dave reaches the cab, activates the doors. They sling shut. '*Stay down,*' he hisses.

'What happened?' I say.

Dave tries to explain. '*It's their Deadly Force policy. Fire on suspects without warning; we could all be carrying bombs. We didn't stand a chance.*'

Holly?

'Should have guessed when the coverage went down. *I should have bloody guessed.*'

'*But Holly?*'

'Holly.' His voice breaks.

Silence. Dust swirls.

'Stay down. We've got a tiny bit of time.'

A bullet zips past at the exact moment I drop to the floor.

'The surprise element's gone. They'll try to fool us, pretend to negotiate.' He seems to be thinking aloud. 'But they'll still fire on us.'

'What can we do?' I gasp.

'*Get upstairs.*'

I don't ask why. I just do it. I dive clear of the windows, and crawl along the floor. The police sirens scream out. The dust devil swirls. So much dust. Can't see. Gunshot echoes from brick and glass. Windows rattle. Air blasts. More gunfire. More dust devils. I get a hazy flashback to the cellar. Abrupt vertigo.

They've just shot Holly.

I look round for a support. I grab at seats. The bottom of a handrail. I crouch low. A line of bullets rattles along the side of the bus. I swing into the stairwell. My pulse shaky. My heart hammering. I glance through the window, see Holly lying there. My legs buckle. I don't know what to do.

HOLLY.

The door flaps crumple under a new barrage of gunfire.

'*GET ON THE TOP DECK.*'

The bus lurches.

'*MOVE – MOVE!*'

Dave?

'*FOR CHRIST'S SAKE GET TO THE TOP.*'

Dave's in the driver's seat. The bus is moving. I can hear the engine. We're getting away? Where to? I fumble. I try to hurry. My feet are clumsy. I grab the stair rail. *Holly?* Swing, bash my elbow. Drag myself up the stairs. I can do it. The bus sways wildly. Hits a pothole. Bumps. Jolts over something.

Dave's driving the bus. We're heading for the dock.

I start screaming. I make the top deck. Open air.

We're heading for the fricking dock.

We jerk away from Holly, away from the army jeep, the police marksmen. A siren splits the air. A low wall blocks the way ahead. I hang on to the bus rail. Duck. A burst of many sirens. More gunfire. A new rattle of holes down the side of the bus.

Holy shit.

A scream, a crash of metal tearing through stone.

The police are shooting.

Keep your head down.

Jesus. Dave is driving the bus straight at the wharf. He's going to drive us into the water.

I don't look up. I don't look down.

Water on the vest. How does that work?

The dock is right there. Black water. Dark. Deadly. The bus hits the edge of the brickwork. Tips. Lurches. My arms flail. I hold the side rail.

Hold the bloody side rail.

I plunge forward. I grip the chrome bar. *Bullets.*

Off the wharf.

This is how it ends. *Please, don't let it end like this.* My eyes fill with sudden hot tears. I'm screaming. The noise. Nobody can hear me.

Just the lonely sky . . .

And the jolting bus . . .

And the bullets whispering past my cheek . . .

We plough through the brickwork of the wharf. Sharp pieces of stone. A bullet ricochets, hits the front window, smashes something with a terrible, flattening, clattering sound.

And as if in slow motion, we tip.

I look back, just a glimpse. People run. Cars screech. A shape lies on the concrete in a strange, awkward, crumpled heap.

In the confusion I turn and see the water of the Thames rushing up towards me. The sky above.

I spin back.

We're toppling on the edge of the dock.

I can't hold my balance.

I'm falling.

Falling off the edge, off the quay, into the dock. I kick out. I paddle the air. I scream.

And the bus takes me down.

My scream hangs in the air. The water below me.

Deep water.

And I can't swim.

17

Experience Zero Gravity

AN IMPACT WAVE SWEEPS OUT. Crashes. Metal on water. I'm flung forward. Off the top of the bus.

Falling.

And I can't stop.

I hit the water so hard I scream out before the air is cut off.

And I'm tangled up in my scarf, thrashing my arms, kicking.

Holly's scarf.

And the vest is heavy. It drags me down.

I flail my arms, force my legs to kick. I'm held by the drag of water. The pull of the sinking bus. *I must breathe.* Relentlessly the water tows me under.

And I'm going down.

Down into the deep waters of the dock.

And I can't swim.

And I open my mouth. And I can't breathe.

I can't breathe.

And I think of Holly and how I will see her soon and of Naz who I will never see again. And I think of when we read Romeo and Juliet *and Naz called me his Juliet and told me he would scale a mountain, let alone a balcony . . .*

And I'm all tangled up in a scarf and a bus and the water is dark.

. . . and he pushed me in the river and said if Romeo and Juliet could fall in a pool we could fall in a river . . .

I'm in a river now and I can't swim. I open my mouth to scream and there's only water.

And they've killed Holly.

And I'm sinking.

And our love was better than the film and . . .

. . . and he loved me so violently he said it felt like all his atoms were shattered into the universe where they were forever orbiting the earth, shouting out my name . . .

And my atoms may be shattered, but I won't be shouting anything.

And I'm thinking – so this is what drowning is like.

And there's a part of me looking on and shaking its head. Wondering what happens when you drown in an explosive vest.

And if I ever get out of all this, I'm never going to complain about life being dull or the wrong kind of butter.

18

Learn How to Hold My Breath for Four Minutes

'TAKE A BREATH AND TRUST ME,' says a voice. Dave yanks my chin round. I claw at his hand. My chest burns. My throat closes. Something is building up in my lungs and I can't fight it.

I gasp, swallow water.

Air.

I can breathe!

Then Dave drags me under. I try to tear at his hand. But my arms are pinned to my sides. I'm being pulled down. I try to kick out and grab at whatever is drowning me. But it breaks my hold with one firm twist.

I kick and I scratch and I want to scream.

But no air.

No throat.

No chest.

No light.

Dave drags me kicking through the deep. I try to open my eyes, blink out the dark. But it's behind my eyes. And it's swallowing me.

A blow lands on my head.

This is it.

The black has turned deep green.

I feel dizzy.

And then my face is slapped. I open my eyes and I can see. Everywhere faintly green.

I'm above water.

I open my throat to breathe, but I can't. I'm choking in air.

'Take another deep breath.' Dave cups his hand under my chin, pinches my nose, presses his lips to mine and blows. Like a gale blowing through my throat, like a balloon suddenly stretched, my upper body rips open.

A lungful of air. My chest is on fire.

And then I'm dragged under again.

19

Have an Out-of-body Experience

And everywhere is faintly green.

And suddenly I can open my eyes and I am back in the cavern, and I'm below the surface of the ancient subterranean lake. And one of the Moirai floats towards me, dressed in gauze, her light playing in the green depths of the water.

And her face is as pale as bleached bones. And she says:

All hail, Genesis.
We are the Moirai. We the three.
We spin the thread.
We water the tree.
Your birth. Your life. Your death to be.
We are the Moirai.

We the three.
Life and death and destiny.

But she is not the same phantom as before.
And she says:

I am Lachesis, second of the wayward three.
I have measured the thread of your life, you see.
And the second truth you seek is: None Are Free.

She tosses back her hair and it streams away from her pale face like dark seaweed.

And around her throat is a necklace. Each bead glistens like opal stones, like pearls: translucent, iridescent, as if deep inside each a rainbow has been forever caught.

She bends her head; the necklace slips off. She loops it over my head and around my throat.

And I try to understand. None are free?

And I say, 'Then I shall be a firmament in the midst of the waters.' Though I don't even know what a firmament is.

And the lights around her fade.

20

Make Mistakes

I feel a pull around my neck, a swimmy kind of panic, and I clutch the necklace.

But it's not the necklace; it's Holly's tie-dye scarf and I hold on and it's dragging me up.

Something jerks my neck, forces my face upward. I try to wrench free. But I'm so weak. I smash out. I don't want to drown. Something crushes my fingers with one brutal jerk.

And suddenly we're breaking surface.

'Breathe again and this time *don't fight me*,' says a voice.

But it's not the Voice.

It's still Dave.

I barely have time to gulp at air, before Dave tightens his arm around my throat and tows me under yet again.

Dark water. Into the depths, all noise cut off. My lungs

132

stretched, breaking. My throat, my sinuses scorching. Dave pulling me ever down. I open my mouth. Only water.

Choking.

Swallowing.

I must stop him. Fight him off.

He's drowning me.

THE PURPOSE OF LIFE IS TO GIVE LIFE PURPOSE

MIDDAY
THE DEATH LIST

(Twenty Ways To
Become An Extremist)

1

Believe in Personal Victimization and Get Even

(Revenge for real or perceived harm.)

WHEN WE SURFACE AGAIN, we're under the brickwork of the wharf. I glance up. See sky. The huge Millennium Mill with its chequerboard of windows. Dave grabs hold of the coping stones on the edge of the quay and hoists himself up. He drags me towards him, out of the dock. The rough concrete grazes my arm. Stinging skin. I splutter. Jerk forward. Gasp. My whole front heaves.

I'm choking. *And it hurts.* I can't breathe. I swallow air.

'Sorry,' says Dave. 'Just breathe.'

I want to say: *'Can't.'* But there's not enough breath. And it's so *painful.* So instead I thrash the air with my hand. My elbow burns. Tears spring to my eyes. I cough and wheeze and gag.

'Breathe,' says Dave again. He drags me further on to the concrete frontage, bends down, tilts my head back, pinches my nose, presses his mouth against mine and my chest tears open with a fresh hurricane of air.

And I breathe. At last. I open my lungs and despite the tightness and the pain, I breathe and cough and splutter.

And retch water.

I look up at the huge sky. A plant hangs over me, a few leaves growing on its scraggy stem. I look at the clouds. *Holly*. It's going to rain.

They just shot Holly. I just saw her brain explode. Blood and bone and pink.

I just saw it and now I can't think. I can't think about anything, except that it's going to rain. I can't think about the blood and the pink. Not now. Not Holly.

Dave gets both hands under my armpits and lifts me up. I flake against him, try to stand. His body so familiar, so alien. I don't know how to think about it. I will stand. He's panting. His whole front is heaving like he's done an Olympic dash. His face is crimson red. Beads of water roll down his neck.

I look out across the water. And suddenly I'm shaking.

Holly?

'Recover,' he says. '*Quickly.*'

Overhead, dark clouds seem to condense. Inside their darkness I read the truth. *You'll never escape. You'll explode into bone and blood and pink and your head will rip free from your jaw and roll on to the tarmac and they'll kill Dave and you'll all die.*

And it's true. There's no escape. I'm strapped to this bomb and the only people who could've helped me are going to shoot me down.

My chest starts heaving. I start hyperventilating. I can't think. I can't think. And I can't stop – until Dave slaps me hard across the cheek.

'It's shock – hysteria. Don't let it take you down. Get a grip.' He slaps me again, gentler this time. And suddenly I can stop. And I do stop.

'Right. We've swum – across the dock, round the corner – and we need to get to those pillars.' Dave points to the great monoliths holding up the old dock building.

I gasp, suck in air and wince as pain shoots down my side. Some huge gigantic stitch stabs under my ribs.

Holly is still over there.

I slap my own cheek harder than Dave did. Not Going There. Then I struggle to balance. Dave lets go of me and sprints across the open frontage of the wharf. I try to follow. *Get to the cover of the old mill building.* I squelch forward. *Don't give in.* The vest drips and is heavier than ever. *How stable can this explosive stuff be? What does dirty dock water do to it? Won't it short-circuit the wiring? Oh God, please don't let me explode.* I threaten to slap myself again. Force myself to breathe.

Keep going. I stumble on the hardcore underfoot. Weathering has broken it all up. *There's no chance she survived, is there?* Great cement slabs rise. Weedy bushes struggle through the cracks. *It can't be right. They can't have killed Holly.* My shoes squish. I suck in air. I stagger after Dave.

It'll be all right, I tell myself, like we're still in some kind of Dr Who time warp. But nothing is OK. Nothing will ever be all right again. I've just seen Holly's head erupt. I've seen her skull shatter. I've seen her brains in blobbish gluey pink lumps. And the police want to shoot me down too.

At last I make it. I lurch in under the cover of the old mill. Dave just saw me losing it out there. But it doesn't matter. Nothing matters. Just staying alive. It's only cos he's a soldier that he can hold his shit together. I can see from the way his hands are shaking. He's in a bad way. Maybe he's losing it inside. So I don't say anything. What is there to say?

We hide behind the piers, under the lower section.

140

We don't look at each other. I don't think we can. If either one of us speaks, we'll probably both crack. So much unspoken stuff. Now this. So we just dart from column to column, zigzag a path under the length of the arcade. Underfoot broken glass, twisted metal. Crumbling lumps of flooring heaved up, as if by some giant's tread. Plants ragged, sinuous, straggling everywhere.

An L-shaped spur pushes out from the main drag at a ninety-degree angle. It cuts across what must have been an unloading area. It gives us cover. In its shade we creep out. Like ringwraiths. Just shadows ourselves. All empty inside.

Here the bushes have grown up almost to the first-floor windows. We squeeze through the scrub. At the farthest corner the shade stops. The plants have shrivelled. If we step out here, we'll be in open view. Round the corner, the building fronts on to the dock. From there it's a sheer drop into the water.

We peek out. There's a lot of dust. Police sirens. The sound of a crane wheeling its great arm around. Traffic, far away. Police congregating on the far side of the dock.

I stop, catch my breath. It hits me.

Holly's dead.

Good, kind, sweet Holly.

I glance at Dave. Not sure I can meet his eyes yet. His

shoulders sag. Everything about him looks broken. If I can't bear it, how can he? I look away, unable to reach out to him.

Across the dock there's a sudden burst of activity. So many police. Were they planning to take us out all along? That change of driver? The bus evacuated? Those new tourists? *How did we miss that?* And it's my fault. It's my fault Holly's dead. If I'd never walked into her salon. If I'd left her alone, stayed away. Somehow I can't take it in.

Dave grabs my hand. We double back round the side of the L and retrace our steps along three or four of the columns. It starts raining. We duck behind the awnings of some scaffolding. Blue netting down to the ground. Raindrops the size of diamonds.

We leave the dock and the water behind. We leave where the bus went in, where the police are standing. We leave the small crumpled shape on that wasteland of dust devils. And I don't know what to think. I don't know what to feel.

We skirt back round the other side of the building. The mill towers up. At least eight storeys high. It must cover hundreds of square metres, must once have been mega, full of workers and industry. And we keep going. Stay hidden. Stay alive. Dave and me again. Just the two of us. How weird.

They don't realize we're here, on the other side of this marina. Behind us wire fencing stretches back to other buildings, other mills, maybe other docklands, other wharfs. Perhaps storage areas? I wonder if it might be a good idea to hide out there. I catch up with Dave and pant out, 'Let's hide.' Frantically, I point at the ruined wharfs.

'Don't be daft,' says Dave. He's gone into some kind of auto-pilot mode. Horribly calm. Horribly logical. Horribly distant. 'We need to find a way out.'

Above us something faintly whirs. The noise of whining air seems to come at us from far away. I glance up. Through the driving rain and the grey I see it. A helicopter.

Dave sees it too. 'Shit. Thermal imaging cameras. If they get in range, they'll find us.' He ducks back under the concrete awnings, pulls me in after him. 'Just pray they'll focus on the bus. Follow me. Keep to whatever shelter you can. The police over there can still spot us.'

Dave breaks into a zigzag run. Every move calculated. He darts out from under the pillars, across an open square – from one pile of rubble, one clump of straggling willow herb, to another. Sticks to whatever cover he can. The pink blossoms of the willow herb hardly quiver as he passes. I hope I can do it with the same precision.

The helicopter sways in like some gigantic bluebottle. Dave halts. He motions with his hand. Don't come yet.

When it's time for me to move, he drops his palm face down – from clump to clump of undergrowth. Dive down. Behind that rubble. Up. Stop. Run.

And after the last stretch, he catches me in his arms. Just for a nano-second our eyes meet. Vast deserts seem to stretch between us. And then we both skid for shelter.

We get to a perimeter wall, about two metres high. In the blink of an eye, Dave scales it and sits on top. He holds a hand down and hauls me up. I look back. Everywhere's grey. The rain pelts down, soaking us all over again. I can't see it, but the helicopter must be in range now – the sound is deafening. We throw ourselves down on the other side of the wall. Leave the dockland behind us. We crouch behind a parked car on a residential street.

The clouds thin. The helicopter hovers; starts to circle, swoops in low. 'Stand up,' I hiss. 'Look normal.' I've seen those helicopter chases on TV. If they suspect anything, if you run or move dodgy, they'll be on it in a minute.

There's a woman walking a dog and getting wet. A couple arguing in a car. Someone on a balcony, under an umbrella, watching the dock. A delivery van drives past. Someone else collects in washing. I link arms with Dave and we speed walk without a clue where we're going.

The rain eases off. The sound of the propellers

hammers into my poor throbbing ear. The helicopter lurches and circles. Keep walking. Look normal. They'll be scanning everyone.

We keep going. Up ahead is some kind of monument, like an old factory chimney. The helicopter sweeps back – and away – over the dock and the wasteland and back towards the sunken London tour bus.

It hovers low over the water.

Hovers over a small, slumped figure.

2

Get Used to Violence

(Lower those inhibitions and lessen those incentives to avoid brutality.)

WE STOP by a roundabout at the top of the street. In the middle of it is the tall, Victorian brick, chimney thing. The last vestige of some long forgotten factory. We dive behind it into a patch of shrubbery. There's a small memorial seat. It's all wet, but we're soaked anyway, so we sink down, catching huge breaths of air, still coughing. Well I am, anyway.

'Good. Now listen.' Dave thumps my back.

I sit there coughing and spitting. My throat raw. My ear numb. My eyes watering. I try to focus.

'Get your breath,' says Dave, 'and get your senses. I can't run with anyone who's not thinking.'

'But I am thinking,' I splutter.

'Yeah, I know.' He's angry. But not with me. Though perhaps it'd be better if he was.

'You can, though,' I gasp out. I point at the vest. 'Go, I mean.' No need for him to die too.

Not like Holly.

We look at each other. We can't say her name. But at least now we can meet each other's eyes. His hand closes over my wrist. His anger helps. It shocks me back to myself. I remember him gripping my wrist like that on that other rainy day, when he confronted me in Streatham. I remember his words: '*I don't understand, Gen. Make me understand.*'

I don't think I can ever make him understand. So I just repeat, 'You can go.'

'You don't get it,' he says. 'I'm a fugitive too.' He smacks his other hand down on the iron hand-rest of the seat. 'They'll have run background checks on us. They'll see my army training. They'll think I've got a weapon. They'll take me out like a shot.'

He's hurting my arm.

'If we're going to stay alive, we've got to work together.' His grip tightens.

Work together. Stay together. After all the heartbreak between us.

Dimly, at the back of my mind, I hear the words of the

phantom from my dream. *'None are free.'* I nod my head. Swallow. He's a fugitive too. OK.

'I never ever thought the police would do that,' I say.

'Text book,' mutters Dave. 'Somebody alerted them. They think we've got a bomb, maybe three bombs. They got us away from crowded areas, took connectivity down, took no chances.'

All the blood drains from my heart. *That Japanese kid.* Her mum must have called the police.

'We should have done something, let them know you were a hostage.' Dave wipes sweat from his forehead and turns to me, his eyes full of pain. 'How will I ever forgive myself, Gen?'

'I told a kid to call the police . . .' I can't finish. *She had a photo. She knew the bus. Why didn't I suspect? That unscheduled stop. That change of driver. Those different tourists.* 'It's all my fault,' I whisper.

'It's not,' he says. 'You didn't glue yourself into that vest.'

'What do we do now?' I say.

'Find those terrorist bastards and kill them.'

'I mean, right now?'

'Treat the police like the enemy,' he says. 'They won't stop till they find us.'

'We can't outrun them *and* the Brightness,' I say.

'They'll simply take us out.' Dave stands up, paces the short path through the bushes, seems to be trying to recall some distant training procedure. *'Respond to imminent danger first. Remove yourself from the line of fire, next.'* He carries on pacing, repeating himself. *'Police and the firearms units are the immediate danger.'* He paces and paces. *'Locate weapons, contain situation, squeeze them out, take control.'*

I want to say: 'But surely, if we explain . . . ?' My voice trails off. I'm so naïve. We've covered that. Nobody's going to listen.

'I'm so sorry, Dave,' I say.

He stops pacing. Comes near. The lines across his face seem to have welded together. He bends down, grabs hold of my wrist squeezes it again. 'Don't give up. We've come this far; we've survived.'

'Holly didn't,' I say. There, I've said it. The unspeakable. My voice breaks. *'And I'm so sorry.'*

His grip tightens.

'I feel so guilty,' I say. 'It was my fault.'

'Don't,' he says.

'If I hadn't gone to her salon, if I'd refused to let her come with me . . . ?' I stop. I can't speak. I don't know how to tell him how sorry I am.

'Oh God,' he says. And suddenly he's hugging me. He's burying his face in my shoulder and he's tightening his

grip and shaking. I put my arms round him. Hold him. I have to. I want to. I try to say 'Sorry' again and again, but my throat's so dry and he's holding me so hard. I touch his head, touch his hair.

And I am so sorry.

And we stay like that, clasped together, unable to speak.

Until at last I say: 'The bomb is pressing into my stomach.'

Dave lets go. 'Hell.' His voice all hoarse. 'Forgot.' His eyes flicker away. He draws back, gains control.

And we sit there not looking at each other, saying nothing.

'We'll get this thing off you, Gen. We'll nail the bastards who put it there,' he says.

I nod. They have to pay for Holly, for that girl from Inverness. For every girl they've tormented. The whole lot of them. Every Brightness cell in the world.

'Right,' says Dave, 'we've got to get out of here fast.' He takes off his jacket, checks the pockets, wrings it out. Squeezes out the hems of his jeans. 'They'll search all these areas when they can't find us in the bus.' He looks at me. His eyes, huge and hazel-grey. A darkness in them. And he's that familiar stranger again. I put my hand on his.

'And we need a car,' says Dave.

OK, a car.

'Like "borrow" one?' I say.

'If you mean shanghai it like in *Grand Theft Auto* . . .' Dave shakes his head. 'It doesn't seem fair to drag some mum out of her hatchback and into this, and it's too risky. If we let her go she'll report us.'

But the idea of hijacking a car sticks. 'I know where we can get a car,' I say. 'And it won't be from a local mum.'

He pulls a frown.

'I can't wire one,' he says. 'No tools.'

'Better than that,' I say. 'A car that won't get reported.'

'We can't hire one. There'll be road blocks on every route into here by now. No minicab will get through.'

'We'll shanghai that gold car that's been following us.'

Holy shit. What am I saying? I must be mad.

I point down the street. 'I watched them every inch of the way. They turned up here. If there're road blocks everywhere else, they'll still be here. Watching everything from a safe distance.'

Dave seems to mull that over. 'They won't like that,' he says. A spark seems to wake in his eyes.

'And they won't go running to the police, either,' I add.

'And they won't expect it.' Dave balls his fist.

I look at him. He looks at me. 'You're pretty much a

genius, Gen,' he says. He cuts off what he's about to say next, straightens his shoulders, looks away.

'So you'll run with me?'

Dave nods. 'Yep, run with you till the end.' He smacks his fist down on the memorial seat like that's some kind of promise, puts on something that is supposed to pass as a smile. 'Right, let's see how much *they* like sitting next to a bomb.'

3

Identify With Group Grievances

(Perceive harm being inflicted on the group you belong to.)

'RIGHT,' says Dave. He looks back at the wharf. 'See if you can spot the car.'

I brush off the water trickling down my forehead, and peer up the street. The rain has stopped. The sun is out again and making up for it. The tarmac steams. Such weird, changeable weather.

'Sure you can make out the right one?'

I'm sure as hell. That gold car is photocopied into every brain cell I have.

I sneak a look out from behind the old factory chimney thing and concentrate. I shade my eyes against the sun. Down the dockland side of the road, there're breaks in the walling. I scope through them, search the whole quayside from where we fetched up, to the point Dave drove the bus into the dock. I squint into the sunshine. Police cars all over the frontage. Some other vans too. Above the drowned bus a helicopter is still circling.

I look back up the two streets heading off from the roundabout.

Nothing.

'Are there residential areas on the other side of the dock?' I ask. 'Where we came in?'

'You mean over by Silvertown? I guess so.'

'Could they have driven over there after the bus went in?'

Dave thinks about it. Shakes his head. 'They'll have blocked the entire North Woolwich Road,' he says. 'This whole area would have been cordoned off in minutes.'

'So they can't go anywhere, until traffic starts moving again?'

'Not without going through a road check.'

'And around here's the best place to get a view?'

Dave thinks about it. 'Nearest they'll get,' he says.

'Let's try down there then.' I point down one of the two streets – Rayleigh Road.

We set off. The vest rubs damp around my ribs, reminds me that even if we can get out of the area, we'll just get back into mobile coverage again. Swap one form of Certain Death for another. I shiver. What happens then? I don't mean After Death. I mean After Rayleigh Road. That phantom was right. No one is ever free. Just stick to the plan, I guess. Army style. Respond to imminent danger first. Keep watch. Keep going.

Across the road are new builds; cute residential rows with circular dormer windows. High glass elevations, black ironwork, white-walled gardens, little balconies with glassed-in sides, bistro tables and chairs. Buzz-in entry systems with smart engraved names. Like *46 RAYLEIGH ROAD: Flats G–L: Mikki Faraz, Tony Bence, Joshua Pickering*. Dave points at them, seems to be wondering if it's worth trying to ask for help, decides against it. They'd *definitely* call the police.

Lovely gated communities. Lovely young couples.

Little safety for us.

The other side of the road is even worse. Boarded up walls and beyond them wasteland, leading back on to the wharfs. Scrub, and nothing else. That gold car is here somewhere though. Must be. This is the only place you can watch the dock from.

'I get it,' says Dave. 'They're going to wait until the police restore coverage. Then they'll know exactly where you are.'

My heart races. When the police restore coverage that

part of the nightmare begins again. 'Then we must find them first,' I say.

'Yep, they won't want to blow themselves up,' snorts Dave.

'But they're terrorists. Won't they think of it as martyrdom?' I ask. 'Will they care if we threaten them?'

'Martyrdom is a serious choice. Takes months, sometimes years to get to that point, Gen. Even though the Brightness may call for the Ultimate Sacrifice, it's only very few who embrace it. The driver of that car will definitely care. He didn't volunteer to carry the vest, did he?'

A woman with a pull-along shopper walks past us. She looks up at the tall chimney and then at us. She shakes her head.

'And they won't want to be discovered either,' I say. I remember someone saying that. One of Naz's Brightness friends. Some idiot who thought extremism was well cool. '*Hardest part of any mission*,' he'd said, '*getting it done and getting away with it.*' Like duh.

An exploded car would not only mean a failed mission, but it'd lead straight back to them.

'Any point in trying the side streets?' asks Dave.

'We could check while we're at this end,' I say.

We scoot up the first turning, down a crescent boxed

in with new builds. Apart from kids racing down a pavement on bikes, nothing. There's no viewing anything from here, anyway. Not unless you're on a fourth-floor balcony.

'Let's go back to Rayleigh Road and keep going down there,' I say. I watched that gold car drive all the way down that street. It's gotta be there somewhere.

We retrace our steps and start combing the road down from the brick chimney. Car after car. But at last I see them.

At least, I think it's them.

A gold saloon, parked up bang opposite an opening in the boarded-up wall. Scrub poking through. Sycamore. Brambles. Metal railings. Next to one of those yellow signs lining the dockland boundary: *ENTERPRISE WARNING. PROPERTY PROTECTED.*

It's them OK.

'There,' I say.

Dave ducks behind a parked van, pulls me down. 'The watchers are being watched,' he whispers. Then he bends over me. 'Bloody genius,' he repeats. And for a minute I think he's going to hug me again, or say something, maybe acknowledge that desert between us, but he stops short, checks himself. 'Are you sure you wanna do this?' he says.

'What choice have we got?' I say. 'We can't walk out of this place – like walk past a police cordon – in this.' I tug at the front of the vest. 'There's no Tube for miles. The buses won't be moving. We can't call anyone. You can't do anything about jamming airwaves until they actually go up – and your mates send you data. If we wait until the coverage is back on, they'll either blow us, or come looking for us. Unless the police locate us first.' I glance up at the helicopter. 'Great. Right now we're at everyone's mercy. Let's do something while we still have the advantage.'

The sun goes behind another cloud. A gust of wind stirs the leaves through the railings opposite. Drops of rain patter off them.

'You wait here then,' says Dave.

'No,' I say. 'I'm going with you.' I point at the car.

'No,' he says. 'You wait here – where the connectivity is down and the vest can't be detonated. I'll shanghai the car. And if it's safe, I'll call you over.'

My palms go all sweaty. My ear hurts. I've skinned both elbows and, yes, I'm safe. But I shake my head. 'Thanks for being chivalrous and all that,' I say, 'but no thanks. I've got the power right now and I'm going to use it.'

'The power?'

158

'I'm the only one who's in control of the detonation right now,' I say.

'I don't follow?' he says.

'Locate weapons, contain situation, take control. That's what you said just now, back there.'

'O-K.'

'I'm the weapon,' I say, 'and once I've made up my mind, I can use it.'

He looks at me and blinks.

'Use it on them,' I say.

'But that would mean using it on you too?'

I just look at him. 'And you,' I add. I don't say it like I don't care. Just plain matter of fact. Like death is a necessary part of life. Like no one is free. Because that's where we've got to, isn't it? That's what we've decided on. And I don't even shudder. It's like there's even a learning curve to wearing an explosive vest. I'm getting used to the unthinkable. Getting used to the new appalling powers it gives me.

He takes a moment. 'You're right,' he says. 'We're going to walk over to that gold car and get in it.'

'Exactly.'

'And if they don't like it, we'll blow them up.'

'You've got to mean it,' I say.

'And you,' he says.

What other option is there? There's no way I can get out of this vest, unless I turn the tide. And there's no way to turn the tide, unless I take charge.

And because of them Holly's dead.

Holly, who trusted everyone.

And Dave has said he'll run with me till the end. And I'm glad about that, though I can never make him understand what happened to us. *I* don't understand. It wasn't just Naz I ran to. I ran away from him.

There was something so final about the way Dave loved me.

So that's it.

'Yes,' I say. 'We'll get in their shitty gold car, and if they don't do what we say, we'll blow them up.' And I think of them, driving like cowards behind the bus. And I think of Dave and Holly, so brave.

I look at Dave and nod. His chin is firm and square. His eyes are steady. I shiver. There's something totally pitiless in them.

'Let's do it then,' he says.

'Yeah,' I say. 'Let's go and blow the bastards up.'

4

Slide Down the Slippery Slope

(Be gradually radicalized through activities that
slowly narrow your social circle and mind-set.)

'RIGHT,' says Dave.

I glance across at him. So calm, so remote. I remember
the days, down by the park. How tough he always was
on kids who tried to push Holly and me around.
I remember the days when it was just me and him. How
safe I felt. A sudden pang catches my throat. A swift
rush of some half-forgotten longing. Things gone forever.
I blink them away.

'Yeah,' I say. 'Let them sit next to me, and see how *they*
like it.'

'Sure it's our man? Car details?'

'Gold BMW,' I say. I dig into my memory through
those awful miles. 'Customized number plate: EC21 PSE.'

'Impressive,' says Dave. 'Right. Wait here. They don't know me, so I'm going to scout – double-check everything.'

'I'm not staying here,' I say. 'Let's go there.' I point to the lane beside the gated community where a delivery van is parked.

He checks the path. 'Good. OK.' The sun breaks through again. 'But if I say jump, please jump. If I say hit the deck, go down.'

'Let's get going,' is all I say. Then I'm on my feet. And we're off, sliding like shadows down the walkway.

It's the car all right, parked outside the last new build. There's one man inside. He's got his driver's window wound down, his head half poked out. He's holding field glasses, and through a gap in the fencing, he's watching the far wharf. He's picked a good spot too. From there he can see it all. He's oblivious to everything except the drama unfolding across the dock: the divers, the police launch circling, the helicopter hovering.

'Stay here?' Dave points to some scaffolding, where a boarded area shelters the end of one of the building developments. 'Just to please me?'

I shake my head.

He shakes his head too. 'Please?' But I stare him down. We're in this together.

'OK. Then when I say, you jump in the back.'

'Better,' I say.

'Right, as you jump in, grab the driver by his hair, pull his head back and tell him that if he moves a muscle you're going to rip your vest open and blow his entire crap to hell.'

'No problem,' I say. And strangely, I'm not even frightened – although I haven't got a clue how to rip the vest open, or even if it's possible. It seems glued up tight everywhere. 'If I knew how to, I'd put him in a headlock too,' I add, filled with a sudden ridiculous bravado.

'Right. A choke hold,' says Dave. 'Lock your arm around his neck and get your two fingers under his windpipe, like this.' Dave suddenly grabs me and before I can do a thing, I'm on the pavement. 'Then, if he struggles, pull up.' I feel the pressure on my throat, feel the air cut off.

Dave releases me.

'OK,' I gasp, 'I'll try.'

'Just kidding,' says Dave. 'Don't even bother trying – grab his hair and threaten him. Let me in on some of the action, too, eh? I'm going for his arms, in case he's armed,' (Dave doesn't even raise an eyebrow) 'as soon as you've got his head?'

He holds up his hand. 'On the signal then. When I let you know.'

'Yup,' I say.

I glide forward, dart down the pathway, crouch behind the boot of the gold car. My heart thrashes about at the base of my throat. *What if we bungle it? What if he's got a gun?* My legs feel like jelly. I forget to breathe.

Dave moves in. With every step, his training shows. Like a great cat he pads his way into the street and down to where the car's parked. In full view of the driver he approaches, nonchalant. Just another rubber-necking pedestrian, trying to get a better look at whatever's going on.

He leans over the driver's window. The man looks up at him.

'What's going on over there?' shouts Dave, as if he's a simpleton. 'Did they kill someone?'

The driver flaps his hand. Like: *go away*. He tries to pull his head in, roll up the glass. Dave doesn't take any notice. He sticks his right elbow into the closing pane, leans on it and bashes on the window again with his left. He faces the driver. 'Hey mate, what happened?'

The man winds the window down a bit and tries to push Dave's elbow out. But as he does so Dave, in one super-fast movement, reaches forward and opens the back door with his left hand. Then he shoots his right arm straight through the open window and grabs the

164

driver by the neck, pinning him back.

The driver half screams. Dave flicks the back door fully open and jerks his head.

And that's my sign.

I race out from behind the boot of the car and jump in. I grab the driver by his shock of yellow hair. Dave doesn't loosen his hold one bit. I try to get my arm around the driver's neck, get a bit more of a grip, not really a headlock, but something like that.

And then it all unravels. As quick as a flash, the man twists his torso. I try to wrench harder on his hair. He half swivels round and punches me in the face.

Crunch.

My nose.

I let go.

I taste blood.

It was the first sort-of headlock I've ever done. And I failed. And that makes me sooo mad.

After everything I've been through. I get a rush. *I am The Bomb.* Nobody punches The Bomb in the face.

'Right,' I scream, jerking his head back again and again, until I hear the hair tear. 'If you move a muscle, I'll rip this vest open. I'll blow you to fricking kingdom come.'

And I bloody mean it.

5

Embrace All Rules

(Advertise outwardly-visible compliance in
dress, diet, language and social interactions.)

THE DRIVER OF THE CAR doesn't know what to do.
He makes as if he's going to scream, but he checks himself.
I drag his hair right back and tug at it. Violent. Angry.

'I think you heard her,' says Dave, coldly. 'So listen up.
You lot just got the police shooting at us, so right now we
don't give a shit. One wrong move from you – if she don't
rip her vest open, I will.'

There's a note in Dave's voice he'd be mad to ignore.

The driver hears it. He nods, croaks out, 'OK, mate.
Easy. You've got the wrong car.'

'Wrong answer,' says Dave.

In one smooth motion Dave bunches his right arm,
balls a fist, punches it in through the gap in the window

and knuckles the man in the side of his head. The guy lets out a funny, choked scream. His head snaps sideways. I feel the tug. He sags a little. Dazed.

Dave retains his hold, tight on the driver's throat. I give another demonic yank. The guy's head comes back up. He reaches round, tries to smash out at me. Dave punches him in the side of his head. *Again.*

This time the guy sags properly in my grip.

Dave pulls his left arm back out of the window, and in a split second opens the driver's door. He jerks the man forward, slaps his hand on the man's chest. Very quickly, very professionally, he frisks him. From under his belt in the small of his back, Dave finds the gun.

'Right,' says Dave, 'asshole.'

The driver twists up his head. A look of fury.

Dave hisses back at him, 'Don't even breathe.' His saliva sprays the man's face. Quickly Dave checks the gun, then presses it into the guy's neck. 'Wrong car, eh? Move over.'

The driver slides across to the passenger side. I ease up my hold on his hair, but not much. Dave gets in behind the wheel.

My heart's pounding so hard, I think it's going to detonate the bomb all by itself. I glance up the street. Nobody seems to have actually noticed our little 'shanghai'.

The tarmac still steams. The leaves still drip. Across the dock, blue lights still flicker, police cars still wait.

I lean forward and say, 'The police will bring back mobile coverage soon. And I'm going to get blasted in my ear, or blown up. And you're sitting right next to me. So what I get, you get. Get it?' I give his hair another enraged yank. 'When the phones are up again, this is what you're going to say.'

I break into a sticky sweat. I look over at the far quay. They've started clearing the wharf. There's a huge space on the dock apron, as if they expect an underwater explosion any minute. We're only just in time.

Suddenly I'm intensely angry. 'When they make contact, you'll say: IT'S OK. I'VE GOT THE GIRL. I GOT HER OFF THE BUS. THEY KILLED THE WRONG PERSON. THE POLICE DON'T KNOW WHAT THEY'RE DOING. Got it?'

The driver nods. Dave holds the gun steady. He says, 'Right. Raise your right hand if you understand her?'

The man holds up his right hand. Dave relaxes slightly. The driver sits there gulping in air. Then tries to adjust his position.

'No you don't,' warns Dave. 'That was my sister who got shot. So you can do as I say, or I'll break your goddamn neck.'

'And as for me,' I add, 'I can't think of anywhere I'd rather be blown up than sitting here with you.'

The man gets it. He sits still. If he moves, Dave will get him. If he indicates to the Brightness he's being held hostage, Dave will get him. And if he doesn't manage to say exactly the right thing – his own people may blow him up.

Yeah. LIFE IS A TRAP: NONE ARE FREE.

'OK,' he says, 'I'll do what you say.'

'Good,' says Dave. 'You'll do as we say. When we say it.' He nods at me. And he releases the driver.

Dave holds the gun out to me. 'Here, hide this out of reach.'

I hesitate. I've never held a gun before. It might go off. I might shoot it by accident.

Dave thrusts it further, abrupt, impatient. Gingerly I take it, hoping I've got it the right way. My hand shakes. I stash it out of sight, under a jacket on the back seat.

Dave flicks the ignition. As the car starts up, he turns up the hands-free set, mounted on the dashboard. Turns off its Bluetooth setting. 'Let's see if we can't hear everything that's going on,' he says.

'Look mate, why don't you just take the car and let me go?' whines the driver.

'Shut up,' says Dave. 'As soon as they make contact,

you reassure them you've intercepted the girl and saved the mission. You hear? You've got her and the bomb in the car. You will be *very* convincing. You understand?'

The driver nods his head.

The engine kicks into life. We pull away from the kerb.

'And,' I add, 'we've got road blocks to get through – so *stay* convincing. If the police think we're suicide bombers, they'll put a bullet through your head too.' I don't let my voice shake. I don't let either of them hear how scared I am. Instead I focus on my new found power.

LIFE IS AN EGG: HARD ON THE OUTSIDE, SOFT IN THE MIDDLE. ONCE BROKEN, FOREVER BEYOND REPAIR.

Dave does a three-point turn. And we drive back down Rayleigh Road, parallel to the dock.

'I need answers,' I say as we slow down to take a speed-bump. 'While we can still talk. Who are you? Why me? And what the hell *is* the mission?'

'We are the Brightness—' he starts.

'Not good enough,' I say. 'Cut the rhetoric and tell me what.'

I don't know if he would have told me. If he'd have suddenly turned round and explained exactly why cells like his take teenage girls hostage, why they'd chosen me and what massive bombtastic event they'd planned on

170

sending me to. I don't know if he'd have come over all Do Your Damnedest, Torture Me With Thumbscews, Stretch Me On The Rack But Not A Word Will Pass My Lips, or if he'd have fessed up to everything there and then.

I don't find out.

Because we haven't gone two speed-bumps more before the whistling starts.

6

Become a True Believer

(Get so serious about political, social and religious beliefs that you can take The Next Step.)

SLICING PAIN. Like red-hot wire thrust into every brain cell I possess. Even Dave and the driver wince. *My poor eardrum.* I clamp my hand down hard over the side of my head.

'OK,' I whisper. 'Enough.' The whistling stops. The ringing carries on. I'm left with a buzzing dizziness and watering eyes. And I shudder involuntarily inside my wet explosive vest.

'Await instructions,' says the Voice, all Totally Evil.

'I'm sorry,' I croak. 'It wasn't my fault.'

Suddenly the hands-free set on the driver's dash crackles. Dave flicks it on to loudspeaker.

'*Come in Exodus One?*' says the Voice. The driver gets the good, chocolatey tones – except it doesn't sound very smooth and creamy right now. More peanut brittle.

And I do a double take. Where's it coming from? In my ear? In the car? The Voice booms out from the driver's handset. Even that hurts. I grit my teeth as the volume sets up a painful zinging, weirdly coming through my back fillings.

'*Exodus One – come in,*' the Voice says.

I lean forward and prod the man. *He better be convincing.*

'Peace be with you,' whispers the driver. 'Exodus One here. Everything's under control, Apocalypse. We're back on track. All praise and thanks to God. Don't detonate.' A trickle of sweat runs down the side of his face.

What kind of a weak response was that?

'Do better,' hisses Dave.

I shake my head, clutch at my ear. Better – not louder (please).

'*Peace be with you,*' says the chocolatey Voice (dark and bitter almond). '*Exodus One, please report – full update.*'

'She's here.'

No wonder he got the job as a driver.

'*We are preparing to terminate. May the Holy One be praised. Advise, are you in vicinity of target?*'

'*SHE'S IN THE CAR! SHUKRI, FOR GOD'S SAKE DON'T DETONATE,*' shrieks the driver.

My eyes water, my head rings. My ear goes mental.

'*Code names only, Exodus One.*'

'SHE'S SITTING IN THE CAR WITH ME.'

I groan. There's a pause at the other end of the line. The driver looks at Dave. I look at the driver. I understand. He's such an incredibly weak link that the Voice, this Evil/Fruit & Nut Case Apocalypse Guy, would probably give his future career as a Brightness Cleric to bomb-blast him into early paradise.

A sudden chill seems to shiver through my gut. *Maybe he is expendable.* The image of my severed head, plummeting down on to a pavement, bouncing in little sickening thuds and rolling to a standstill, flashes before me. Bloody limbs tangled with car doors. I shut my eyes, clench my teeth. Feel sick. The ringing and the nausea conspire together in my saliva glands. *Don't throw up.*

'EXODUS ONE HERE.' The driver's sweating like a pig. Beads of water are running down the back of his neck. 'WE HAVE THE GIRL. THE MISSION IS NOT COMPROMISED. WE ARE EXITING THE CORDONED AREA.'

I try to think of something, anything that will give us the edge, but my mind is deadlocked. I tap Dave on the shoulder, indicate I want his mobile. I need to tell him: *This guy's a disaster. They may not mind blowing him up if they think he'll spill. He's screwed their plan. Will coverage still be down behind us? Can we go back?* He passes the mobile to me. But before I can tap anything in, like: *We need answers from him, let's turn round*, we come out of the industrial area into a line of traffic. Blue and white tape. Lights flashing.

And suddenly we're boxed in with vehicles front and back.

Bang ahead is a police cordon. Three police vans. Two officers directing traffic. Yellow and blue checkered cars. High visibility neon vests. Orange traffic cones. Blue lights. Cars on the other side of the road being turned away. Cars in front being stopped.

POLICE – DO NOT CROSS THIS LINE.

Oh God help us.

The driver sees it. 'SHUKRI,' he yells. Voice shrill, panicky. 'POLICE CHECK.'

This guy is seriously not cut out to be a terrorist. Even I'd make a better one. I wonder vaguely how he thought he could make it. I wonder why any Brightness cell worth its Extremist Ratings would let him in on a mission. And that's kind of a weird thing to be thinking when you're strapped to a bomb.

'*Complete the police check. May peace be with you,*' orders Apocalypse.

'BUT THEY'RE CHECKING ALL THE CARS OUT OF THIS AREA,' squeals the driver.

'*I am turning transmission off,*' states Apocalypse. '*They may monitor communications in the area. You are on your own. Remember God loves those that lay down their lives for his glory.*'

I hear something in my ear click off. The driver twists his head, seems to be looking for a way out. Now he's on his own and he doesn't like it. Frantically, he turns the handset off and on and off again. 'Come in, come in?' he says.

Is it OK to speak now? I wonder. I'm not sure. I keep one hand clamped over my earpiece, to muffle everything I can (just in case), then listen out with the other.

The driver reaches out his hand to the radio, as if he's going to start switching *that* on and off too, but Dave knocks his hand back and turns the radio on himself.

'. . . *A senior Foreign Office source has reported citizenship-stripping in the EU is rising, due to the numbers of foreign nationals travelling outside their borders to support the campaigns of Brightness extremist cells . . .*'

'We're going through this road block – like everyone else,' says Dave, the sound of the radio masking his voice.

'You,' he turns to the driver, 'put something over your hair. And is that handset completely off?'

The driver pulls a durag from his pocket and puts it on (so that's how they tone down their look). Then he passes his handset to Dave. Dave checks it, seems satisfied.

'. . . *known Brightness sympathisers will have their travel documents temporarily revoked. They may even face relocation orders inside the UK to move them away from known cell locations . . .*'

'Tell me *now* if this car's hot.'

The man doesn't answer.

Dave turns to me, hisses: '*The gun. Hide it.*'

I shove the gun under the carpet in the foot-well. *I need to hide the vest, too.* I pull the jacket off the seat. It's a guy's. I put it on. It's a bit big, though not a bad jacket, actually. Black leather. Quite cool. It completely covers the vest. I run my fingers through my hair, untangle the knots, slick my wet fringe up and back. I give up, snatch the driver's snap-back that's fallen into the foot-well and twist my hair into a roll, shove it under the cap. I pull a few curls out to cover my ear. God knows what I look like. Not myself, that's for sure.

'*We break the programme "What Next For Britain's Home-grown Terrorists?" to bring you an update. The police have released a statement on the Docklands terror attack at*

177

Gallion's Point, only half a mile from London City Airport and two miles from the crowded O2 Arena. Chief Inspector Derek Hawkins has confirmed that a woman was shot at the scene and a number of suspected suicide bombers are still unaccounted for. The police advise against all travel to and from the area . . .'

'Let me worry about the where-to and the where-from, here,' says Dave. He shifts down the gears.

'*. . . despite public concern, London police confirm that the Deadly Force policy of shooting potential suicide bombers without warning will continue to take effect . . .'*

'We are going to chat normally,' says Dave, 'and be relaxed.'

Two police vans are parked at an angle across the road. All the incoming traffic is blocked by the blue and white tape. Cars approaching on the far side are told to turn round and go back.

On our side, the exit traffic must pass between the cones. A police person on duty stops and checks each vehicle. A little way off, a different officer speaks into his walky-talky. Two more, in bullet-proof vests and full riot gear, stand with weapons at the ready. A police van nearby seems to be running number plate checks.

'Is this car clean?' hisses Dave to Exodus One.

'Yeah, it's clean,' says the guy.

'It better be,' says Dave, 'or we're all for it.'

It starts raining again. The policeman on the driver's side of the car stops us. His face set, unsmiling. Clearly he's used to drivers obeying him.

'Can you show me your driving licence please, sir?'

My heart pounds. The debate on the radio continues. An MP is talking now: '. . . *You can't just take away rights from people – whether you like them or not. This is dog-whistle politics. It's about sounding Tough on Terror when the Government doesn't have the power to do anything . . .*'

'Haven't got it on me,' says Dave.

The officer turns and signals to the nearby van. The policeman inside nods.

I sip in a tiny breath of air. His walky-talky crackles. Can't hear what it says. But the policeman seems satisfied. The car plates must have checked out.

'Is this your car?' the policeman asks Dave. 'Nope,' says Dave, 'it's his.'

'. . . *new proposals, widening the use of banning orders against extremist groups; and a new anti-radicalization duty for public bodies . . .*'

Once again the officer signals to the parked van. I wait, gnawing my cheek, every second crashing around me.

The guy in the van nods. The walky-talky crackles again. I realize I've chewed into the side of my tongue.

The car insurance has checked out too.

'Any identification?' the policeman asks Dave.

I stiffen.

'Nope,' says Dave.

'Where have you come from?'

'Rayleigh Road,' says Dave.

The officer nods.

'Where are you going to?'

Where are *we going?*

'See a mate in West Norwood.'

OK. We're going to West Norwood.

'Purpose of journey?'

'No purpose, just catching up.'

'Anyone else in the back?' The officer leans in and looks suspiciously at me. 'Your name, miss?'

'Clara.' I'm nearly fainting.

'How old are you?'

Someone in the queue behind peeps a horn. The rain suddenly starts really chucking it down. Something tells me to keep my age as young as possible. 'Fourteen.'

'Would you mind getting out of the car, sir? We just need to check you. Routine.'

Dave gets out of the car, starts getting soaked all over again. *I cross my fingers, cross my arms, pray.*

'I've asked you to step out of your vehicle under the

stop and search powers granted to me by the state, under Section Sixty of the Criminal Justice and Public Order Act 1994. This is Officer Four-three-eight of Dockland Police Force conducting the search. I'm searching you as a routine matter, because you cannot provide me with identity, are driving through an area under surveillance, and as part of our ongoing anti-terrorism efforts. There has been serious terrorist activity in the vicinity. A valid S-Sixty authority is in place. You have the right to remain silent but anything you do say may be taken down and used in evidence.'

Dave spreads his legs and places his arms on the top of the car.

'Can I have a home address?'

'Forty-six, Rayleigh Road.'

'Postcode?'

'Only just moved there – forgotten.'

'Not to worry – I'll find it,' says the officer.

The officer pats Dave down. The line of cars behind grows longer. *If I jumped out now? Begged for help? Would the police still shoot? Would Apocalypse detonate?*

Not Going To Find Out.

'Your clothing's a bit damp, sir, can you explain why?'

'Like apart from going out in the rain, being caught in the rain and standing here in the rain, you mean?'

The radio blares: '. . . *radicalization is about young men believing that extremism is cool and will impress their peers. It's a chance for them to carve out an identity, which will not only define, but demonstrate their masculinity . . .*'

'And your name?'

'Joshua Pickering.'

God, Dave's good! Ice cool. I imagine him under enemy fire. In control. The police enters the details in his hand-held machine.

'Is that Flat H? Sir?'

'They're actually numbered on the Roman numeral system,' sighs Dave.

'Right you are. I'm only getting alphabetical listings up here. It says you're at Flat H?'

'OK,' says Dave. 'Can I go now?'

'Yes,' says the officer. He ticks some boxes on a receipt and signs it. 'This is your search record.' He hands the paper to Dave.

Dave gets back in the car. The policeman waves us on.

And we pull out!

I'm sitting on my hands to stop them shaking. Through the traffic cones, past the police vans.

Dave turns round to check I'm OK. '*Roman numerals?*' I mouth.

Dave makes a shrugging gesture, like: *Didn't know*

if he was trying to trip me up.

Thank God for new builds and secure entry systems.

And then we're through. We're back on the high road. My hands are slick with sweat. My heart's in my mouth. I realize I'm holding Dave's phone so tightly, it might crack. Up ahead the dual carriage is nearly empty, and Dave is swearing.

'Shit in a bed,' says Dave, 'that was worse than being under fire.'

'What do we do now?' I mouth.

'Get the hell out,' Dave replies.

And then?

Dave jerks his thumb at Exodus One. 'Get some answers from him.'

7

Develop a Tight-knit Group of Friends

(Who share religious, economic, social and sexual bonds.)

ABOVE US THE SOUND OF THE HELICOPTER is gone. Behind us the street is strangely empty. Everywhere's empty. I guess they're diverting traffic as far away as Canary Wharf.

Dave clicks his tongue. Seems to be searching for something. I'm too scared to talk. The transmission on the driver's handset from Apocalypse is still off, but I'm taking no chances. Someone might try listening in through my earpiece.

Dave pulls the car over into a huge supermarket car park. At the barrier entrance he turns to look at me. *Time to get some answers?* We pass some of the staff who've come out to gawk at what's going on. They stand in little groups, smoking fags, peering down the street, trying to figure out if they're going to get to see anything.

We drive across the car park towards the line of recycle bins at the far end, where it's pretty empty.

'*Gun,*' mouths Dave.

Cautiously I give it to him.

I point at my ear and raise my hands as if to ask a question. I'm trying to indicate to Dave: *Not sure if they're listening.* He gets it and nods; he's clocked that already. Exodus One is as white as a sheet. He's finally figured out things are Not Looking Shit Hot for him.

'*I'll check the boot,*' I mouth to Dave. '*Try to get him to talk.*' I want answers too. But I don't want to be heard getting them, so very quietly I ease the back door of the car open and slide out.

Dave prods the gun into the driver's ribcage and points to him to get out too.

The driver does as he's told. He must be totally crapping himself. And I think he's more afraid of his own lot than us. He's got that If-I-Knew-I-Was-Getting-Into-All-This-I'd-Have-Stayed-Out look. Dave checks around. Nobody near, nobody watching. Dave gets out too and thrusts the gun into his pocket, aiming it at the driver through the cloth of his jacket.

I get out and open the boot.

I watch as Dave walks the man round the side of the recycle bins. Beside the bins is a patch of shrubbery. Rose things and low, flat, spreading conifers. Bark chips. We're out of view of the supermarket building here, too far away to alert anyone. The driver makes like he's going to shout, but the car park is too huge and empty. Plus in London? Shouting? Please.

Dave forces him to walk as far away as possible from the car. Then faintly I hear him say, 'Who are you?'

The man at first makes like he'll be difficult then suddenly he seems to crumple. 'It wasn't me,' he whines. His voice hardly audible. 'They forced me to do it. They got my mum and sister in the house. They'll kill them, if I don't get everything right.' I keep my hand clamped over the earpiece.

'Bullshit,' says Dave coldly. 'Who are they?'

'Them, you know – the Brightness.' The man seems to be pleading. 'I don't know who they are.'

'Why did they put a vest on her?'

'I *don't know*. I ain't one of them.'

'OK, we do this the hard way,' says Dave.

And I think Dave is going to make him kneel and put the gun to his head and make like he'll execute him there and then. (Or beat him into a bloody pulp.) And I watch. I can't believe I'm just watching. (To be honest, I'd prefer the bloody-pulp thing.) But I keep my gaze steady. And I'm not going to intervene. Or even discourage Dave in the slightest. And I never thought I'd be able to stand here and just look on while someone got pulverized. But I find I can. I'm even thinking: *Instant justice. Cheaper. Quicker. What they all deserve.* And I'm kind of appalled at myself. Appalled at Dave. And then I think of Holly. And figure Exodus One *does* deserve it. And I hope Dave gives it to him.

But then I think, Holly wouldn't have wanted that. And I start to run over, waving my arms at Dave, making like we should stop.

But the driver has no intention of going through a mock execution – and he's definitely not up for pulping, any more than giving us answers. He suddenly ducks and darts back towards the recycle bins. He's quick too, but not as quick as Dave. Before he's gone two strides, Dave is on him. He flicks out a balled fist. It crunches into the driver's head. One brutal uppercut under the guy's chin, and he drops. Knees give. And he crumples into the conifers.

Dave shoots a look at me, like: *OK, we need to get out of here now.*

My jaw goes slack. For a second I don't see Dave at all. Just something male shaped, raw, scary, ruthless.

A crawling in my throat. I quash it. Blink. God, Dave's hard. That guy had it coming though. Quickly, I check the contents of the boot. Not much there. Just a tool case and a plastic draw-string carrier bag. I grab both.

Dave gestures impatiently to me, like he wants to tie a knot.

This draw-string? I hold up the plastic bag. *Is he going to throttle him?*

Dave shakes his head. 'Check the tool kit,' he hisses.

I open the tool case. I hold up a pack. *Cable ties?*

Dave nods, beckons with his hand. *Chuck them over.*

I throw Dave the whole pack of mixed-size cable ties. He clicks their casing open and takes out two long ones. He restrains the driver. Hands and feet.

Paper, pen? Dave makes a scribbling motion.

I dig around in the tool case. *Pencil? Felt tip? Any good?* I hold up a fat permanent marker and a stubby pencil.

Dave points to the marker, gives me a thumbs up.

I throw the marker at him. He catches it with one hand, pops the top, bends down and writes something across the guy's forehead. Then he arranges the foliage over the limp figure and within seconds is vaulting back into the driver's seat. The ignition's still running.

Can you help with this? Dig it out? I indicate the earpiece in my ear.

He shakes his head. Types into his phone: **No time to reroute the signal – we need to get going before someone discovers our sleeping beauty.** He jerks his head in the direction of Exodus One. **It'll hurt and bleed too,** he warns. **Plus we need it right now.**

I look at him and understand. This is the tough bit.

This is when we must face Apocalypse.

8

Participate in Nonviolent Activities

(Justify criminal acts for radical purposes, invoke radical purposes to justify criminal acts.)

DAVE MAKES A 'LET'S TALK' SIGN with his hand. He points at his phone, hands it to me.

I type in: **Exodus?** I hold up the phone so Dave can read it.

Dave makes a sleeping gesture. One hand held horizontal, cradle-like against his tilted cheek. Then quickly types into the phone messenger. **Dead men tell no tales, nor do terrorists – not to the police anyway. But he'll have fun trying to explain.** Then he adds, **One down, Gen, and I reckon another two or three more to go.**

How's that? I twist my head at him questioningly.

He jumps down from the car, walks a few paces off. Holds his phone to his lips. Records a voice memo. He walks back and shows it to me. These guys work in cells – small teams – never more than five. It's safer – less likely to be discovered and gives everyone a chance to shine. This cell must have: 1) an explosives guy who can tap into a weapons supply chain; 2) a driver, or an on-the-ground person – we've dealt with him; 3) a central command operative – that's Apocalypse and 4) maybe, I reckon, a techie or resource person. Four at the max. Maybe only three. Maybe Apocalypse is the techie too.

I put the draw-string bag down on my lap.

Dave types. I'm going to get them all, Gen. You watch.

Only three or four people? Somehow in my head they'd multiplied into hundreds. Massive, international networks of terrorists, backing every threat worldwide. Whole suites of the latest technology at their fingertips. Access to everything I do, every thought recorded, every noise understood.

Although – of course – it would only take one to send me to Bombshire.

Dave records another voice memo. They'll have a hub somewhere: could be the back of a van, a garage, a rented flat, somewhere they won't be disturbed. They'll have a couple of fast computers and smart phones. I reckon that's about it. Their technical know-how is not impressive. Dave indicates the handset.

Just a handful of people. The whole nation terrorized. Why is it like that? Why does one Evil Plan have the power to destroy so many others?

'*What happens next?*' I mouth.

Dave pauses. Then records: This is the tough bit, Gen. We have to get them to keep their mission going. We have to tell them Exodus One is out of the picture. They'll have a choice to abort or carry on. I haven't received any data from my mates and we've changed coverage zones. I can't jam airwaves without precise info or some proper kit. I keep flashing my phone to vary the wireless carrier, but unless I hear from them it's all hit and miss.

He adds: We had no choice with Exodus. He wasn't going to tell and would have sabotaged us if we'd kept him along.

By the way, I wrote I AM A TERRORIST. ARREST ME on his face.

I nod. In a different life that would be kind of funny.

I grab his hand, then take the mobile and type in, OK, let me do it. I'll speak to them. Then I add, You can walk away now, Dave. Please?

My throat goes dry. A fleeting image of my decapitated head. Severed hands, fingers curled in. *Please Dave, just go. I didn't know I still cared about you.*

Dave shakes his head and mouths out: *'Two brains stand a better chance.'* I want to thank him, smile and refuse. But I can't.

'We go?' mouths Dave.

I nod. What else can I do?

He flicks the handset on and off and on.

Immediately: 'EXODUS ONE – COME IN?' says Apocalypse.

I'm not ready. I don't know what to say. *Think, Gen. Think.*

'Exodus One?' says Apocalypse.

'He's not here,' I say. *'Please don't kill me. I'll do whatever you want.'* And suddenly I'm sobbing and gulping and sucking air and I can't speak.

There's no reply.

'It wasn't my fault.' My voice is cracking. I'm spluttering. The words can hardly come out. 'He just got out and ran away,' I sob. My throat has closed up. *Don't cry. Try to breathe. You must explain. You must make them carry on with the mission.* 'After we got through the barrier,' I gulp in air, *'I don't know what to do. Please don't hurt me.'* My throat won't open. I'm sniffing great gulps of mucus.

And I can't think of another word. I should be saying something, convincing them, but all I'm doing is crying.

There's a delay, the only noise my weeping. Dave sits there, pale, clenching his teeth. Then he looks at me, his eyes totally focused. He makes a driving-the-car motion.

'I drove the car to this car park,' I sob. 'I'll drive anywhere you want.'

Dave nods, his eyes stay steady. There's a long pause. Every second crashes around me like a dead weight. One more second. Maybe the last. I'm holding my breath. I'm dizzy. I'm so terribly dizzy. The severed head on the tarmac seems to roll and twist and look at me. Its pale, dead eyes reproaching.

'*PLEASE*,' I plead, '*I'll do anything.*'

The earpiece crackles.

'*I'll finish the mission. I'll do anything – anything.*'

The Voice in my ear. Electronic. Worse than evil. I draw in a huge moan.

'Go to Heathrow Terminal Three Departure Hall. You have one hour. If you arrive on time, we may consider sparing you. If you do not, you will be detonated automatically, wherever you are.'

'I'll go.' I gulp. 'Thank you, thank you.'

'And no more communication. We do not negotiate. We will not speak to you again.'

9

Feel You Are Succeeding in Society

(Come from a disadvantaged family, have a low IQ, be of poorer socio-economic status.)

DAVE JAMS THE CAR INTO GEAR. I hear the roar of the engine. We're on the road; shooting out of the supermarket forecourt. We cross the river and start ring-roading it west.

Dave says nothing. The clock on the dash says 11.45 a.m. One hour. I try to catch my breath. Wipe my nose on my sleeve. Stop myself from hyperventilating. I pull open the string on the carrier bag. Inside is a bunch of papers, a wallet and some cash. Maybe there's something here. I open up the wallet. No credit cards. Just bank notes folded in an envelope. I put the wallet back. Dave points at the radio, turns it up.

Some music plays. I flick channels till I can get an update on the news. I pull out the papers. A police spokesperson is being interviewed. '. . . *when identifying and confronting suicide attackers, avoiding risk to police officers and members of the public outweighs all other concerns. Police officers are instructed to open fire on suspected suicide attackers without warning and immediately, but only when they are at a safe distance . . .*'

I swallow something in my throat that threatens to choke me.

Holly.

She didn't stand a chance.

'. . . *Extreme-Threat Tactical Commanders have been advising the nation to stay vigilant since terrorist Lumin cells affiliated to the Brightness Brotherhood announced today as an End Time Day of Action . . .*'

It could have been me or Dave. How do I live with that? Random selection? It doesn't make sense. Someone as special as Holly. Dead for nothing.

DEATH IS A LOTTERY: PAY YOUR MONEY AND HOPE TO LOSE.

And my fault.

The news changes. '. . . *in America, Federal forces are on Critical Code Red after a suicide bomb exploded at a crowded train station on the Mexican border with Texas. It seems that a teenager was taken hostage and used as a walking weapon – forced to travel the state and post images of herself in crowded public places. We leave this programme for a live update . . .'*

Dave whips round, looks at me. My mouth goes dry. I can't seem to take it in. A clawing feeling starts to mushroom inside me. *It's not just me.* There are others out there: across the UK, across America. How many of us are being forced to walk around in suicide vests right now? Forced to walk into train stations, into airports and stand there – stand by lovely people like Holly – and kill them?

I can't do it. I can't. If they want me to walk into Terminal Three and blow up holiday makers, I just won't. I won't blow up Dave either. As soon as I can, I'll get to an empty spot. I'll run away. I'll hide. I'll wait till 12.45 and that's all.

'*I'm coming, Holly,*' I whisper. '*I'll be with you soon.*' And in a way it's a huge relief. I can let go. I don't have to be so precious about my little life any more. If you'd asked me yesterday if I could feel ready to die within twenty-four hours, I'd have thought you were mental.

I watch the grey tarmac of the road ahead disappearing like smoke under our wheels. Is this how heroes feel? Ready to give up the fight knowing it will save others? Sad that, after all, life has no more meaning than death?

I glance at the clock: 12.07. Not so long. I look out of the window for a place where I can Walk Off Into The Sunset. If I'm going to go it alone, I'd like – at least – to make a bit of an exit. A desert would be fine. Cactus and rattlesnakes. But there're just streets, shops, pavements and pedestrians. People everywhere. Nowhere to walk off into. NO SUNSET. I smile; these days you can't even find a place to die.

Whilst I'm thinking of Death Scenes and how I Want to be Remembered for Doing the Right Thing, I open up the bag and pull out the folded papers. One of them reads:

May the Brightness ever be with you and may the Sun be darkened in preparation for the End Time. Praise be.

End Time Day of Action

Glorification and Celebration to the Line of Totality

Cell Group E

EXODUS ONE

Detail for the Messenger-of-Fate Mission

- **Set up capture, locate dump point. Check wake-up timings. Coordinate.**
- **Set in place [on the ground operative] used car/**

untraceable cash/untraceable mobiles [Exodus One].

- Whistle alarm wake up [Apocalypse].
- Set tour in motion.
- Voice/report/coordinate Apocalypse exchange.
- Record all interactions.
- Film/photo all movements.
- Follow on tour bus to all key London targets.
- Including all transport hubs.
- Coach/bus/trains/underground/airports in Cell E zone/all key tourist points on route planned.
- Follow selected operative on round trip in London to:
- Heathrow
- Windsor Castle
- Reading Hub
- Film and photo and upload to @theUKbrightnesscellE #EndTimeDayofAction.
- Follow on rail communications to final destination.
- Bristol Hub Temple Meads Railway Station.
- Retire.

The second paper reads:

The Line of Totality Day of Righteousness Action Cell E
The sun will be darkened. The End Time is upon us. The Door of Repentance for sins will be closed and will remain

closed until the Day of Judgement. The Hour of Illumination is Nigh. 444

- Attack installations, cause explosions,
- Create Brightness.

Footage

1st release on ALL LONDON TOURS in real time.

2nd release of PS explosion in time with the LOT to cause the maximum chaos.

Desired Goals

Create panic

Create fear

Waste authority time/ resources

Show strength

Strike fear in heart of society

Glorify the Brightness

Give cell group cosmic afterlife

Strike blow against the West

Leave confusion

Create terror

Explode SFP at PS

Leave impact for decades

Promote cohesion

Look strong

Brother Proverbz Operative Schedule

Routes

Details of tides

Ordnance

Details of explosions

Communications

YC and equipment

Details of SFP location

Details of local knowledge

Maps included

I don't understand much of it at all.

It's puzzling, but as I read page one through again, I figure out that I'm looking at Exodus One's work schedule. And that's *very* weird: a terrorist's work schedule.

LIFE IS A TIMETABLE: GET BORN; STAY ALIVE; DIE.

My imagination goes into overdrive.

EMPLOYER: Good morning, would you like to tell us why you've applied for this specialist job?

TERRORIST: I've been employed now for the last two years in the terrorist industry. My CV reflects that I can confidently complete missions at every stage: from obtaining illegal C-4 explosives to the successful blowing up of twelve targets, including a succession of teenage girls. I'm quite handy at a bit of solo rape and pillage if needed, but prefer to work in a team.

How bizarre. I read the page through yet again, paying close attention to each point. Then I reach for Dave's mobile.

And I get Twitter up.

I search for @theUKbrightnessCellE. I press my lips together and wait. The search engine whirs round – a little wheel of small spokes.

And then it loads.

The UK Brightness Cell E @theUKbrightnessCellE
@Exodus1 Praise be @theUSbrightnessHub @theEUbrightnessHub our
Messenger of Fate at the start of her final journey #EndTimeDayofAction

I scroll down.

All the blood in my veins seems to freeze. My lips go dry. There, posted on the page is a picture of *me*. Me: this morning, standing by the SEE LONDON TOURS bus stop. Me: surrounded by tourists. Me: with the bus in the background and a close-up of the vest.

I scroll further down, my hands shaking, my blood going past freezing into sub-zero chills. Posting after posting of me – on the bus outside the Shard; at Waterloo; through the bus window at London Bridge, even me sitting on the top deck by the Globe; by Tower Bridge – Me. Just *me* everywhere. There I am again, standing by tourists, sitting by tourists. Me: white faced, with guns superimposed into my hands, black angel wings

202

cartooned into my shoulders, me looking like I'm the angel of death and loving it. Even one of Holly, right beside me, waiting at the bus stop. All with the message: WE CAN GET YOU: ANYWHERE; ANYTIME; ANYPLACE #ourbombergirl.

I pass the open Twitter feed to Dave.

I can't seem to take it in.

There I am, in real time. *The Messenger of Fate.*

My hands start to shake. I feel ill.

Dave indicates I should open up one of the conversations under a post.

The EU Brightness Hub @theEUbrightnessHub
#EndTimeDayofAction @theUSbrightnessHub @theUKbrightnessCellE
to blow or not to blow that is the question. lol.

↩ ⇄ ★ •••

The US Brightness Hub @theUSbrightnessHub
@theEUbrightnessHub @theUKbrightnessCellE #EndTimeDayofAction
BLOW BLOW BLOW! BLOW HER! BOOM!

↩ ⇄ ★ •••

Blood is the Way @bloodistheway
@theUSbrightnessHub @theEUbrightnessHub @theUKbrightnessCellE
Love that VEST! #EndTimeDayofAction

↩ ⇄ ★ •••

Dark Sun @DarkeningOfTheSun
@BloodIsTheWay @theUSbrightnessHub @theEUbrightnessHub
@theUKbrightnessCellE Save the VEST for last! Lol. #EndTimeDayofAction

↩ ⇄ ★ •••

I let the phone fall from my grip. I stare forward. I can't seem to function. The vest is suddenly heavy against me. That last post: *Save the VEST for last!* I scrabble for Exodus's work sheet. Frantically I run my finger down his list. Where does *last* come?

- Coach/bus/trains/Underground/airports in Cell E zone/ all key tourist points on route planned
- Follow selected operative on round trip
- Heathrow
- Windsor Castle
- Reading Hub
- Film and photo and upload to @theUKbrightnesscellE #EndTimeDayofAction

Follow on round trip. (That must be the London tour.)

- Heathrow

On my way there now.

- Windsor Castle
- Reading
- Bristol Hub Temple Meads train station

Heathrow isn't the last stop. There are three more afterwards – three more before they 'save the VEST for last'.

Sadistic bastards. Suddenly I don't want to walk off into that sunset any more. I want to blow their plans sky high. I want to mess up their heads and post *that* on Twitter. And I'm in with a chance now. I've got a little bit more time to play with – because as long as I make each destination in time, they're going to string me along.

LIFE IS A STRING: YOU JUST DON'T KNOW HOW LONG IT IS.

I wave the paper in front of Dave. He points at the clock. 12.21.

10

Isolate Yourself From Friends and Family

(Nobody understands, so why not associate with completely different parties, including political, religious, or cultural radicals?)

12.44 P.M. AND I'M STANDING IN HEATHROW TERMINAL THREE DEPARTURE HALL. There's a massive snake of passengers lined up for a Virgin flight to New York, right in front of me. Dave waits out of sight. I take up a position as central as possible. My heart is doing some crazy thing inside the vest, but I ignore it, because I'm thinking, *God, I hope I'm right. They must know I'm here. Their tracker will tell them. Won't it?*

And I'm really jumpy. If I thought they meant to detonate the vest here, I'd never have come in, but Exodus

One's schedule has kind of cast everything in a new light. The whole point of me being here is *not* to blow me up – not yet, anyway. Isn't it? *Oh God, I hope it is.*

12.45 and my earpiece crackles.

'Stand in front of the New York check-in desk and snap a selfie. Email it to TheEndTime@hotmail.com. Make sure we can see the Virgin signs above the desks. You have five minutes.'

'But I don't have a phone!' I cry.

But Apocalypse has clicked off.

I don't know what to do. Borrow Dave's? Maybe they have someone watching. Maybe Dave is wrong about the cell being so small – maybe there're hundreds of them, all focused on me.

What if he is wrong?

I can't risk letting them know he's here. Out of the corner of my eye I see a security guard. He's looking at me suspiciously. *Oh God don't let him come this way.*

OK, move Gen. Move. Be creative.

Shops upstairs! I race away from the check-in desks. Hit the escalators. Race up them. Which shop? Boots? WH Smith? Where can I buy a smart phone? I've got Exodus's draw-string bag. His cash! I open up the bag, rip the plastic. In Phones4Less there's a deal on for a Samsung. I pull out the wallet. Tug a sheath of twenties out of it.

Stuff the rest back into the wallet. Drop it back into the plastic bag.

There's a queue. Shit, hell and damnation. *Let me past.* One man looks like he's going to be assy. *Idiot!* If you stop me, I'll blow you up. You'll die. '*Please*,' I say. I'm frantic. I'm near tears again. I don't want to kill anyone. I really don't.

Next in line.

'Can I buy that phone?' I gasp.

The attendant's impossibly slow. She creaks around, has to unlock the security cabinet, asks me dumb questions, like Do I want a chip? Which mobile provider do I prefer? Do I want a top-up? *Of course I want a chip! And what use is a flipping phone without a top-up?*

Only two minutes left.

I throw the money at her, snatch the phone. She starts packing everything in a carrier bag. *Forget the carrier bag!* 'It'll need to be charged,' she remarks, so do I need an additional charger or an international adaptor?

Would I like insurance too?

I burst into tears. '*HAS ANYONE GOT A PHONE I CAN BORROW?*' I scream out, frantic, sobbing.

'What's the rush?' drawls a tall guy in the line.

'I've got to post a selfie, or I'm out of the game. I've only got two minutes left,' I say, sucking in gasps of air.

'Here.' He chucks me his mobile. 'Why didn't you say so? It would've been a whole heap quicker. We've all got planes to catch, lady.'

'Thanks,' I gasp. I grab the bag off the sales girl, and race out of the shop. I pose by the balcony over the check-out desks below. I snap myself with the Virgin signs in the background – then I send it to the email address.

I go back to the guy. He's totally cool about it. I hand him back his phone. My heart is racing like I've run a marathon. 'Thank you,' I breathe, 'thank you.'

'Sounds like a fun contest,' he says, and hands me his card. 'Count me in on the next round, I'm a real kickass hero when it comes to scavenger games.'

'Thanks,' I gasp out again.

I leave him in the queue. Make my way back downstairs to Dave.

LIFE IS ALL ONE BIG, FUN GAME: MISS YOUR TURN AND THE FUN'S OVER.

The Voice crackles in my ear. 'Excellent.' Its tone is almost hazelnut swirl. Sweet on the outside, hard in the middle. And I don't know what to make of it.

'Will you let me go then?' I ask, nervous, wary.

'Get to Windsor Castle by one twenty. Main entrance. And we'll see.'

Why did I even bother? I'm surprised at myself. I've

never been a slow learner before.

'Do not communicate with us again. We will issue no further instructions.' The Voice clicks off.

I pick myself up and dust myself down and set off at a run.

11

Allow the Group's Mind-set to Affect You

(Discuss, interact with and experience a
radical group to find yourself more committed
to the cause than ever.)

BACK AT THE CAR, I throw myself in, sick and dizzy.
'*Windsor Castle. One twenty,*' I mouth at Dave, who has
followed me back to the car. He hits the spur road, clocks
up over eighty, and soon we're speeding down the M4. I
rip at the packaging on the new phone, tear into it with
my teeth, struggle to get the back off and the battery out.
I pull the charger free and pray that the charge plug on
the car works. I fumble with the chip, nearly drop it, my
fingers all slippy with sweat. *I need a working phone.*

Don't bother, indicates Dave by shaking his head. *Take*

mine. He holds his phone out.

I shake my head. Too risky. They mustn't figure out I'm not alone. If anyone is going to do any figuring – it's got to be me.

For some reason I think of Naz. Of figuring things out. Of being alone. How we used to do crossword puzzles together. LIFE IS AN ANAGRAM: ANY WHICH WAY YOU ARRANGE ITS PARTS, IT DOESN'T MAKE MUCH SENSE. EFLI; FIEL; FILE; IFLE. Of Naz and being alone, and not alone. Of being here with Dave, and not with him.

I never felt alone with Dave. Not like this.

I see Dave's grip on the wheel of the car, the way his knuckles have turned white. He's doing all this for me, isn't he? He could've bailed long ago.

I blink. *Oh God. And I treated him so badly.*

And I never regretted it.

And I think of Naz. His dark eyes, those wild boat rides. And I still don't regret any of it. Oh Naz. *Why did you stop seeing me? What happened?*

I suck in my breath. *Stop it*, I tell myself. *Just figure things out. Get going. Start from a fact, then interrogate its meaning. Any fact. Start with LIFE and what its meaning might be. What can you figure out from still being alive?*

The fact that I am alive suggests:

1. *They have nobody else following us (or they would know about Dave).*

2. *Exodus One has not been found. Or handed over to the police. Or is not awake. Or is dead. (Or he would have called them and warned them, wouldn't he?)*

3. *They have a definite plan for me and a final destination (which I obviously have not reached yet).*

4. *They cannot hack into closed circuit CCTV security systems like Heathrow and motorway traffic (or they'd see I wasn't driving the car).*

5. *They may be coordinating something else, as they seem to go 'off air' for periods of time. (Like what is all this WE WILL NOT BE COMMUNICATING WITH YOU AGAIN STUFF? Or maybe there is only one of them at the command centre and he goes off to look in the mirror and faint in admiration?)*

I manage to pop the chip out of its case and into the new mobile. Now I've got to call up the mobile provider to get it up and running. I key in the number. Some annoying voice tells me I'll have to wait for three text messages.

I stare out of the window, willing the networks to work for me. I fiddle with my hair, feel the vest for the hundredth time in the hope of discovering some missed or entirely new magical button or catch which instantly lets me take the whole thing off.

I think about taking it off. What would that feel like? In some weird, masochistic way I've almost grown attached to it, like one might grow fond of a birth mark or a set of false teeth. Already it feels moulded to my skin. It's become a part of me, like it's some huge bombcancerous scab – all carcinogenic, deadly, and all mine. And as I run my hands again down its concealed bumps and canisters, I can almost feel it growing and growing, drawing on my energy, feeding on my life blood – swelling up until it reaches some inevitable critical mass where it will burst and release its poison and take over all that's left of Genesis Wainwright.

'*Use this one?*' Dave whispers. He holds up the mobile that belonged to Exodus. '*Change the old chip?*'

I blink. Oh my God. So simple. Of course! I'm not thinking. Thank God Dave is. Change the chips! I pick up Exodus's phone, swiping the code I saw him use. His mobile screen blinks into view. His smart screen registers fourteen missed calls. All from the same number.

I show Dave.

His face lights up. Like: *At last the Red Sea parts!* I'm not sure why he's so happy, but he rolls up his sleeve, and gestures to me to write the number down on his arm.

I grab the permanent marker and write it. Then I

remove Exodus's old chip, place everything carefully in a well near the gear stick, and click the new one into place. I turn the phone over and swipe it open. And it works. *It actually works.* I wipe the sweat from my chin and get Safari up. Within half a mile, I've got an email app and I've signed into my account. Then I check the Twitter feed from the Brightness.

I know what I'm expecting to see and I'm not disappointed. There I am in Terminal Three, Heathrow. I look dreadful. Huge scared dark eyes, tear tracks, dishevelled hair. Stupid, stupid huge stupid leather jacket. Two superimposed guns, drawn-on death wings, and the Virgin sign over the departure check-in desks behind me.

Beneath the picture it reads: *TO FLY OR DIE, THAT IS THE QUESTION.*

I hope Mum never sees that picture. Nobody who ever loved me should have to see it.

I know what they're doing. I'm certain. I try to imagine what will happen tomorrow. All the analysts will pore over this picture, dissecting every pixel, trying to establish who took it and when and where. And was I a willing participant or was I under duress. And what does that mean in terms of the new trend of radicalization – are girls as much a threat as boys already? Is the fact there's a VIRGIN sign in the background a message? THE NUNS

WITH GUNS debate will be broadcast into every living room. Parents everywhere will shake their heads and say, 'This is serious. It could have blown *there*. Or *there*. With all those passengers.' And then they'll scroll back through the feed and see all the other could-have-beens. And under each one will be the message:

You're next. Anywhere. Anytime. Anyplace.

And there will be complaints and recriminations on how the police were TOO SLOW and how they should have got to London Bridge or Heathrow SO MUCH MORE QUICKLY. And there'll be an inquiry and someone will recommend a change in the law, so police can access CCTV without having to seek permissions, and someone else will say the Freedom of Information Act is not fair, or that unsupervised police access to all CCTV cameras contravenes civil liberties and the freedom of the individual – and we are in danger of ALL being under surveillance ALL the time . . .

And the police will plead: How could WE KNOW where or even WHEN the images of her were taken?

Maybe they were taken weeks ago?

How could WE BE SURE she wasn't entirely complicit?

And the debate will carry on with WAS SHE IN ON IT?

YES, SHE WAS; NO, SHE WASN'T.

And the Brightness will be laughing.

Because they were one step ahead.

And that cool guy in the checkout queue will be sorry he ever lent me his phone. His name will appear on every terrorist blacklist forever. And Virgin shares will take a huge market tumble.

And Mum? She won't believe I was ever one of them. But her bosses might. Will she lose her job? She loves that job. She won't care about the job if she loses me.

It seems however much I try, I will still leave a trail of devastation behind me. I'll make it count, though, everyone. I swear I will. Today hasn't ended yet. And I'm so sorry.

I squeeze my eyes tight. Force all tears away. Because for all that to happen, Apocalypse will have had to have blown me up first.

12

Indulge in Group Isolation

(Allow the group to exert a totalising influence over you, or face social death.)

1:16 p.m. AND WE'RE ON A SIDE STREET IN WINDSOR – just a quick jog up to the castle. Here there are plenty of tourists too. CONQUER THE TOWER TOUR. IT WILL BLOW YOU AWAY. I double check the job detail for Exodus One.

- Windsor Castle
- Reading Hub
- Film and photo and upload to @theUKbrightnesscellE #EndTimeDayofAction.
- Follow on rail communications to final destination.
- Bristol Hub Temple Meads train station.
- Retire.

No special details for Windsor Castle. And it's not the end of the line. Not yet. I close my eyes. I pray I'm right.

I get out of the car and start jogging. As I turn into the long drag up to the castle the Voice crackles in my ear. At the same time I get a text.

1.19: This is a confirmation SMS: welcome to EE.

1.20: Snap a selfie with the castle and the tourists in the background. Upload it to the email address, and we'll give you extra time to get to your next destination.

Extra time. Big Deal.

Definitely Smooth Milk Chocolate.

My heart's banging. My back is slick with sweat. The mobile hasn't got a lot of charge left on it. But the extra time has to be good.

Though not as good as the rest of my life.

I crouch, poise, snap the picture. Check it has the castle in it with the flag flying. I send it to the email address.

'Good,' crackles the Voice. 'Now get to Reading Railway Station by three.'

So that's my extra ration of life is it? One hour and forty minutes.

'But,' I say, 'you said . . .' My voice trails off.

'We do not negotiate. We will not communicate again,' says the Voice. Predictably.

'But . . .' I try again.

This time all I get is a blast from the whistle.

Back in the car, I type to Dave: **Reading Train Station 3.00.** Then I add: **Can you get the receiver out of my ear? I've had it with the whistling. I don't care any more about how much it's going to hurt.** I make a hopeful face.

Dave looks thoughtful. He puts down his phone. At first he shakes his head. Then he examines my ear and nods. He points to me, then to himself, then makes a talking movement with his fingers, opening and closing them like 'Yappity-yap', then he makes a 'No' gesture, shaking his head sternly. Does he mean he just called for help and there's none out there? Does he mean we should talk about not cooperating? Does he mean the police have put a trace on his phone and he daren't use it any more?

I don't know. I don't understand. And it doesn't matter. I want the receiver Out Of My Ear. That's as far as I can think. I want to get clear of Windsor. Get to somewhere. And try. I've got one and a half-ish hours to get to Reading and that's plenty of time to stop and rip out my ear canal. Hopefully. If my head does get blown off, I certainly want there to be some sign left on it that I fought back.

While Dave gets the car heading west again down the motorway. I check Exodus's job spec. Yet Again.

- Reading Hub
- Film and photo and upload to @theUKbrightnesscellE #EndTimeDayofAction
- Follow on rail communications to final destination
- Bristol Hub Temple Meads train station
- Retire

Bristol Temple Meads train station, my final destination. I turn the page over in the hope there might be more. But it's still as blank as it was the first time I turned it. I check the second page too. No fresh clues. That's where they'll blow me up then.

My Last Resting Place.

13

Exhibit High-risk Behaviour

(Cement your pathway to status:
re-construe stupidity as bravery and
commitment to the cause.)

WE DRIVE A SHORT DISTANCE until we hit signs to a service station.

I type in a message. **Please?** I point at my ear again. Dave seems to calculate. Then he nods.

The radio says: '. . . *latest figures suggest millions may travel to Bristol today to see the eclipse, which will only be visible for a short time along twenty miles of the Severn Estuary* . . .'

Bristol. Temple Meads.

It all falls into place.

Today the station will be packed. Tourists will be streaming through, travelling west for the eclipse – not just hundreds, but thousands. Maybe even more. And it's strategic too. Blow up a train station and everyone will be scared to travel anywhere by train ever again. Security will go through the roof. Possibly the whole infrastructure of Britain will start to crumble. It'd be easy to police Windsor Castle's one access road; Heathrow already has massive security – but railway stations?

How do you tighten security on hundreds of thousands of miles of track? That whole, huge network? And all the zillions of stations that are the gateways to it?

So that's it. Bristol Temple Meads.

We take the exit. The forecourt to the services is massive. Parking bays stretch for a hundred metres under the blossoming trees. There's an aisle of raised flower beds between the furthest parking spaces and the service station. We head there.

We pull into a bay and keep the engine running.

A family in their estate car pull up too. A dog, steaming up the back window. Kids jumping out the car. Mum and Dad yelling. The kids run around the car and screech, 'We want doughnuts!'

How simple life was when you were a kid and the only thing you wanted was a doughnut. And you were on your way somewhere – going on holiday down to the south-west, to that caravan on the cliffs, overlooking a wide blue ocean; a sandy beach – and you just hoped it wouldn't rain, so that you could go out and build a sandcastle and even when it did rain, it was fun to go to the shopping centre with Mum and look at all the things that were different . . .

I blink, suck in my lip, chew on it.

LIFE IS A SANDCASTLE: ONE HIGH TIDE AND IT'S ALL OVER.

Dave quickly moves the car further off. We swing in under more trees. Spring is already here. One tree is coated in white. Petals caught in the breeze drift like snowflakes across the tarmac in front of the car. Almost like it's snowing. Or someone just got married. And on the grassy bank ahead: daisies, clover.

I wish I'd noticed how beautiful the world was before.

'*Come here*,' mouths Dave. He pulls me to him, lifts the hair back from my ear and examines the earpiece.

Something about his touch, warm and soft. I blink fast. Still so familiar. I haven't felt a touch like that since Naz held me. I try to focus. I look up through the windscreen. *Does he still not understand? Does he still search for answers? I do. Though not about Dave. I'm still trying to understand what happened with Naz.*

The sun's high, heading for grey clouds again. The afternoon is sweeping by. An hour? All the things one could do in an hour.

I reach my hand round for his phone. He places it in my palm. I tap in: **Dig it out. Use anything. Don't care how much it hurts.**

The sun hits the edge of the clouds, a stray beam of light seems to flash off the bonnet and strike the upholstery inside. Dave sorts through the glove compartment, finds one of those tiny screwdrivers for doing electrical work. I bend my head. He tucks the lock of hair back behind my ear, pulls at the device, wiggles it.

The engine runs, the radio blares. I wince, grit my teeth. Is Apocalypse listening, or has he gone off again to admire himself in his mirror? There's no way of knowing.

LIFE IS A MIRROR: YOU ARE THE MAIN FOCUS OF IT.

Dave works his way round the earpiece, lifting it, gently twisting. It hurts, but I clench my jaw tight.

I hold up the phone, tap in: **Can you do it? If so, be quick.**

He taps back: **Not as hard as you think. Only glued into the outer ear canal. Might hurt. May rip the skin.**

He holds my head steady, runs the screwdriver in another exploratory turn around my inner ear, pressing deep. A sharp, stabbing pain shoots from my earhole down the side of my jaw. My teeth suddenly seem to be grinding ice.

Dave cups my face with his other hand. '*Going to be*

225

OK,' he mouths. '*Believe it.*'

I feel the lumps of explosives tight against my ribcage. But I don't contradict him. Dave lays my head on his chest. Nearly face down. Damp cotton. Smell of sweat. I hear his heartbeat. Steady. Strong. I slightly lift my chin to breathe. Dave digs the screwdriver in again, works his way between flesh and plastic. A bead of sweat trickles down my face. The sunlight through the windscreen shines in pale, dappled patches. Unearthly. Beautiful. Another bead of sweat.

Dave turns my face a bit to the side. That stray curl untucks itself, falls across my lips. I blow it away, remembering how I gave my clip to Holly. I look up at him, sideways. Firm mouth, chiselled cheekbones, straight nose. He's frowning.

There's a lump in my chest, and a sudden longing. I wish – somehow, magically – he could wave the earpiece out. Slip me out of the vest, and we'd be on the road – *just driving till we hit some great highway, heading off to that caravan in the south-west, to some crazy place, with a beach and a dog and a bag of doughnuts* . . .

Out of the blue I catch myself imagining what it might be like to be with him again.

Before I have time to bite down, Dave rips the earpiece out.

A wave of nausea hits my throat, shoots into my back, across my shoulder. My stomach clenches up. And I scream. I can't help it.

There's an ear-splitting whistle. The Voice clicks in.

I bite the scream off. Dave holds the earpiece close, and I whisper into the bloody set: 'Sorry. It's nothing. I just bit my tongue, and knocked the earpiece by mistake. I'm so hungry, I've gone hypoglycaemic. I've stopped, to find food. I've got to eat . . .'

There's another short sonic blast. Then the Voice says, 'You have your mission. Every second you waste reduces your chance of success.'

So they were listening.

But suddenly I don't care. I feel like laughing. *The thing is out.* My ear is bleeding like crazy. And I Don't Care. I press Dave's hand in thanks.

Dave examines the receiver. He sorts about in the side pockets of the car, pulls out a tissue, wraps up the earpiece in it. He holds it at arm's length, whispers to me, 'Well done, Gen, you were spectacular.' He wipes the blood from my cheek with the front of his T-shirt. And in a brotherly way he kisses my forehead.

So weird to feel him kiss my forehead.

'If we muffle the earpiece and whisper, they won't be able to hear us,' he whispers.

And suddenly I feel like a naughty kid, whispering after lights out. And so grateful. Because we've freed ourselves – just a bit.

And I've got my voice back.

14

Compete for Who is the Hottest

(Become radicalized as a form of group competition.)

'I ACTUALLY DO NEED THE LOO,' I whisper.

Dave doesn't look happy. 'Can't you go behind a tree?'

I shake my head.

'Well, hurry,' he says. Then he adds, 'If you can, get some crisps, chocolate, whatever's quickest.'

I take the earpiece from him and unwrap it and lodge it into my good ear. I hurry across the car park. At every step, I feel the vest tight against me. I break out into a sweat. I shouldn't go near people really. But I've *got* to pee. Wash my ear. Sort myself out.

I reassure myself with the certainty that they want me on that train, and blowing me up in a Chicken'n'

Fries outlet on the M4 isn't exactly going to strike terror into millions.

As long as they think you're on track, it'll be OK, I try to tell myself. Have Faith.

I get to the end of the car park. A huge horse chestnut is struggling to burst into blossom. I can see each bud, like a candle-tip, ready to flower. How beautiful. How amazing. I think of Holly. My eyes start to well up. I love life. I want to cling to it. I'm so scared of dying. And that's the worst thing – *I'm so freaking scared of dying.*

And this stupid jacket is way too big. I can't even fold my arms across my chest. I let them hang limply at my sides. I walk on the white lines of the car park. Try not to step off them. Walk down the next.

Stay on the white, you'll be all right.

Step on the black, break your back.

LIFE IS A BALANCING ACT: ONE FALSE STEP AND YOU'LL REGRET IT. I think of Dave kissing my forehead. I think of Naz. I think of my search for the ultimate metaphor for life. Me, forever making up one-line LIFE IS poems.

I miss Naz so much.

I reach the motorway facilities. I see myself in the sliding glass doors. Strange. Scary. I swing my arms a little. My hair's gone completely mad. It's all standing up. My body looks odd. Spookily padded out in the wrong places. My skirt stupidly short. The leather jacket is not all that shit hot after all. It looks like HELL'S ANGEL MEETS THE HOMELESS SHELTER. The doors slide open. Behind me people press past. I step to one side, scared that they may knock into me, dislodge something.

Inside the precinct. I head to the ladies. I catch another glimpse of myself in the mirrors. Beyond dreadful. I haven't even got a brush, haven't got eyeliner, no lip-gloss. NO MAKE-UP. Holly would HATE me going around looking such a mess. I smile at myself: *like you've got nothing else to worry about, Genesis?*

I get to the loo. I've been so scared, I haven't realized how much I *do* need it. After I've peed, I just sit there in the closed cubicle. My head in my hands. Trying to think my way out of this. Trying not to think at all.

I wash my hands. I remove the earpiece. I clean it as best I can and wrap it in loo roll. I put it in a great wodge of tissue in a zip pocket of the jacket. I splash my face. I squint at my reflection in the mirror. How much longer can I do this?

Then I set about bathing my bad ear. Gritting my teeth, I trickle warm water into it. Slosh it around, tip my head and roll it from side to side. *God it stings.* I even punch the soap dispenser and splosh some of that in too. I clean out everything by half ducking my head under the tap. It hurts like hell. My eyes water all by themselves, and I'm not even crying. It starts bleeding a bit. I dab it dry with more loo paper. Then roll up a tissue plug and pack it into my ear.

A girl comes out of a loo cubicle, shoots me a questioning look, then makes straight for her stuff. I back off a little, with a: *wasn't-going-to-touch-your-bag* look. She washes her hands, starts doing her eyes. I look on jealously, as she brushes mascara into her lashes. Wistfully I stare at the cosmetics bag on the tiles in front of her. She looks up, sees me and raises her eyebrows.

'Yeah, I know,' I say, 'a train wreck.' I run my fingers through my hair, trying to make it settle down.

'Oh sort it,' she says and nods in a conspiratorial way at the make-up bag. 'You can't go around looking like *that,* girlfriend.'

'Thanks,' I say in surprise.

I grab the make-up bag. I shouldn't really. No time, for one thing. 'You sure?'

'Go ahead!' she laughs. 'And don't thank me. It's not mine! I was worried it was yours! I've already taken advantage. Some dumbster left it there! She's probably in Bristol by now.' She holds up a tube. 'A girl's first duty

232

is to wear the coolest shade of lipstick, right?'

Quickly I raid the cosmetics bag, find a comb, tug at my hair, find lip-gloss. Put some on. I find more mascara, make my eyes look better. After that I put it all back.

'Woo, speed make-over,' says the girl. She pulls out some perfume from her own bag and sprays me: a wonderful, fresh spring smell, like freesias and grapefruits. She points to the leather jacket with the vest underneath. 'Call out the fashion police,' she laughs.

I look at it in the mirror.

Ugly. Horrific.

'Yeah,' I say. 'Tell them to arrest me!' Then I'm gone. Out into the foyer, ducking into a stationery shop. Cold drinks and sandwiches are tucked behind the magazine aisles. Up near the counter is a coffee-dispensing machine and snacks. I love coffee. But no time. If I race, I can beat the three people heading for the till. A woman in her sixties. An old man with his old wife.

I jump in front of them. I grab two bags of crisps – cheese and onion, salt and vinegar – and two Mars bars. The old man looks pretty grumpy. He gives me a look designed to deflate. I ignore it. I could blow him up with the flick of a wrist. I pay for the things. I take the bag and head out.

Under four minutes.

Back at the car. Dave says, 'Wow.'

I don't answer. Instead I take the earpiece back out of my pocket and put it on the dash.

15

Provoke Governments to Crack Down on You

(Legitimize further violence by making the enemy strike back.)

'I'M GOING TO TRY AND DO SOMETHING TO YOUR RECEIVER,' Dave says. 'And I've set up a rendez with some mates to look at the vest. Don't worry, it's on our way – but don't get your hopes up too much.' He picks the earpiece off the dash, and carefully unwraps it.

Of course my hopes SOAR. A rendezvous! They'll look at the vest and find a way to get it off me! I want to ask: *Do you think that* . . . and *Does it mean this* . . . but I'm too scared to even go there.

'What mates?' I say instead. I try to remember who his mates were. Will they remember me? Or has he moved on so completely since we were together that they'll be strangers? New mates, new dreams. Maybe a new girlfriend? I realize that hurts. He's not allowed to have a new girlfriend. How bizarre. As if I still want him for me.

'Ex-army, bomb-disposal guys,' he says. 'But – honestly Gen – please don't. These things can be complicated.'

'OK,' I say, my mouth suddenly dry, my heart fluttering like a moth's inside it.

Dave turns the earpiece over. After a close examination, he seems satisfied about something. He copies down some coding on the inside of it, into his own handset. He hands the earpiece back to me. Quickly, I wrap it back up in the tissue. Dave works on settings in his phone.

'Bluetooth it?' I ask, still really wanting to ask about his bomb-disposal friends and where we are meeting them and what he's told them.

'Better than Bluetooth.' He holds up his handset. 'This unit has wireless communication technology. I can connect it with any other device – it can even connect *itself* to any other device that accesses remote radio waves.' He gets that geeky look, so I stop him mid-stream.

'Won't Apocalypse realize?' I whisper.

'It'll transmit files and contact details between multiple devices, intercept ongoing transfer of data . . . with a bit of luck we can divert any detonation commands too. You'd be surprised at how simple detonation is. Just one number. One phone call. If I can trace that number I can re-route it through my handset. Then I'm in with a chance.'

If he can trace the detonation call, he can re-route it. My God, he can re-route the detonation call! *Can it be true? Can I be so lucky?*

How bizarre to feel lucky when you're strapped inside a suicide vest.

But I am lucky! I'm lucky to be here with Dave. Lucky he loves technology. Lucky to be in with a chance.

And I try to imagine how it might be. How I'd feel if, suddenly, we could miraculously intercept that detonation call. *How one day we might come back here, to this same car park, with crisps and Mars bars and see the flowers on the horse chestnut in full bloom.*

And then I'm confused. If getting the earpiece out was all it took, why didn't we get it out before?

And I say so.

'It wouldn't have helped us before,' whispers Dave, 'because we didn't have the command centre's mobile number until now, so I had no way to get in.'

'The command centre's number?'

Dave shows me his bare arm. The black inked mobile number.

'It must have been Apocalypse who was calling Exodus One.'

And I realize he's right. Those fourteen calls must have been from the command centre.

'If I can hack this number and download all its recent usage, and re-route all the numbers through mine, I can work out which one is the detonation one.'

'How?'

'Process of elimination. Plus, they must have done dummy trials on the vest, and each trial would need a call, and each call would only last for a split second. Can't be many numbers on the call-log with that profile.'

My heart lurches with a sudden crazy hope. I pull out a chocolate bar from the plastic bag. I rip off the paper. I bite into it and start at the way saliva spurts into the sides of my mouth. I didn't know I was so hungry. I give Dave one.

'Meanwhile I'm going to try and amplify volume by sending the input to this earpiece through the car speakers.' Dave puts the Mars bar down on the dash tray. 'If we can hear more background detail, we can listen for clues, hopefully figure out where they might be.'

I stop chewing.

'Every network has its own fingerprint. And every street its own sounds. Plus, they may give themselves away. If we can pinpoint their command centre – I know it's a long shot,' the vein on the side of Dave's jaw pulses, 'but I'm going to get them, Gen. I really am.' He plugs some wires from his phone into the car's media centre.

I crowd forward, try to peer at what he's doing, watching in admiration.

'Give me a bit of space, so I can read the settings on this thing.' Dave gently pushes me out of the light. 'We're short on time.' He takes the earpiece out of its wrapping and turns it over.

I draw back. Give him air. Give him light.

And then I hear a ping, a new kind of sound, as if all the phones in the neighbourhood are being turned off, or put on hold.

Then Dave punches the air. 'Got ya!' he hisses.

He adjusts something. Some new frequency? He taps in different details on his handset. And suddenly, through the speakers in the car, I hear talking. Some sort of call centre? In the distance, strange voices. Clicking. I can definitely hear a voice giving out instructions and someone else being told to keep moving. Familiar echoes.

And suddenly I can identify it. *It's the hub.* The room they're operating from.

'Let's see what you're up to, then,' mutters Dave. He leans forward and turns up the volume on the car radio.

Another voice comes on the line. Then the clicking again. I hear the Voice, Apocalypse, in the distance, going over some location details. In the background, a familiar kind of howling noise – or maybe screeching – like air trapped in a wind tunnel.

And someone else.

Someone whose voice I recognize.

Oh my God.

'We're through to their command,' says Dave. 'This is getting interesting.'

Very quietly, I sit back in my seat.

Dave turns, sees me. 'You're very pale,' he says. 'Stay strong. Small steps – we're spying on *them* now. *And* I've stopped this little beauty from transmitting too. They can't hear us any more. All they'll get is interference and a bit of radio.' He places the earpiece on the dash tray. 'Information Technology, Gen,' a note of pride swells in his voice, 'is what I do.' He unwraps the chocolate bar and devours it in two bites.

I can feel all the blood draining from my heart. My knees going all shaky.

'I'll crack the detonation code. I swear to God, Gen, I'll keep you safe.'

'It's not that,' I whisper.

Dave holds out the other chocolate bar. My appetite's

completely gone. 'I've contacted my mates. We'll try our best to get the vest off you, even if we can't stop them.'

The transmission crackles. And I hear his voice again.

Must be someone who just sounds like him. Mustn't it? People do sound like each other, don't they?

But I'd know that voice anywhere, even if I lived to be a thousand.

I've heard it in my dreams.

I never imagined I'd hear it in my nightmares.

'What is it?' asks Dave.

My mouth goes dry. I can't swallow.

'*It's Naz*,' I say. 'That's Naz talking on the transmission.'

16

Help Your Radical Group Gain Legitimacy

(Produce backlash so that the existing political order loses credibility.)

I SIT THERE, stunned. It can't be.

'Tell me about Naz,' Dave demands.

I lean forward, turn the volume up to its loudest.

'Tell me everything,' Dave says.

But I don't know what 'everything' is.

'Ev-ery-thing,' Dave spells it out. 'Our lives may depend on it.'

There he is again.

'I can't help you if I don't know what the hell's going on.'

It's definitely him.

He flicks the engine into life.

'OK,' I say.

I take a deep breath. Tell him about Naz. But what do I know about Naz? The Naz I loved and cried over? The Naz who loved me back, promised to be mine, forever?

And suddenly the world is spinning. *Naz is not the Naz I used to know. How can he be? The Naz I used to know loved me.*

How can that be this same Naz?

It can't be.

A Naz who straps me to a bomb?

I blink, suck in my bottom lip. 'OK,' I repeat.

We pull out of the service station and get back on to the highway. I sit there, biting my lip.

'Where did you meet him?'

Breathe. 'At school, in the sixth form.'

'OK. Where's he from?'

I take a deep breath. 'He's from Newport.'

'So he's Welsh?'

'I think his parents just moved there.'

'Parents?'

'Quite rich,' I say. 'Got a stepdad, he doesn't like him much.'

'Who did he live with?'

Small stones spray up behind us as we race up the slip road.

'An uncle, I think.' I realize how little I do know. Why was he in school in London? Why not an arts school in Cardiff? I never asked. I didn't need to. I just loved him.

'Getting into drama school is a big deal,' I say. 'And if you have to leave home to take up your place, that's part of it.' I just supposed he was like me, mad about performing, thrilled to be in London.

Through the wing mirror, I see a car pull off the hard shoulder at speed. Looks like a patrol car. It comes racing up the outside lane, straight after us. I look across at Dave in alarm.

'Shit,' he says. 'We've got company.'

I freeze, hold on to my seat belt.

'Try to remember everything,' he says. 'Let me concentrate on driving.' Dave flicks up the sat nav app on his phone, tosses it at me. 'Get the map up.'

A blue light starts flashing behind us. Some kind of patrol car. Dave hits the accelerator. 'Map-read us to High Woods.'

A siren suddenly splits the air. We zoom forward. 'Hope this car's got good tyres,' Dave says, and we streak off, like a plane down a runway.

I'm holding my breath, but not like before. I can't work

it out. Even as I press myself tight against the car seat, I still can't work it out. How can I? All I can work out is a whole pile of nothing.

Why would Naz join an extremist group? I know all about dying your hair and wearing Lumin-cool stuff. Being a 'Brightness Brother'. I mean, that's one thing. Not that it's OK to glamorize terrorism. But it's just fashion – isn't it? I mean, boys like all those guns and things and I understand that. But to buy into the whole deal? To take it to the max – to actually think about killing people? *To think about killing your girlfriend.* Wouldn't he stop and question what he was doing?

Didn't he care about me?

So did I never know him? But how can that happen? How can you see someone every day and *not* know them? So if I knew him, why didn't I see that he was changing inside? How could I have *no* idea that a new and toxic conversation was playing in his thoughts? Have no idea that, after everyone was asleep, he was waking up and signing in to online terrorist chat rooms, learning to hate, learning to kill?

And why me?

Why kill the person who loves you most?

'Hold tight.' Dave yanks his seat belt. Belts the gas.

I don't understand, Naz. Make me understand.

We hit the speed limit and go past it. The road whizzes beneath us, a grey blur. I love speed, it's like a total sugar rush. But we're hitting the death zone. I hardly notice.

How did it get to this?

Dave checks the mirror, cuts into the very inside of the slow lane and overtakes a coach on the hard shoulder.

'Stay with me, Gen. Think it through. Start at the beginning.'

I hold my breath. I try to focus, think back to the beginning, *to that boy who smiled at me on the first day, at sixth form. How we sat on the college steps in the sun, and shared his bag of tortilla chips. We didn't share my squashed tuna sandwich – I was too shy, too embarrassed. Soggy bread. Oozing tuna.*

Sirens wail. Lights flash. We pass an exit. Dave checks the mirror, says, 'Highway patrol. They won't shoot. Hold on now.'

Then suddenly he slams on the brakes. I rocket forward. *Highway patrol? They've tracked us down. How're we going to get out of this?* My seat belt crunches into me. We swerve on to the hard shoulder. My head smashes against the side window. *Holy Shit. That hurt.* The wheels of the car screech. A plume of tyre rubber whirls up. We turn *completely* round. *360 degrees.* The coach ploughs past. *For frick's sake. That was close.*

Then we race *back* down the hard shoulder *the wrong way*. My pulse explodes like a firework. My head pounds. The patrol car shoots past on the outside lane, sees us too late.

I rub the side of my face. Dave changes down through the gears. Hits the brake. A terrifying squeal. Then we take the exit.

We shoot out of the slip road, race across the roundabout at the top, ignoring traffic lights. *Holy Mary.*

My mind's a whirl. Switching crazily between Naz and why that patrol car was so on to us? Has Exodus One been picked up? Blabbed? Were the number plates on this car dodgy after all? Something's up for sure. And now a description of our location and probably what we had for breakfast last weekend will be circling nationwide.

At the flyover we send one driver into a skid. Horn blasting. We swing right. Over the motorway, head out towards Reading.

'By now they've matched us to the car check at the police block. We *need* to change cars.' Dave hits overdrive.

I check the sat nav. We're OK for High Woods. 'If we keep straight along here,' I say, 'we'll reach a right turn. Take it.'

'Who did he hang out with?' Dave says.

'Naz?'

'Yes, Naz. Talk about Naz.'

'There was a group of boys, all very full of themselves, being badass and whatever. Some guys, you know – trying to be hard.'

My mind races over that. They were trying to be more than hard. They must have been fantasizing about killing even then. *Why would they do that?*

Because it's fun and addictive? KILLING SOMEONE – THE ULTIMATE BUZZ. I think about the way Naz was hooked into gaming. POW. POP. BANG. Blood splatter. YOUR LIVE RANKING IS IN THE 100 PERCENTILE. YOU HAVE KILLED MORE ZOMBIES TODAY THAN ANYONE ELSE ONLINE.

LIFE IS A FANTASY: DEATH A FULFILMENT.

'Anyone in particular?'

'Not really. Not amongst his friends.'

'Try harder, Gen. Remember everything you can. Naz is our way into this cell. We need to know who we're up against. What their screwy plan is.'

I rack my brains. I go over the way Naz and I held hands in the corridor, how we had our favourite spot on the campus, how we texted each other in class. How we hung out after school behind the sports and dance facility. My eyes suddenly itch and I have to tilt my chin up.

'They'll download every inch of CCTV footage, from

every camera across London, every mile of the M4,' says Dave. 'It may take an hour, but no more. They'll be on our tail *very* soon, so please try.'

'But like what?'

'Search wider. Anyone at all in the school – anything?'

The sports and dance facility.

And I remember.

'Yes,' I say.

'What?'

'The football coach.'

17

Embrace Good and
Evil Thinking

(See the enemy as less human, so that they
don't trigger your inhibitions against violence.)

'THE FOOTBALL COACH WAS ONE OF THEM.'

'One of who?'

'Them. The Brightness. He had that dyed yellow hair. And all the Lumin-cool gear. Though I never saw any tattoos round his wrist.'

'You're sure?'

I nod. 'Yeah, but it doesn't always follow that dyed hair equals total Lumin extremism, does it?'

'Just tell me.'

'Well, Naz was trying out for rowing. The guy, sir, Mr Farringdon, thought he was junior Olympic standard.'

'And?'

'Turn right here.'

'Give me the phone.' Dave takes the turn, slows, checks the map. 'OK,' he says. 'They'll be updating local police. We've got very little time. Hold on. Shut your eyes if it helps to remember. And talk.'

'You just get us there,' I say. I need to think.

And I shut my eyes and I do remember – when Naz stopped coming round to be with me. Skipped the chats and went straight to rowing. When he started doing a lot of praying: sunrise, sunset, before exams; asking weird questions, like, was I prepared to follow 'My Man' even if he had to marry other childmakers? Like where did that word 'childmakers' come from? And whoever mentioned marriage?; like, 'would I shave my head and get his name tattooed across it?

And other weird, stupid stuff.

Dave belts the car forward, and we race through a labyrinth of country lanes. My seat belt tightens against the vest. Hedgerows whirl, like in a blender. 'Tell me about the rowing club.'

'Mr Farringdon selected boys who were keen.' I pause. *Did he?* He selected Naz and Johan and Cadiz and Jake and Nathan. Were *they* keen? I don't remember them being very keen on anything except looking hardass and slacking off. Cadiz was a total waster at everything except acting. He couldn't row to save his life.

'He collected boys who were losers,' I say. *Was Naz a loser?*

Dave nods.

We whizz past pooled water, send a spray tree-trunk high.

'OK. So what did you do with Naz: before, after, during. Everything. Any detail – where you went, who you met – anything could save our lives.'

I feel the weight of the vest. Still damp. I breathe in. I know how close to death I'm sailing. *Sailing.*

Sailing up the River Severn. That picture of us above my bed – when we were so happy. Naz liked sailing. He loved boats. That's why he tried out for the rowing.

Naz, how could you? We were so happy.

'We went to his favourite place,' I say. 'Down past Gloucester, across from Chepstow. His family had a flat in Bristol; we stayed there. Naz "borrowed" the key to it. He liked doing that sort of thing, in secret, a surprise.'

'And behind someone's back.'

'Suppose so.'

'And I bet it was his stepfather's old place, wasn't it?'

I glance at him. How did he know that?

'Because he didn't like his stepfather, did he?' Dave

takes a corner at such speed the back wheels of the car slide across the road. 'You meet them all in the army; certain types that're always looking for a way to get back at someone, for something. Imagined or real. They're all haters, eaten up with anger.'

'No, he wasn't like that,' I protest.

'So what was he like?' Dave suddenly laughs. 'No need to answer that,' he says. 'Maybe I'm jealous. Beautiful girl like you. Scum of the earth like him. Just tell me about his dad's place.'

Beautiful girl like me.

Suddenly tears well up. I think of the girl in the service station mirror. I glance down at the jacket. Ugly. Horrific. And Dave sees beyond that. He always did.

He still sees I'm beautiful.

I suck in my lip, squeeze my eyes tight, swallow the tears in tiny sniffs. Is he still jealous? 'We went there one weekend.' I force my voice to grow steady. This is so dreadful. *How can I be telling Dave this?* 'A studio flat in Bristol, right near the train station. And we went sailing at Oldbury. Just a bike-ride away.'

And I was so beautiful then. There, with you, Naz. How could you have turned me into this?

'We had motorbikes. Well, Naz had a motor bike.' I don't say: *He taught me to ride a motorbike.* I wish he'd never taught me anything. I wish I'd learned to swim instead. Oh God. This is so embarrassing. I try to change the topic. 'We were researching our social studies project: "Longevity – Why Some People Live Longer".'

That was Naz in the hub. It really was.

'Go on.' A vein pulses down the side of Dave's jaw.

'There's this group of people in the far south of Gloucestershire that reach amazing old ages. One even made a hundred and ten. It used to be a place they sent people to convalesce during the Second World War. Tortworth area. We were supposed to be researching it. But . . .' The vein pulses again. He's really angry. He's driving too fast.

'But what?'

'We spent most of the time at this marina. Naz's stepdad had a boat. That's what Naz liked doing best – speeding up and down the Severn Estuary.'

Oh God.

I check the time. A tractor appears on the opposite side. The road's too narrow. Dave doesn't slack off the speed. The tractor tries to pull as far off the road as it can. I grit my teeth, brace myself. We shoot by, scraping the car on the hedge, knocking the wing mirror flat.

My heart crashes around somewhere against my breast bone.

'Don't lose focus,' says Dave. 'Remember what you can.'

I remember the tearing spray, the wind in my hair, the salt tang on my lips, speeding through a wave of water up the river. How I stood up, like I was on the Titanic, *and shouted out, 'Gonna close my eyes, now.' How I nearly fell in. How Naz dropped the rudder and the wheel and the engine cut and he pulled me down into his arms and we tumbled on to the deck – and the boat did a huge curve too near the coast . . .*

And the seagulls were shrieking. And the spray was spraying. And we were laughing. And I loved speed and I loved Naz.

I remember.

'Rich kid. No love. Hates stepdad. Steals keys and boats. Sociopathic. Sporty but not good enough . . .' Dave seems to be ticking off a mental list, cutting Naz down to size.

Why didn't I see it?

'But . . .' I start.

Dave glances at me.

But he must have been like that, mustn't he? I bite my lip, look away. I wonder for a fleeting instant if Dave ever liked speedboats. If he'd ever have taken me on one.

'When did he become a Lumin?'

'Pretty soon after we met,' I say in a very small voice.

255

'Dyed his hair?'

'Yes.'

'Started being, you know, about girls?'

'Yes,' I say.

'It's OK,' says Dave. 'Whatever you did with the guy in his family flat, it's OK. I don't need those details.'

I bite my lip. Those few days, so blissfully alone, so blissfully in love.

I wasn't going to give him 'those' details.

Although they're imprinted on my brain forever.

18

Desire to Die for a Cause

(Pursue martyrdom as an absolute value.)

'WE'RE NEAR THE PLACE,' says Dave.

'How much further?'

'Not far,' he says. 'See that clump of trees? When we get past them, there's no wireless or mobile coverage.'

I look up at woods clinging to the hillside, standing dark against the horizon. I hold my breath, bite my lip.

'Here, look, just hang on.' Dave chucks me his mobile phone. As we climb the slight rise towards the trees, I look down at the connectivity bars on his phone. They blink out. A brief message flashes on to the screen: Searching . . .

'See,' says Dave. 'The police won't find us easily up here, and the Brightness can't detonate. We're safe while we take a good look at that thing. Believe me, I know.

My mates wouldn't have agreed to it otherwise.'

We crest the top of the hill. The bars on the mobile don't reappear. Instead it reads: **No Signal.**

'I come up here with the lads when we want to get a few things done – you know – off the radar.'

I try to imagine all the things he must have done since we parted. The continent of Dave. Sudden new, uncharted territory. I glance away – out of the window across the rolling plains of Berkshire. I chew the inside of my cheek, try to focus on the horizon, settle the churning in my stomach.

'But will we still be able to get to Reading?'

'Worst case scenario? We've got forty-five minutes.'

'Let's hurry then.'

I realize I'm trembling. Dave pulls the car off the road and into the woodland. Huge trees. Silver-grey trunks. Dappled shade. We bump between foliage. Ferns. Nettles. Crumbled tarmac. Potholes. We take a left fork on to a dirt track. Grass growing down its centre. Thin branches scrape the sides of the car, brush across the roof. Dave pushes on until the trees give way to a small clearing. A low composite-walled building stands there, green with algae. Some kind of barn? Outhouse? World War Two bunker?

'Base camp,' he says. 'We'll hide the car first.' He points

into the woodland where the undergrowth is at its densest with spring foliage. 'Far side. For a quick getaway.'

'Do you always think of everything?' I ask.

He laughs. 'Always look for your way out, as soon as you find your way in.' He flashes me a sudden sad smile.

Oh dear God, let them get the vest off.

We drive past the old building. Close up, I can see it's not as abandoned as it looks. Somebody has obviously repaired it. The roof looks in good nick – though still covered with a kind of green mould. On the far side, we turn a sharp right behind a giant beech.

'Over there.' Dave points out a jeep, well camouflaged behind a pile of logs. The jeep is angled out for a clean downhill run on to a field, just near the verge of the woodland. 'Marco and Bill. Dead professional.'

Dave aligns the car next to theirs. 'Just in case,' he says.

I'm so glad he's with me, so lucky to have him here. I make a mental note to always be on Dave's team in future. If we have any future. A wild hope starts to beat at my heart. *Please let me have a future.* I hold my breath. I flex my fingers. I can hardly believe. This may be it. The end of the nightmare. Then I stumble out of the car. The vest has dried a bit, it clings to me. Heavy. Frightening.

Dave takes my elbow. 'C'mon, no time to waste. Let's hope it's nearly over.'

Please, I breathe, *please let it end.*

We run, ducking through the trees, towards the low hut.

Inside are two guys. They're in civvies. One of them is rolling a cigarette. The other is sitting on a bale of very old and very mouldy hay, chewing gum.

They both stand up, like I'm royalty. It makes something catch in my throat.

'Sorry about your sis,' says the tall one to Dave.

'Meet Bill,' says Dave.

'It's shit,' says the other – Marco, I presume, 'and we wanna help.'

'And sorry about your friend.' Bill nods at me.

'Meet Gen,' Dave says. 'She's pretty special, and she's been through a lot.'

The tears just well up again. *Beautiful* and *special.* Oh Dave.

'We'll do what we can for you,' says Bill.

'You poor kid,' says Marco. 'I'd give you a hug, but I'd like to get that bomb off you first.' His smile is genuine and warm.

I'm not sure what to say. I'm not sure I won't cry. So I just say, 'Hi,' and wave a hand at them. Then I feel at least I should try: so I say, 'I'd give you both a hug, if I wasn't in this.'

Bill crosses over to Dave, puts a brotherly arm over his shoulder. 'I'm really sorry, mate,' he says.

Dave just nods. His chin stiffens. His lips go tight.

Bill sees. Moves back. Turns to me. 'OK, Gen,' he says. 'You're in safe hands. We've dismantled bombs on the side of roads, under enemy fire. We've tackled ordinances attached to the wheels of armoured jeeps, just ticking away; and once we took a suicide vest off a kid sent to the barriers. We're trained, and I want you to know we update our training to keep abreast of every new IED trick being used. Especially since the advent of the Brightness.'

'Improvised Explosive Device,' explains Dave.

Bill's eyes are so sincere. His voice so steady.

'And although we served with Dave, we've been demobbed. Marco and I are freelance now – EOD specialists. Explosive Ordnance Disposal. We work mainly for commercial outfits now – BombRisk and the like. Dave was lucky to catch us, we've only just got in from the Middle East.'

He says it like it's his usual induction talk, all kind of formal and friendly and professional, but I don't mind. I prefer it really – it makes me feel safer.

'Thank you,' I whisper.

'We'll do what we can, but we've limited equipment with us and no time to go for backup.' There's a note in his voice warning me not to get my hopes up too high.

'So if you'd just like to come and lie on the couch,' Marco points to some mouldy hay bales, dragged to form a ledge under the window, 'we can see what we're dealing with.'

I bite my lip. *Oh God please let them get it off.*

Dave takes my hand, squeezes it. 'Believe me, they're the best,' he says. 'If they can't remove it, they'll tell us.'

Suddenly it's really hard to reach the hay bales. Dave catches my elbow. Bill puts out his cigarette. I lean on Dave, dizzy, my heart skipping every other beat. I lower myself on to the hay. Marco sets up a device on the floor and links it up to a car battery. It winks in steady green flashes.

'Hey-ho,' says Marco after a few seconds.

'What's wrong?' asks Dave.

'Here we go round the merry-go-round.'

'What do you mean?' I look up at Dave, at Bill, at Marco.

Bill moves over and takes a look. Marco points out something on the device. 'It's complicated with these homemade explosive vests,' Bill tries to explain. 'Because the components the bombers use are put together in a way not intended by their manufacturers, the method of producing the intended explosion is limited by the science, and by the imagination of the guys who built the vest. So it's not always possible to follow a step-by-step approach.'

'So sometimes we have to get creative too,' adds Marco.

I suck in air. I can tell by their tone that that's not what they like doing.

'The first principles of explosives is to try and deduce what the perpetrator has done,' adds Bill by way of an afterthought.

A wind seems to have sprung up outside and some kind of bird lands on the roof of the hut with a crashing, scuttling noise that spooks me out.

'Also, some IEDs are set up to deliberately target IED operators,' Bill adds.

'Pity you couldn't have brought her in properly,' says Marco. 'Roadside recovery is never as good.'

'Also,' says Bill with a very serious note, 'the presence of chemical, biological, or nuclear material can't be ruled out.'

'Well I think we can rule out nuclear,' says Marco. 'The Geiger counter's not biting.'

'OK, check connectivity,' Bill says to Marco. 'We don't want some idiot to detonate it here.'

'It's down. And gonna stay down. Out of range by three miles,' says Marco.

'Turn on the THOR?' says Bill.

'No – save the battery, there's no coverage.'

'You got a THOR here?' says Dave, a sudden note of excitement.

'What's a THOR?' I ask.

'The THOR III is awesome,' says Dave. 'It's a man-portable, counter-radio-controlled improvised-explosive-device jammer.' The geek look clocks up to full strength in Dave's eyes. 'It uses three transceivers – low, mid, and high bandwidth – to jam radio-controlled IEDs. And it's mobile, mounted on a backpack – you can take it with you anywhere.'

'Just stops them detonating, Gen,' says Marco kindly. 'And sucks a lot of juice doing it.'

'If we can't get her out of the thing right now, can I take the THOR?' Dave says.

Bill nods. 'You'll just owe us hundreds of thousands if you don't bring it back.'

'How much power has it got?' asks Dave.

'There's a battery pack that'll last you about an hour,' says Marco. 'It'd be too heavy to carry around more.

The THOR alone, with just that pack, will weigh about thirty kilos.'

Gingerly I sit there. 'Should I stand up?' I ask.

'No, don't,' says Bill. 'First, I want to see how they've attached it at the back.'

Bill turns me, so my back is towards the light. He examines the vest. Carefully, he slits through some outer material, prods and pushes around at the packaging of the device underneath. Dave comes round to the front, squats down and places my hands in his. 'It's going to be OK, Gen, try to believe that,' he says. 'You've been so brave. And they have a THOR.'

A lump rises in my throat, a strange fizzing starts inside the bridge of my nose.

'Not very sophisticated,' Bill says. 'Though shit-kickingly lethal.'

'Cheap,' says Marco. 'Those guys are always so cheap.'

'But *that*'s not cheap,' says Bill, prodding something.

I feel them tapping around below my collar bone. Marco fetches the monitor.

'Get into your locker gear, Marco,' says Bill. 'Dave, you get back to your car, or further. This is a well-designed piece of kit. It'd take a truck over it before it triggers, but there'll be a catch; always is with these bastards.'

They've found something. Something they don't like.

Dave shakes his head, doesn't let go of my hand. 'Forget it,' he says, 'I'm staying put.'

'What is it?' I say. I've never heard my voice sound so weak, so faint.

'It's just a bit more complicated than we thought,' says Marco.

19

Be Committed Until Death

(Display outsized demonstrations of loyalty at all times.)

STRIPES OF SUNLIGHT sparkle on the dust of the old window pane. I stare at the grime and motes floating in the sunbeams. I focus as hard as I can, so that I won't move or scream. I look up into Dave's face. His eyes hold me steady.

We could be blown apart – right here and now – everything else means nothing – this moment – right now – Dave and me – maybe forever.

'We're going to have to cut the straps,' says Bill. He touches my shoulder, and immediately I freeze up.

'*Is this it?*' I ask, biting down too hard on my lip. Is this the moment when my brief little life is over? It feels so short. Too short. So many things left undone.

'I mean your bra strap,' Bill mumbles.

I hold my breath.

'We're going to see if we can find any sensors,' says Bill. He starts patting the vest. He holds a monitor over it, moves it slowly up and down, just like a sweep search at the airport. Methodically he runs it the length of my top. The green light on the device blinks and blinks – sometimes faster sometimes slower. Lets out a series of high-pitched squeals.

Marco snips at my clothing.

'OK, I've cut the bra straps, and your top – across the neck line,' he says. 'Is there anything else you wear under your top?'

'No,' I say, 'only a chain.' The chain Naz gave me with the little pendant sun on it. I don't need his chain any more. 'Cut it off,' I say. If only I could cut him out so easily.

'Gonna have to,' says Bill. 'Don't want it to catch on anything. The idea is, that if we can cut away any clothing that might snag us up, we can examine the inside of the vest without taking it off you. We're going to try and use this device.' He shows me a flat, ruler-like thing. 'It's just a scanner. It'll tell us where everything is on the computer. Gives us more detailed information.'

'Opening up the vest, at this point, is not something

we're going to go for. Trust me about that.'

'OK,' I gasp.

Bill rotates the vest. It's still very tight. He eases it from side to side and up and down a bit.

'Sorry,' he says.

'OK,' I say.

He snips and continues easing the vest very slightly until everything underneath is clear. Then he slides the scanner down my back.

Dave turns to me, his face anxious, pale. 'You're doing great, Gen,' he says.

'Can you hold your arms straight above your head and hold very still, Gen? There could be anything going on under the wiring – we've only got limited equipment here.' Bill waits for me to raise up my arms.

'OK,' I say. I keep my arms straight above my head.

'Hold still now,' Bill says. 'We've got a problem.'

I hold still. Very, very still.

'I see what they've done, cheap bastards,' curses Marco.

'What?' Hands still straight above my head.

'Shit.'

I hold my breath.

'*Shit. Shit. Shit. Double bastard shit*,' swears Marco.

'What is it?' I say, my voice so small it's hardly a whisper.

269

'What?' yells Dave.

'Tell them,' says Marco.

'They've wired a timer in—' explains Bill.

'How long has she got?' demands Dave.

'– and jamming the airwaves won't stop it,' says Bill.

'How long?' I say.

'Just spit it out,' yells Dave.

'And we can't stop it. Not with the kit we've got.'

'OK,' I say.

'And we can't take the vest off either,' adds Bill, 'well, not here.'

'I'm so sorry,' says Marco.

'We need to take you in, or go for a lot more equipment.' Bill is looking really worried.

And that's when we hear the police sirens.

'Great – backup troops already here,' says Marco.

'Thought you said this job was off radar?' says Bill.

Dave jumps up, runs outside. Within seconds he's back. 'Guys, we've only got a few minutes. The police will come armed and ready to shoot. Police counter-terrorism. Deadly Force Policy. They shot . . . Holly – like that.' Dave bites down on his lip.

'OK,' says Bill.

'Copied,' says Marco.

Bill looks at Marco. Marco looks at Bill. Dave says, 'You

don't have to suck this up, guys. You get going – get clear.'

'Not the way it works,' says Bill.

'It does this time.'

'Dave, you're a bastard, you know,' says Marco.

The police sirens howl out much louder.

'Way I see it,' says Bill, 'you guys are under fire. We're your decoys. You take the THOR and retreat. We'll give you cover, hold off the advance.'

'See if you can negotiate?'

'As always,' says Marco.

'Stop shitting us around,' says Bill. 'Take your bomb and get going, or we'll all be screwed.'

'I'm stuck with it, aren't I?' I say. *It was too good to be true. There was never any escape.*

'I wish I could wear it for you,' says Dave. And I think he really means it.

'Thanks,' I say, 'but this is my mess.'

Bill kneels beside me. 'This is hard, Gen,' he says. 'We very nearly got it off. Sometimes it's like that. Now you have some choices to make. This bomb cannot be removed here or at any roadside point. You need proper equipment. It's set to detonate by a timer or, earlier, by a mobile phone call. The only way to stop it is to reprogramme it from the hub – or get yourself into an EOD centre.'

'If you can, try to get to a facility near Exeter – Dave

knows it – that's probably best. We can set it up, and bring you in.'

'And I will,' says Dave, 'if I can use the THOR and get the police to hold fire.'

'Before the THOR battery dies,' I say.

Dave goes grey.

'Or the timer times out,' I say.

How long exactly have we got?

Marco looks at me. 'It's not good,' he says. 'It's set to explode at four forty-four p.m.'

20

Start to Take Action Based on Your Beliefs

(Prepare for an Act of Furtherance.)

IT'S 2.40 P.M. NOW. Barely two hours.

If a helicopter swooped us up in the next few seconds and travelled at top speed – with a good wind – straight to the facility in Exeter, we might just make it with about twenty minutes to spare.

But there's no helicopter in sight. And if there was, it'd be far more likely to shoot us down. And even then we'd have to get more battery life for the THOR, which we haven't got here. That is obvious to everyone.

So right now I've got a choice to make.

And I don't know what to do. My heart is banging and tumbling around from my throat to my legs. I think I might throw up. I'm slippy with sweat, but it's like a cold sweat. I think I must be in shock. I have to decide: to walk off into the woods and wait for 4.44 p.m . . .

Or what?

Or carry on running? Following orders from Naz? Until I blow up a multitude of others?

I don't think so.

There's no choice then. There's no way I can get to Exeter in time.

'Is there any other centre we could get to?' I ask.

'There's Edgware,' says Dave. 'That's the closest, but it would mean coming in, setting it up, briefing an army team. It might take longer than a clean run through to Marco's place in Exeter.'

'And we have no mobile coverage for three miles and sharp shooters and still no helicopter,' I say.

I look from Dave's strained face to Marco's to Bill's. Each one of them says it loud and clear.

'If we'd had the THOR, known about the timer earlier . . .' says Dave.

'Guys,' I say. 'It ends here. I'm going for a walk in the woods. Don't follow.'

THE PURPOSE OF LIFE IS TO GIVE LIFE PURPOSE

THIS AFTERNOON WHAT IS LIFE?

(Twenty Things It Could Be)

1

Life is a Dream: Sometimes Good, Sometimes Not, But in the End It's Over

I stumble to the door. Somehow I open it, stagger through. I let out a noise. Not a sound I've ever heard before. It's not a plea for help or even a cry of despair. It's just the sound of something breaking. And I'm half jogging, half floundering. Oh Mum. I wish you were here. And I don't know where I'm going. *I don't know.* I just don't know.

The branches whip at me. It's sodden underfoot. I want to find a hole under the bushes. Somewhere to crawl into.

Behind me I hear footsteps. I hear them, but they don't register.

'Hey,' calls Dave. 'Don't.'

I hear, and I don't hear.

'Gen!'

And suddenly Dave is swinging me round and crushing me against him and holding me tight. And he smells sweaty.

And my throat's hurting.

'Please,' I whisper. 'Let me do this.'

'No,' he whispers. 'I can't.'

'It was my fault,' I say. 'It was me who got involved with Naz.'

'All that was yesterday,' says Dave. 'You're with me right now.'

'There's nothing else I can do.'

'There is,' he says.

'Please, you have a choice,' I say. 'Just leave me.'

'No,' he says. 'If you're going to let them blow you up, then you'll have to blow me up as well.' His voice breaking under a new weight.

I raise my eyes to look at him. His eyes so dark and troubled. He means it.

'Genesis,' he says, 'we have a chance. Don't let Holly die in vain.'

The sound of her name is like a wound I can't escape. It hurts. It forces me to listen. I stand there, trembling. Dave stands there. Sirens wail. The police are nearly here.

A bead of sweat drips off his chin. He wipes his forehead with the back of his hand.

'We carry on,' he says. 'We don't give up.'

'But I can't be responsible for killing all those people.'

'No,' he says, 'you won't be. We'll find another place if it comes to that. Another wood, another patch of wasteland. We'll face it together.'

'But . . .'

'There's still a way. We've come so far.'

'There isn't. You heard Bill: *The only way to stop it is to reprogramme it from the hub – or get yourself into an EOD centre.* And there's no time left to get to an EOD centre.'

'What if I can find the hub, Gen? What if I *can* reprogramme it?'

It's such a long shot, I almost want to laugh.

'We've got a THOR. I've got their command centre mobile number. The papers that driver left say this was Cell E. These guys are territorial – that means Cell E operates around here: between London and Bristol somewhere. Most importantly, you know Naz better than maybe he knows himself. He must have been to that hub often. There's still a chance. *Please* – let's try?'

And I don't know what to do. But he's conjured me with Holly's name. And he's stayed with me every step of the way. And he's ready to stay till the bitter end. So that means I owe it to him?

'I don't know,' I say.

And he takes that for a 'Yes'. And he hugs me closer. Kisses the top of my head.

'Let's move then, quickly.' He grabs my hand, drags me back towards the shed. And I don't resist, though it's all so hopeless. 'Whilst there's still some chance of making the three o'clock deadline in Reading,' he says.

'As long as when the time comes you'll let me go it alone,' I say.

Back in the shed, Dave swaps his tee for Marco's, chucks his old one at me. 'Put that on. We need to change our look a bit.'

I pick up the tee and pull it over my head – it's yellow and too big and it smells of raw, male sweat, deodorant and dock water.

'Thanks,' I whisper.

'For nothing,' says Dave. He pulls on Marco's jacket. My heart catches.

'We'll deal with everything here,' says Bill.

The sound of screaming sirens echoes into the woodland.

'Sort out the police if you can; it'd make life a lot easier,' says Dave.

'Consider it sorted,' says Marco.

'Let's go,' says Dave.

'We'll give you a head start,' says Bill. 'We'll come out and surrender when we're sure you're away.'

'They may shoot,' I whisper.

'Not through these,' says Marco, and I realize both of them are wearing protective body suits.

'Or them.' Marco points at their bomb-disposal helmets.

'OK,' says Dave.

I stand at the door. Sunlight streams down through a canopy of leaves. There's nothing I can see out there. No glint of marksmen yet.

'Here – take the jeep,' says Bill. 'May confuse the scent for a bit.' He chucks Dave the keys.

'And get going,' adds Marco. 'By the way, I removed this from Gen's vest.' He holds up a small electronic device.

The tracker.

Suddenly I think of a zillion reasons why we should leave it behind. And another zillion why we should take it with us. Marco drops it in my hand.

Dave picks up the THOR, groans a little as he shoulders it, grabs my hand.

'See ya,' he calls at Marco and Bill.

'Thanks,' I say.

'You both take care,' says Bill. He gestures like he's drinking a pint. 'On you.' His face is set. His eyes give nothing away.

'And good luck,' says Marco.

We run out of the hut, through the undergrowth, down, away from the track. We dive into the scrub where the vehicles are hidden. Leafy shoots smack at me. Dave is going at an impossible pace, despite the THOR rucksack – its square bulk bouncing on his back like a mountaineer's backpack; its radio-transmitter antenna poking up, snagging branches.

When we get to the jeep, I double up with a stitch.

Dave goes to the BMW, collects: Exodus One's handset, the earpiece, the tool kit, and dumps them in the drawstring bag. I climb into the front of the jeep. He springs in beside me. He bangs the gears into neutral, releases the hand brake. We coast out of the brush, into an open field, on to a sharp downhill slope. Dave bump-starts the engine.

'And, just for the record, I didn't have a choice,' Dave says.

'Sorry?'

'I didn't have a choice about going with you before. If I hadn't run too, the police would have shot me, like they did Holly.'

I suddenly realize he didn't; at least, maybe not at first. 'Would you have run with me if you had had a choice?' I ask.

He looks at me. 'With your big brown eyes and total death wish, you mean?'

I feel blood mount to my cheeks.

'Would be mad not to.'

I blush as I buckle myself into the front seat of the jeep. I don't know what he's trying to say. 'You have a choice now,' I say. 'You don't have to run with me any more.'

'No,' he says. 'You're wrong. When it comes to you, Gen, I've never had a choice.'

2

Life is a Book: Every Day a New Page

WE HEAD OUT OF THE WOODLAND at speed. The track twists between tall beeches. Low overhanging branches look like they'll behead us. They loose a flurry of leaves, as we hit them with the roof of the jeep. Twigs whirlwind up from our wheelspin. Dave smacks on the wipers, clears the debris. And we bounce.

Dave pulls on his seat belt. 'Tighten yours,' he says.

I yank my belt taut, plant my feet firmly on the jeep's flooring. Brace my knees against the front. Dave swerves and weaves the jeep through the trees.

'Check the rear,' he says. 'Can you see them?'

I twist in my seat and see nothing except a plume of mud and grass, the sway of greenery and our tracks through the leaf mould. Just a trail of whirling undergrowth.

'Nothing,' I say.

'We've got a few minutes' start on them; longer, if Marco and Bill keep them talking.'

Maybe.

'And we'll be back in coverage soon.'

'Can we still make Reading by three?' I ask.

Dave jerks his head towards the THOR. 'We'll use that if we can't.'

We take another turn, lose the woodland, emerge on to a farm track. A rabbit scoots out of nowhere, disappears into the hedgerow. The jeep lurches. Suddenly we're across a field and out into open countryside.

'Put the radio on,' says Dave. 'Let's update ourselves before we have to deal with the Brightness.'

I flick the radio on, press search. The whole nation must be buzzing with our movements.

'*Police are still dragging the dock at Gallion's Point in search of a number of unknown terrorists, as the attempted bomb plot on London City Airport takes a bizarre new twist. One suspected suicide bomber has been shot dead at the scene. Recent leads suggest the others may have got as far as Wiltshire . . .*'

The radio starts to crackle. 'Try to keep it on,' Dave says. He crashes the gears down, swears. 'Bloody jeeps.' Then he cuts across a ditch, out of a gate, and we're on a country lane with high hedges. I hit the search button again.

'Listen for any update on the Marco and Bill situation,' says Dave, as he roars down the lane.

We get to the end of a song on some local channel and then: '. . . *the police have been called out to a local, isolated spot, where it's believed sympathisers of the well-known Lumin extremist group affiliated to the Brightness are hiding. It's believed at least one of them is suspected of carrying explosive devices. Police have cordoned off roads leading to the area.*

'*We're leaving this story now to hear the latest on the solar eclipse in the Northern Hemisphere, due to overshadow Dallas, Texas in the next few hours . . .*'

'Cordoned off the roads?' says Dave. 'We'll have to go across country again.'

At the next bend he pulls off the lane into a field of young corn. 'Trouble with no connectivity is I can't use my phone's sat nav.' He sounds frustrated.

'Maybe they've got a map?' I say. I flick open the glove compartment of the jeep. There's a handbook on car maintenance. No road map of Britain.

'Don't worry,' says Dave. 'It's been dry, apart from a few showers; these vehicles can go anywhere. We'll chance it. I'm going to head west and up there, see if we can spy the land.' Dave points to a peak about two fields away.

We bounce off, taking the tractor furrows through the corn, until we reach the gate to the next field. I get down to open it.

Then I see something I really don't want to see.

Blue lights tearing down the lane we just left. My heart rate trebles in the space of five seconds. 'They've found us.'

Sirens blast through the still air, and instinctively I duck behind the hedgerow.

Dave leans out of the jeep. 'Three cheers for local radio stations,' he hisses. 'And barley.'

'Barley?'

Dave points to the field around us. Sage-green barley. Army-green barley. Tall, green barley, nearly up to the bonnet of the vehicle. 'Couldn't have asked for better camouflage.'

I open the gate and get back into the jeep.

'I want to listen to the eclipse stuff,' I say. 'There's something that keeps nagging at me.'

Dave manoeuvres the jeep down the field behind the hedge. 'We need to be prepared for the Brightness by the time we get off these hills.' He looks over to the lane. He seems to make a decision and we turn right through a field of yellow rape.

I turn up the radio, glance at the dash clock. Only about twenty minutes left till 3.00 p.m.

We come out of the cover of the rape field on to a slope. Dave releases the hand brake, the jeep rolls down the hill and we're out on the lane.

Right into the path of an oncoming police car.

3

Life is a B-movie: You Don't Want to Leave in the Middle of It, But You Don't Want to Ever See It Again.

'*Shit.*'

Dave spins the jeep, heads west towards the sun. Windscreen wipers. Blur of hedges. The wheel spinning.

'Spoke too soon.'

Sirens.

'Hang on, Gen,' says Dave. He changes into second gear. The jeep growls out a response. The tyres shriek. We surge forward.

'I want to know the rest of what happened with Naz. Especially where he went. If we're going to have to locate that hub. But right now we need to deal with this.'

We race down the lane, swerve a pothole, screech round a bend.

I try to search back. For how long had Naz been planning all this? And how come I never noticed *anything*? By the time we did the last part of our project, he'd already joined the Brightness – or at least was doing the ultra Lumin-cool look. I remember the first day he turned up at college with his hair dyed yellow; he was in a black T-shirt with all the swag.

'This jeep is no good on the level,' says Dave. 'They'll out-race us.

'Is there any hope we'll make Reading?' I repeat.

'In any engagement with the enemy,' says Dave, 'you play for time.'

'OK,' I say.

'And you source every bit of intelligence you can.'

The police cars behind seem to have multiplied. I glance in the wing mirror. *Three now*.

'Can't we call the police and at least try to reason with them?' I say.

'No,' says Dave. Voice curt, dry.

Sirens wail into the afternoon

'But why?'

'One: no mobile coverage. Two: no time. Three: Deadly Force Policy states: fire shots to the head

290

without warning. No negotiation.'

'But surely? If we try and explain?' I know he's right. I just don't want to believe it.

'Gen,' says Dave. 'I'm not making this up. Suicide bombers are likely to detonate their devices on realizing that they've been identified. Police act covertly where possible, and use tactics to ensure immediate incapacitation – to give the bomber no opportunity to detonate the bomb. It's simple. They'll shoot first and say sorry afterwards.'

A bird on the road. I shut my eyes. They're gaining on us. No crunch. We missed it?

'Tell me what happened after Gloucestershire.' Dave shoves the jeep into overdrive.

'Gloucestershire?' I gulp in air. 'Naz joined the Brightness,' I say. *They'll really shoot first. I don't know why I keep hoping – something we could say; something we could do.*

Naz.

I remember how it all went wrong. I grip the dash, grit my teeth. Those days when his phone was off, or he didn't pick up. How the lies started. The sudden outbursts of temper.

'Tell me facts,' says Dave. 'Places, dates, names, timings, anything I can use.'

Oh my God.

At the end of the lane another police car appears.

In front of us.

We're trapped.

'Don't look behind you,' says Dave.

Three behind, following. One in front, approaching. We're totally fricking trapped.

Dave speeds forward, takes a sharp right. We skew right. We skid. We leave the lane. We bounce across a ditch and hit a wooden gate. It bursts open, timbers crunch. Splintered slats fly. We hit a field of cabbages or greens or something.

And behind I hear the head-on collision.

Police car against police car. The one coming in front against the three chasing behind. The smash of glass. The screech of brakes on tarmac. The roar of metal buckling. Metal on metal on metal. The sirens wailing on. Hysterical. Manic.

Dave puts the transmission into four-wheel drive. 'That's screwed them,' he says. They won't be following us anymore.

I don't look round. *Holy shit. That was close.* I hope no one's hurt. I think I've bruised my knee; I've been pressing it so hard against the front. *They're really going to kill us now.*

We surge up the slope. I realize I'm holding my breath. The jeep likes the change of terrain. We hit the crest of the hill.

'When we reach there,' Dave points to a mobile phone tower up ahead, 'connectivity will be on. We need to be ready.'

We take the downward curve along a dirt track. A farm route. We see Reading spread out below.

'But at least the police can't follow us here, even if they get clear of the gate.' Dave jerks his chin skywards. 'Although *they* can.'

I lean out of the jeep. Above us, almost touching the tree tops, is a helicopter. It's so close I can read its model number – *MD 902*. My stomach contracts like I've swallowed concrete. This is it then. There's no way we can outrun a helicopter. I think of Mum, of Aunty Gill, how my death will break them. *I'm so sorry*, I whisper.

The mobile tower behind the trees looms nearer. The helicopter sways over us. The police sirens wail. There's a high, lost pitch to them. A wind whips over the slope and the trees to our right shiver.

I look at Dave. Long clouds overhead chase the sun. Dave shakes his head slightly. 'They can follow. They can skyshout at us. They can relay images of the chase to police in Reading. If they have Cessna technology they can intercept our mobiles. They could even use Tasers,' he says, 'but they can't do much else.'

OK, I think. *Do they need to do much else?*

'Back to Naz. We need to locate their hub, urgently.'

A huge lump rises up in my throat. 'He asked if I'd go to Brightness meetings with him, meet his new friends.'

'Did you go?'

'Once,' I say.

'And?'

'I didn't like it.'

'Where did they meet?' asks Dave.

'In London, but that place can't be the hub. It was huge. Had lots of groups from all across the UK there.' I remember the huge hall. The crowds of young men going in to meet. The separate 'waiting area' for women. 'They don't like women, you know,' I add.

We hit a puddle. Muddy water sprays up the jeep.

'OK, so that's not it. Let's try this from a different angle.'

'What angle?'

'What happened in Somerset? Was he interested in your family?'

'Only my mum. Naz was really interested in her job,' I say.

'Does she still work at the power station?' The helicopter

loops low in front of us, seems to be about to land. Then it jerks and dips and suddenly swerves up again.

'Yes, Hinkley Point. She's now Head of Spent Fuel.'

'Spent Fuel. Explain.'

'SFPs are storage pools for used fuel from nuclear reactors.'

'Details.'

'Spent fuel pools hold the fuel assemblies taken out of the reactor. The pools are quite deep – about twelve metres. Mum is in charge of all assemblies of spent fuel rods. All the pools in fact.'

'What do they do with the rods?'

'They're massively radioactive – they store them underwater near the nuclear site for up to twenty years before they get sent off for reprocessing.'

I watch Dave's face as he mulls this over.

'What did Naz talk to your mum about exactly?'

'About how and where they stored the spent fuel.'

We race past a field with a knoll of trees in it. The helicopter climbs higher.

Suddenly I see Naz's interest in Mum in a new light. *How stupid.* I thought he wanted to get to know her! *Wanted to become part of my life.*

'OK, what about the project?' Dave says. 'Just the basics.'

I swallow. 'We went to a few villages, interviewed the oldest people there; asked them some questions.'

'What did they say?'

A flock of smallish brownish birds fly up, wheel overhead. The jeep speeds down the farm track, through a pasture of thick grass, wild tansy. The helicopter starts up its skyshout. 'IN THE JEEP. STOP. POLICE.'

I clap my hands to my head. The skyshout's so loud, my bad ear starts ringing all over again.

'Don't stop,' says Dave. 'I'm not going to.'

I try to collect what I'd been going to say. The project? What keeps people going in the face of adversity? 'Some said it was love that kept them alive – all kinds of love: their families, their children, love for the hills, you know, that was the conclusion of the study.'

'And what did Naz make of that?'

I press my lips together. 'He seemed very interested in the afterlife,' I say.

The clock on the dash says we've got seven minutes. The helicopter whirrs a great circle round us, blasting the undergrowth.

'He was particularly interested in their vision of heaven; the rewards for their deeds on earth.'

'Men and women same?' asks Dave.

'Ha ha,' I say.

'Typical,' snorts Dave. 'Only the men are going to get rewarded in paradise; the woman are just there to serve them.'

We turn on to a long lane. Tarmac at last. A sign says something like *Green Lane*. The helicopter tries another skyshout. 'STOP. IN THE JEEP. POLICE.'

'Was he different with you?'

I nod. *How the hell are we going to get away? How does Dave stay so focused?* The concrete in my belly seems to have solidified, glued all my intestines together. And my throat is so dry I can hardly croak.

'Tell me?'

'It wasn't as if he was tired of me, it was more as if . . .'

'*What?*' says Dave.

'He didn't treat me like a real person.'

'*Didn't treat you like a real person?*' Dave's eyes seem to enlarge. Then he mutters, '*What a jerk*,' then swallows a snort.

Five minutes to go.

'Maybe by then he'd already marked you out, or agreed with his group that you would carry the bomb,' says Dave. His self-control is back.

'But—'

'That would make you kind of holy,' says Dave. 'But not in a nice way – more taboo.'

I shake my head, try to swallow. *Did Naz agree to that?*

'Now think carefully. Around that time, did he go away? And where? This is really key, Gen. He'd have had to go somewhere to nominate you as the messenger – he needed your family profile. He'd have done it in person, so it would be after the Somerset trip, but before you went back to London?'

And I do think. I think as hard as I can. 'He only went back to pick up his motorbike from Bristol,' I say. 'Nowhere else.'

'Then the hub is in Bristol,' says Dave.

I think of that day, of him going to Bristol. Leaving me writing up our joint project. I turn my head. Watch the barley in the field swaying under the rush of the helicopter. Other girls get dumped or cheated on. They get passed over for the latest babe in town. I get strapped to a bomb. And I don't have a clue. I don't even know it. I just sit there happily doing his coursework for him.

So why did I carry on loving him? I must've been mad. Is that what love is?

'Hey,' says Dave. 'No time to get upset; let's do that together over a pint with Bill and Marco, after we've shut these bastards down.'

And that's just funny, with a helicopter screaming at us and a police car pile-up and a time bomb ticking.

LIFE IS A HELICOPTOR: YOU CAN SEE WHAT'S GOING ON BUT YOU CAN'T DO A DAMN THING ABOUT IT. EXCEPT SCREAM.

'I've got an idea,' I say.

'Right?'

'If we can lose the helicopter and make the station . . .'

'We'll try.'

'. . . we'll tell Apocalypse we'll do whatever they say. We'll promise to get the bomb to Bristol. We'll do what it takes and obey.' I remember how pleased the Voice sounded when I grovelled.

'And?' he says.

'On the way, you locate the hub, use the THOR and all that. I'm going to read through Exodus One's papers again. There's something there and I need to figure it.'

'And?'

'We leave the tracker on the train and go in search of them instead.'

'Right.'

'And if we run out of luck – we just do.'

4

Life is a Game: What You Get Depends on How You Play It

Up AHEAD after so many fields are the first houses. Instantly, connectivity is restored. There's a long, ear-splitting whistle, it's so loud that even though it's coming through Dave's phone, it catches us unawares. I duck my head down and cover my ears on instinct.

Before they even speak I have my line ready. '*Please, I'm nearly there,*' I start. '*You have to listen. I'm being chased by police. There's a helicopter. Please – it wasn't my fault I went out of coverage. I'm really really sorry.*'

The jeep tears on up the high hedged lane. Dave puts his foot down. Apocalypse doesn't waste time with threats. 'You had one chance to get this right,' he says.

'*Please,*' I continue, '*I'll make the rendezvous point. I will. I promise.*'

'You have your instructions. Get to Reading Railway station before fifteen hundred hours.'

Dave fiddles with the tuning. I'm terrified he's going to tune Apocalypse out and I'm going to miss something. But instead of the Voice fading, it gets louder. We can even hear the noises in the background better.

They must know I'm nearly there. They must be tracking me.

'You will go to Reading Train Station and board the train to Bristol Temple Meads. You will use the travel pass provided,' says the Voice. 'We will be watching. You will stand in front of the drinks dispenser. You will not look round.'

'OK,' I say. I look at Dave. Why would they want me to do that? My eyes are wide with alarm.

Dave nods at me, as if to say: *They're bluffing*. It's a control thing. He makes a gesture with his hand like he's stirring his tea. *Carry on. Carry on.*

'OK,' I say again. 'But you promised if I get to Reading, you'll let me go.'

'You will board the train and get off at Bristol Temple Meads.'

We hit Reading. Traffic. Red lights. Signs to the railway station. Prospect Street. Roundabout. Church Street. Overtaking. Overspeeding. Police sirens. They pull out

301

after us. Too late. *We're nearly there.*

My hands are shaking.

'We will not make contact with you again,' says the Voice. 'For any reason whatsoever.'

'But if I make it to Bristol?' I ask.

'Then your mission will be over.'

5

Life is a Bar Of Soap: Once You Think You've Got a Hold of It, It Slips Away

READING TRAIN STATION. 2.58 p.m.

Dave swings the car into an underground Aldi supermarket car park, right out the back of the train station – no barriers, just a camera. I grab the draw-string bag. Dave's got the THOR and before the police behind have time to swing in after us, we're out of the car and running.

Straight through the automatic glass door. Straight up the slope escalator into the brand new shopping area. We hold hands, race through the food section and then walk.

We walk right through the mall and out into the back of the train station. There are boards everywhere. Behind us we see the police cars streaming into the car park, above us the helicopter whirls. All around people mill. There are signs pointing the way to platforms one to three. Looks like the whole place is undergoing some massive renovation.

'Go first,' says Dave.

'Which way?' I say.

How the hell are we going to find the right platform in time?

'Hang on,' he says.

I dip my head, tight-lipped. He moves to the side, peers over a boarded barrier. 'Shit, shit, shit.'

'What is it?'

'They're closing the station.'

A trembling starts right under the canisters packed against my stomach.

'They've got police at the barriers; they're stop-searching everyone going on to the platforms.'

I look around. *There must be something we can do. There has to be.* But everywhere are narrow walkways between wooden boardings. There's a disabled-access ramp towards my left. A white metal handrail. I hold on. I steady myself. *What the hell are we going to do?* A bridge over to the main entrance. *How long have we got?*

'Come on,' says Dave. 'This way.'

He grabs my hand and yanks me through a temporary door in the boarding. It's got *NO ADMITTANCE* on it. It slams behind us. And we run. Down some steps. Round a corner. Race round piles of sand. *It's a fricking building site.* One guy in a white protective helmet and high-visibility work vest is having a fag behind a barrier. He jerks his thumb at us. Points to another boarded-in walkway.

'Platform for Bristol?' asks Dave, like we're lost or something.

The guy points the other way. 'Taking first exit left,' he says in an accent I can't quite place. He draws on the fag. It glows red. He throws it down, stamps on it.

We take the first exit left and run. The boards sway a bit; a yellow foot ramp wobbles as I pound up it. And then we're out through another temporary wooden door.

On to a platform.

I hope to hell it's the right one. The one with the drinks dispenser. The one going to Bristol Temple Meads.

Dave scopes the length of it. He gives me the thumbs up. He points to my right. 'Down there. You stand in front of the drinks dispenser. Choose a drink. Look casual. Like we just walked in, did the whole stop and search thing. I'll watch your back, check for anyone. The police will have the jeep by now, they'll be all over Aldi, but it'll take some minutes for them to check CCTV to see where we went. We can make it.'

'But . . .' I start. I want to say, *I need to remove the yellow*

T-shirt, because it's so noticeable. But the explosive vest is all exposed at the back. So I don't bother. 'You don't have to do this,' I say. 'You could still go.'

God, I don't want him to go.

He twists a strange, sad smile. As if something hurts him at the thought of going. As if being with me is all he wants, even at the peril of his life. 'Pass,' he says. 'I'll be near, but we're safer apart. The police are looking for two people.'

Then, almost invisibly, he drops out of sight. How does he do that? For an instant I imagine him on campaign, out there on the dusty streets, in foreign parts. Was it there he learnt to disappear so quickly? Was it that constant closeness to death that makes him so focused?

Suddenly I gulp at how much I've underestimated him. I pull his T-shirt close around me. *In future*, I warn myself, *you're going to see Dave very differently*.

The platform is full. Commuter-land. That's good when it comes to helicopter imaging; bad if the bomb goes off. Nobody seems to care about a dishevelled teenager. I take stock; I look back to see if the police are moving this way, see if I can catch a glimpse of Dave. There are two policemen in full riot gear standing by the barriers at the far end. Another two on the platform opposite. Workmen are being herded off, metal barriers erected. There's a middle-aged man with a backpack and shoulder-length grey hair blocking my view to my left; an Asian couple checking a phone. The couple move off. The man sits down on a bench. More people. I can't see a thing. I check for the helicopter, glance up. All clear. Only the sound of an unseen aeroplane gently roaring.

Are they really here?

Beside one of the iron pillars holding up the fretwork of a fascia board, is a drinks dispenser. Dusty, pockmarked, with spots of rust through chrome and black. Murky glass. Crisps. Chocolate. Cans. On auto, I move towards it. *Are they watching? Why would they want to check now? Do they suspect? Will it be a replacement for Exodus? Will they follow me on to the train, film every last step of my journey?*

I stand facing choc chip and cola. I can see the reflection of myself in the dim glass. Behind me people, clouds. Patches of sunlight. Dirty smears across my face. I don't know if that's the glass or me. I peer into the reflection, straining to see if someone's watching. Only my pale face stares back. Eyes huge. Mascara smudged. Hair all gone wild again. Yellow blur of T-shirt. I wait to catch a glimpse of the face of the other, of the enemy. Shock of dyed hair? I wonder if *he'll* come?

Naz.

Would you want to see me one last time? Would you, Naz? Would you want to see me again before you splatter me into oblivion?

I wait and wait. *It must be gone three by now?* Have we missed the train? All these people. We can't have. At last I can't bear it. Somewhere to my right the tracks shake; something rumbles in the distance. *Stand firm*, I tell myself. The pale faces of the Moirai flash into my mind. '*I am the handmaiden.*' That's what I'd said in my dream, or whatever it was. '*I shall be the firmament in the midst of the waters.*' Another weird flicker of déjà vu.

'*You have been chosen.*' That's what Apocalypse said.

A strange feeling of destiny. A sense of purpose, but to what end I don't know.

I turn away from the drinks dispenser, look over my shoulder. I can't see anyone watching. I start to panic. *This is it then.*

No, there is still some job left for me to do.

LIFE IS A TRAIN RUMBLING ON THE TRACKS: YOUR JOURNEY IS SET. IT HAS MANY STOPS, BUT YOU MUST STAY ON IT TO THE VERY END.

I want to see Dave again. I want to see his face. I realize how much I've grown to need him. There's a rushing. I hear the track whining. As I look down the platform the train glides into view. The people crowd forward.

And then, like a miracle, there he is. Suddenly in front of me, appearing just as quickly as he disappeared. His face set. Strange tension in his mouth. His eyes all steel.

'Was there anyone?' I whisper.

'No,' he says.

I look at Dave. Something of the conflicts he's seen, something of the cold mountains and the endless desert, is still hovering around him, clinging to the set of his jaw, the way he holds his hands.

I'm so glad he's here, so glad he didn't bail out. *So glad.* I look into his face. He's so much older than his nineteen years. His eyes so tired.

If I could live things over again . . . have another chance . . .

Was he always The One, then?

I glance up at the departure board. *THE 15.00 TRAIN TO BRISTOL TEMPLE MEADS HAS ARRIVED AT PLATFORM 2.*

'The police have already cordoned off the back of the station. They're evacuating Aldi. They're stop-searching everyone, even those leaving the platform now. After this train they'll close the station.' Dave adjusts the backpack.

We step forward, press towards the train doors. My back is completely wet. *We've done it. We got here. There is still a purpose to everything.*

Dave grabs my hand. I step up. We squeeze through,

get on the train. *We're on.* We move down the coaches. Sticky back. Sweaty palms. People file ahead. No seats just yet.

The station whistle blows, the train shunts forward. As we pull away from the platform, I see the police running over the footbridge, moving on to all the platforms. I don't know if I've won or lost. Next coach. More space. We pass seat after seat.

And that's when I look at the information scroll by the luggage rack.

NON-STOP TO BRISTOL TEMPLE MEADS.

There's no way we can get off.

We're taking the bomb straight to where they want it.

We're going to blow up hundreds of people. Maybe thousands.

And there's nothing I can do about it.

6

Life is a Taxi: the Meter Just Keeps A-ticking, Whether You're Getting Somewhere or Just Standing Still

LIKE IN SOME WEIRD KIND OF FILM, we move down the carriages, through the packed seats to the canteen car. There's a guy serving behind a high counter.

'Two coffees please,' says Dave. I pick up a sandwich and place it on the counter. The sight of the pink ham and the slice of cheddar squashed between the two slices of bread makes my stomach growl. Dave picks up a huge, filled baguette.

The guy busies himself with the coffees. Such beautiful, ordinary things: to drink coffee, to eat sandwiches. Did Paul W. Tibbets, the pilot of the *Enola* Gay, who dropped

Little Boy on Hiroshima, reach for a sandwich before he pressed the release button? Did he bite into ham and cheese, 44.4 seconds before it detonated? Did he chew a little as 60,000 people died instantly? Did he swallow, 31,000 feet above and ten and a half miles away from them, as he felt the shockwave? Or glance back at the mushroom cloud, 13,716 metres high. He always asserted he felt no regrets.

444. The number seems to have a fatality all of its own.

'Does your screen work?' Dave asks the guy behind the counter.

The guy looks up. 'Do you mind if we watch?' says Dave, pointing at a coms screen screwed to the wall. 'We're hoping to go and see the solar eclipse.'

I don't know why we have to explain. Maybe because it's off.

'Bit late, aren't you?' says the counter guy. 'Most went down this morning.'

'Thought it was at four thirty-ish?' I say.

'4.44 p.m. exactly,' he says. 'And you'll never get near by then.' He places the coffees down in front of us. 'All the best spots'll be taken. And the roads are packed. My sister and her boyfriend went down two days ago and pitched a tent.'

444. How weird. My timer is set to coincide exactly with the solar eclipse, the exact same number it took for Little Boy to fall on Hiroshima. And Temple Meads is at the exact spot the Line of Totality hits the UK.

I point to the screen.

The guy shrugs and flicks a switch under the counter. 'Just the police, running some message on a loop,' he explains. 'I turned it off; was sick of hearing it.'

The small screen bursts into life. The world rocks. I lean on the counter to stop myself buckling at the knees. Dave catches my elbow. Holds me. 'Shit, Gen,' he says. 'You're as white as a sheet. You seen a ghost or what?'

My eyes must have saucered out. My breath feels shallow. In fact, I've stopped breathing.

I *have* seen a ghost.

Sort of.

There, filling up the screen, right over the counter, right in front of us, is the face of Naz.

Naz. Clean, fresh-faced Naz. His yellow hair and big smile.

'*Please,*' he's saying. '*Please, Genesis, wherever you are, give yourself up. I don't know the truth. I don't know what's happened, but please get to a police station and turn yourself in. I'll come. We'll talk. Whatever it is, we can work it out.*'

I look into those grey-blue eyes. Let my breath out in a kind of sneeze. Naz. His gentle smile, his cute way of clipping Ts as he talks. I shake my head. I can't actually believe this. I catch my breath. In fact I feel sick.

You clever bastard. You treacherous, no good, clever bastard. Covering your own cowardly arse. If I ever live through this. If I ever get to see you again . . .

Anyone can commit murder, you know.

Two can play at that game, given the right provocation. At the wrong time.

'Gen?' Dave holds out my coffee for me. 'What's up?'

I point at the screen.

Dave clicks into training mode. Scopes the carriage. Times the guy behind the counter. Waits till he's moved off to serve someone else. Then stares intently at Naz.

'Believe me,' says Naz. *'I'm still your friend. Please give yourself up.'*

I suck in air. Bastard. I straighten up.

The screen flicks around the interior of the room behind him. A rolling headline banner under him reads: *NATIONWIDE SEARCH FOR SUSPECTED SUICIDE BOMBER, MISSING TEENAGER GENESIS WAINWRIGHT. POLICE COMBING WEST OF LONDON. SOME TRAIN STATION CLOSURES. DELAYS ON MAIN LINES*

EXPECTED. M4 CLOSED AT NEWBURY.

A picture of me from my first London poetry gig. Animated. Inspired. Chin high, mouth smiling. Hair tossed back. Make-up perfect.

Doesn't look anything like me now.

Thank God.

'Drink,' orders Dave. He puts the coffee down. He busts open four packs of sugar, stirs them all into the poly-paper mug. 'Now.'

I sip at the coffee. 'Do you think he's at a police station?' I say. I suck at the coffee. It burns my tongue. 'Do you think they'll recognize me?' I point at the picture.

'Eat.' Dave opens up the triangular pack and plonks the ham'n'cheese sandwiches down by the coffee cup. 'And act normal.' He unwraps the baguette.

'*Please, Genesis,*' continues Naz.

'No, he's not in a police station.' Dave examines the picture. The counter guy moves back our way. We remove our food and drinks and head for a seat.

We can still see the TV. Still see Naz.

'You've got to understand, Gen,' says Dave. 'This is war. He's playing mind games. He isn't in any police station. That's a video link being played on a loop. That appeal he's making could've been recorded anywhere – probably at the hub – and sent in to a broadcasting studio. He could have recorded it at any time – ages ago, even.'

Still can't believe it.

'Can you see anything in the background you recognize? Maybe you went to this hub with him?'

I look over Dave's shoulder at Naz's face on the screen. There is something I recognize. It's a print of Van Gogh's 'Sunflowers'. But there're thousands of prints like that everywhere, so I shake my head.

'Turn yourself in. Be reasonable. I'll be there for you.'

Such lies. That day we pretended we were Romeo and Juliet and jumped in the river. Such stagecraft. He's never been there for me. I look at the steely calm of Dave's eyes. I feel the gentle pressure of his hand on mine. Naz has never been there for me. Not like Dave. Dave wouldn't have asked me to jump in a river. He wanted to teach me to swim in a kiddies' pool.

How come I never saw it all before?

The news comes on the screen.

'As the search for the missing suicide bomber, Lumin convert Genesis Wainwright, widens, two suspects have been apprehended in Berkshire . . .'

More pictures of me.

I can't focus.

The announcer goes on, *'. . . today, designated as*

a Day of Action by the Lumin, the extremist militant wing of the Brightness . . . This afternoon millions are expected to turn out in the south-west to see the eclipse . . . this morning in East London . . . this broadcast contains flash photography . . .'

I just can't focus.

Across the screen, images of the drowned bus being hauled out of Victoria Dock. Pictures of me at the poetry slam. Cameras flashing. Naz again.

The programme is interrupted.

'. . . *BREAKING NEWS . . . A BOMB HAS GONE OFF IN DALLAS, TEXAS. We leave this programme to receive live coverage coming from the US . . .'*

There's a slight pause and a crackle. Dave and I sit up. I'm focusing now. Eyes on the screen.

'*A bomb has been set off at the Comanche Peak Nuclear Power Plant, in Somervell County, Texas. The plant has around one thousand three hundred employees and is operated by a division of Energy Future Holdings Corporation . . .*'

A bomb?

'*It is not known at present how the explosion took place. A national emergency has been declared . . .*'

A nuclear power station?

'*A zone around the burning plant is currently being evacuated . . .*'

444. Nuclear explosion.

My mum works at Hinkley Point.

'*The explosion has disabled the power supply. The cores are feared to be in imminent danger of meltdown.*'

Blown up.

'. . . *eye witnesses report a huge flash of brightness . . . high radioactive releases . . .*'

The Brightness.

'. . . *over one hundred thousand people are being evacuated . . .*'

Naz.

'. . . *so far the death toll is estimated at five hundred and sixty lives lost . . .*'

Me. And a bomb. And Naz's fascination with Mum's job when we were in Somerset. My mum and her job. In a nuclear power plant.

And suddenly I'm terrified. 'Dave,' I say.

'Yep?'

'I think . . .'

'Right?'

'We're part of something much bigger.'

'Go on.' His face goes grey. 'Talk.'

America. Cell E. Those Twitter messages. It's much bigger than just us. Bigger than just the UK. *This is their Day of Action.* Across the whole of the western world.

'Dave, I think they're going to blow up more power stations.'

Why else would Naz have insisted my mum took him on a tour of Hinkley Point?

7

Life is a Tin Of Sardines: We're All of Us Looking for the Key

DAVE TAKES THIS INFORMATION IN. And stays quiet. This time I don't even get a '*Right*'. The news on the TV changes. A scientist is being interviewed about the Texas attack:

'*The most significant danger is in exposing spent fuel to the air. Any loss of pool water in a spent fuel pool could trigger the possibility of a zirconium fire. This risk remains years after a final reactor is shutdown, and in the case of the attack at Comanche Peak . . .*'

Then suddenly the TV screen blinks off. There's a noise of grinding metal. All the hairs stand up on the back of my neck. The train starts to jerk and shudder.

'Shit,' says Dave. 'We're slowing.' We look at each other, as if to say: *Are you thinking what I'm thinking?*

The police must have checked through that CCTV.

The door to the coach slides open. Three burly looking guys march through. They stop, order the guy behind the counter over, demand food. Quickly. While he slides sandwiches, water at them, they speak in low voices and act like nobody can hear them. 'Stock up, this is going to run into hours,' says one.

'Start where?' asks another.

'At the tail and work back,' the lead guy replies.

'Mark unclaimed bags?'

'But don't move them. No headlines. Note down locations, move passengers on a pretext.'

'Police?' says the third.

'Yeah. Driver's been told safest evacuation point.' The first one turns and nods at the others as if to say: *Shush – now*.

'How far?' whispers the last guy.

'Cutting ahead, we need to clear that. We've dropped speed. In about twenty-five minutes.'

They see us sitting there and stop talking. When they leave, I say, 'We need to hide.'

'And quickly,' Dave adds.

'Toilet? Furthest one that way?' I can't think of anything more original.

I grab the draw-string bag. Dave pushes the antenna

on the THOR further down, tugs the rucksack cover over everything, clicks buckles. Then he shoulders the whole thing. Just another backpack.

We slide out into the aisle. I swing past the seats. Each one has a strange yellow knob on the top of it, right where you need to grab. I hope they're there to hold on to. I grab them anyway. Keep myself steady. Holding on to those yellow knobs, one seat to the next, I kind of ski my way down the train.

There aren't many people in the first few carriages. The third one's packed full of school kids. Happy little faces. *Christ.* I feel the jog of the vest. Feel ill.

We get past the children. I break out in sweat. My hair sticks to my neck. Droplets of sweat trickle down my back. *Jesus Christ – a train full of little kids.* My armpits get sticky. My palms slide on the yellow knobs.

In the next carriages, we pass people clutching coffees, working on laptops, talking into phones. One group are sharing vodka in paper cups. An old man is puffing an electronic cigarette, a young one scratching his head.

They bombed a nuclear power plant in Dallas.

LIFE IS A WALK ON A MOVING TRAIN: ONE STEP FORWARD, 330 FEET BACKWARDS.

On, between the seats, holding on to those sunshine yellow knobs. Dave takes the lead. He's good mannered, apologises to passengers. Strides out. I follow. Watching his back. Don't think. Get to a toilet.

Through the first-class carriage. People shrink away, turn slitted eyes on us, screw their faces. One man looks up, angry. I mutter, 'Sorry.' Though I don't know what the hell for. Out of the carriage, across the couplings, into a corridor, empty space, toilets on either side. Keep going.

Dave reaches behind him and holds out his hand.

I put mine into his.

We reach the very last landing. The very last toilet. Dave punches the button on the curved toilet door. The door rotates out. Open door, stale smell of urine, soggy tissue paper on the floor. We step in. Dave shakes his head. The door rotates back, closes around us. Dave swings the door lock on. I flick down the cover of the loo seat and sink on to it. I think the sugar and the coffee must have done something to my blood sugar. I've gone all jittery. *What's going to happen now?*

And here I am, locked in a toilet with Dave. And if it wasn't pretty dire, I'd have to laugh. I'd have to think of the toilet take on life. Write another one-line poem.

A whole seventy-odd minutes left of existence, in a toilet with all the things on my Life List left undone. Like: Go to a Really Good Uni. Become a Famous Performance Poet. Write Important Things About Life. Fall in Love

With The Right One. Make Babies. Be There for Everyone I Love. Live Happily Ever After.

Yeah.

LIFE IS A TOILET: IT STINKS.

And I can't even just sit back on the loo seat and give up. And my mind is jumping between 444 and Temple Meads and Texas and the police about to board the train.

'Dave,' I say, 'something's wrong.'

'Like something worse than hiding out in a train toilet with a bomb?' he says.

I kind of grin. Somehow in the face of everything, that's funny. 'Well maybe,' I say. 'Look.' I pull out the crumpled piece of newspaper, still in my pocket: *A spectacular total eclipse will be seen in the northern hemisphere at 4.44 p.m BST* . . . 'I've been thinking about this.'

Dave takes the paper from my hand.

I get off the toilet and lean over him. 'See, the Line of Totality hits Dallas, Texas at 3.10 p.m. our time. Then in New York at 3.55 p.m. Then it reaches maximum totality in the west of England at 4.44 p.m.'

I run my finger down the trajectory the Line will take. 'At 4.44 p.m.,' I repeat.

Dave holds his hand out in a shush motion. Someone walks past outside.

'Hinkley Point is not on this line,' I say, jabbing at the

paper. 'Though Bristol definitely is – it's exactly where the line hits the UK.'

He nods. 'This is important, but we really just need to focus on how we get out of this jam,' he says. 'Respond to imminent danger first. Remove yourself from the line of fire, next.'

I carry on following the Line of Totality with my finger. 'That gold car number plate was EC21 PSE. That spells *eclipse*.' I emphasize eclipse, willing it to explain something to me. '4.44 p.m. Their time to shine, in sync with cosmicness.'

'If you weren't wearing a bomb we could just evacuate the train like everyone else, I s'pose,' he says.

'Well I am,' I say, 'and that's why we're hiding in a toilet.'

'So it's gonna have to be the window.'

For the first time since Dave agreed to 'run with me', I feel he is not on board like before.

'Why d'you think Naz wanted to find out about spent fuel pools?' he says.

'I get it,' I say. 'They're bringing Brightness to the people who live in darkness. That's the kind of metaphor they'd like. An eclipse like this won't happen again this century.'

Dave looks at me.

'And 4.44 p.m. is symbolic. It's the number of the Vibrations of Archangels. It means, in numerology: illumination. Naz told me that once, when he was excited about—'

'Did you ever hear Naz ask for technical information about the spent fuel pool at Hinkley Point?'

'*Listen*,' I say. 'When Naz was excited about learning I was born on April the fourth at four in the morning—'

'Because he'd have needed very specific details, if that's their target,' Dave says.

'*Illumination* means *Brightness*. *Vibrations* means *explosions* . . . I was born on the fourth of the fourth at four a.m. My name is Genesis . . . and Naz once said "considering all that" I could play "a small role" . . .'

Dave looks at me. 'We should concentrate on escaping first. We could get out through the window, maybe?'

'444 is symbolic,' I repeat. 'Like 666 means the devil.'

'And 999 means the police,' says Dave. 'Who will board the train and shoot through that door pretty soon, if we don't find the dotty mallet.'

'I wish you'd concentrate on this map,' I say.

Dave takes the page right off me. He straightens it out on the wall of the toilet. 'Right, we're here. Hinkley Point is here – and, as you have already identified, Hinkley Point is not on the Line of Totality, which means despite

Naz's interest in your mum's job, Hinkley Point is not the target. So if Hinkley Point Power Station isn't their target – then what is?'

'You mean apart from me and Bristol Temple Meads train station?'

Dave acknowledges this then adds, 'You're the one who thinks there's more to it. I just want to get us off this train.' He moves me to one side and starts searching around the back of the toilet.

'The target is not Hinkley Point, I agree,' I say, 'but the Brightness targeted a train station *and* a nuclear plant in the US. Both were on the Line of Totality there. Look.' I prod the map along the line at the two points in the US: the Mexican border and Dallas. If they are going to do the same thing here, and Bristol Temple Meads is the train station, then logically the next target must be a nuclear plant after Bristol and along the Line of Totality,' I say. 'Where's next on the Line of Totality after Bristol?'

Dave straightens up. 'Naz wanted to find out about spent fuel pools. Right?' He frowns in concentration.

'Dave,' I say. My voice suddenly sounding odd. 'Look. This is where the Line of Totality ends.' I point to the map. 'What if the next target is there?'

'If Naz was so keen to know about spent fuel, that suggests they're going to attack a fuel pool at a power plant,' concludes Dave. 'But there is no other nuclear power plant on the line after Bristol.'

And I suddenly understand. 'BUT THERE IS!' I say. 'Look! This is where everyone's going today. Millions of people will be waiting right here.' I put my finger down bang in Gloucestershire, bang on the place where I spent so many hours by the river with Naz, bang on the now *closed* nuclear power station of Oldbury Naite.

BANG.

'There *is* a nuclear power station here. I know – I've been there. It's just not marked on the map.'

'And now I get it,' says Dave. 'Radioactive waste is stored on site for years – decades – long after nuclear power stations are decommissioned.' And he puts his finger down on top of mine.

Bang on the location of the closed power station's spent fuel pool.

8

Life is a Tube of Toothpaste: I've Yet to Figure Out Why

SUDDENLY I FEEL SICK. All those people. All of them packed out along the Severn estuary, all sitting out by the old power station.

444. Illumination.

Little Boy. Hiroshima.

I am the handmaiden. I am the firmament in the waters. Now I know. *I have been chosen.* The Moirai have singled me out. This is my purpose. I have to stop that explosion.

'There'll be a dotty mallet, somewhere,' says Dave.

And if I'm right about Oldbury Naite, it'll be in those notes. The ones we just didn't understand before. I start to scrabble through the draw-string bag. I pull out the papers. Exodus One's job description and the work sheet. 'A dotty mallet?'

The train judders, grinds on the tracks.

'Emergency glass-break hammer – look for a red plastic-handled thing with a steel ice-pick kind of nose. It'll be stashed in a case above the window, behind the loo – it's got to be somewhere,' says Dave.

I start going through the notes again.

'Look – the window has a red dot, so the mallet must be in here.'

I don't ask why windows have red dots.

'That bomb will kill you and a whole shedload of others, if we can't get you out of that window.'

'Here,' I say. I read one section aloud.

Selection points

Is key radicalization target group? (Your daughter. Your choice)

Has been nominated by cell member as suitable death-spouse by key operative?

Has made contact with cells and been approved?

Is tractable and will follow instructions?

Is easily scared, being female?

Is robust enough to carry bomb?

'Is that me they're taking about?' *Tractable*, *follow instructions* and *easily scared, being female*?

Je-sus!

I read the next bit.

The Line of Totality Day of Righteousness Action Cell E

The sun will be darkened. The End Time is upon us. The Door of Repentance for sins will be closed and will remain closed until the Day of Judgement. The Hour of Illumination is Nigh. 444

- Attack installations, power grids, explode NR,
- Create Brightness.

Footage

1st release on ALL LONDON TOURS in real time.

2nd release of PS explosion in time with the LOT to cause the maximum chaos.

Desired Goals

Create panic

Create fear

Waste authority time/resources

Show strength

Strike fear in heart of society

Glorify the Brightness

Give cell group cosmic afterlife

Strike blow against the West

Leave confusion

Create terror

Explode SFP at PS

Leave impact for decades

Promote cohesion

Look strong

<u>Brother Proverbz Operative Schedule</u>

Routes

Details of tides

Ordnance

Details of explosions

Communications

YC and equipment

Details of SFP location

Details of local knowledge

Maps included

B.P.

Provide means of delivery

Research SFP (exact location)

Local knowledge

Firearms training

Member of YC

Leave hub 3.30 p.m.

Arrive YC

Conduct checks

Leave upriver YC 4.39

Delivery 4.44 p.m.

And now it makes sense.

NR – Nuclear Reactors.

PS – Power Stations.

LOT – Line of Totality.

SFP – Spent Fuel Pool.

YC?

BP?

What do YC and BP mean?

'I know exactly where Oldbury is,' I say.

'So do I,' says Dave. 'In Gloucestershire.'

'No, I mean I know *exactly* – it's just a mile or so up the River Severn from the yacht club where Naz and I went sailing.'

'OK,' says Dave.

'What's the time?' I ask.

'Twenty to four.'

'That girl was blown up at a railway station on the Mexican border at the start of the Line of Totality. That was a kind of *Hello, America*. Now Dallas has already gone up so, if we're right,' I say, 'any power station falling on that line will get hit. Like here.' I squint at the map. 'When the line gets to Indian Point Nuclear Power Station, New York, there could be another explosion. A kind of *Goodbye, America*.'

'Let's hope you're not right,' says Dave.

'Right there.' I point it out on the map. And I start thinking about a *Hello, UK* at Bristol Temple Meads Station and a *Goodbye, UK* at Oldbury.

Dave bends down under the basin. 'I've located the hammer.' He straightens up. 'Who – the frick – is going to look there in an emergency?' He unclips the Perspex casing round the dotty mallet and yanks it free. 'Now the window.'

I take it from him. 'I'll break the window,' I say. I've always wanted to break one. And I may not get another chance. I close my fingers around it.

A sudden lurch of the train. Dave shoots his arm sideways to balance himself. The train settles into a long, slow, braking curve. I raise my hand and am about to smash the glass, when something stirs in my memory. Something about the sound of howling brakes on tracks. I drop my arm back, steady myself against the door.

'That painting,' I say. 'And that howling sound.'

'Try and hit it hard on the red dot.'

'Dave, I think they're using Naz's stepdad's studio as the hub.'

Dave stops what he's doing. Says nothing. Instead he takes off his jacket.

'There was a painting of Van Gogh's "Sunflowers" in his flat. And when we stayed there I could hear the trains.

That braking sound this one's making now. I heard it in the background when Apocalypse was speaking.'

Dave goes pale, then dark, then pale again. 'You sure?'

I listen to the long squealing of the tracks.

'Yeah.'

'Then,' he pauses to calculate, 'I might be able to do it,' he says.

'What?'

Dave suddenly laughs. His first laugh since Holly died. 'Save you, Gen. Dave the Save! Remember? That's what you used to call me! That's what I'm good at. Fricking saving people. If I can get into the place with the THOR. And get into the flat. And get into the computer.'

'That's a lot of "get intos",' I say.

Dave grabs me. The pressure of his hands on my arms almost hurts. 'What's the address?'

'I don't know exactly, but I can describe it. It's on the street parallel to the station.' *Christ, it must be the hub.* They can actually watch Temple Meads explode from there. Explode in time to greet the eclipse.

'Street parallel to the station?'

'Familiar name, like Devon. No, Somerset – like where we come from – and it was the house on the corner with the red bricks that went all the way up. Sort of new bricks. All the rest have a stripy brickwork thing going on.'

'Right,' says Dave.

'Top flat.'

'But I can't come with you, Dave,' I say.

He freezes. Looks lost for a minute.

'Can't,' I say. 'I've got to get off this train and get to Oldbury Naite. Somehow.'

I am the handmaiden.

A look of panic.

'I've got to. There's only an hour left.'

I feel sick all over again. All those people. All of them: sitting, picnicking, enjoying their day off, looking forward to a spectacular solar show.

A spectacular solar show.

'If I get there,' I say, 'I won't go near the people.'

'Right,' he says. I just love Dave for that. You could say anything. Like: *I'm going to take this bomb to a picnic party.* And he'd go, 'Right.'

'Read this bit.' I point out lines on Exodus One's papers.

Brother Proverbz Operative Schedule

Routes

Details of tides

Ordnance

Details of explosions

Communications

Boat and equipment

Maps included

B.P.

Provide means of delivery

Research SFP (exact location)

Local knowledge

Firearms training

Member of YC

Leave hub 3.30 p.m.

Arrive YC

Conduct checks

Leave upriver YC 4.39

Delivery 4.44 p.m.

'That's Naz,' I say. 'That's his schedule. Must be. *Proverbz* has got to be his code name. He'd have loved that. He was always trying to make up "Life Is" ones that were better than mine.'

And YC must be the yacht club.

He's going to take his boat up the river to the power station and somehow blow up all the radioactive waste that way. 'Look.' I point at the schedule.

Leave upriver YC 4.39

337

'But I want to be with you, Gen,' Dave says. 'I promised myself.'

'I know,' I say gently. 'But I've got to stop Naz, and only I know exactly where he moors his boat. You see, the Severn is tidal,' I try to explain. 'You have to move your boat if you're planning a trip, or it gets marooned on mud flats. Naz has this special place. It's hidden, because you shouldn't really damage the eco-system on the river bank . . .' It's just taking too long to explain. 'And anyway, you've got to save me.'

The train jerks in a series of braking stops. Dave reaches out, braces himself on the door. I catapult into him. I look up into his troubled face. 'Is there any hope the police will listen to us, and stop him – if we tell them?' I say.

'We could try.'

'You try. After I'm gone? Promise?'

'Gone?'

'Not *Boom* gone,' I say. 'I mean, after I get going for Oldbury.'

He doesn't look good. A new look of pain in his eyes. His mouth is tight, lips pressed. I've got to help him. How strange to have to help someone choose life, knowing you can't do that for yourself.

'You're going to stay on the train now, take this ticket,

take your THOR and get off the train with everyone else. Get yourself on to the relief train, call the police, tell them about Oldbury, get to the hub in Somerset Street and save my life.' I pass him the All Day Travel Card that the Brightness put in the vest pocket.

'Right,' he says. A flicker of hope briefly glows in his eyes.

'And you take the tracker with you, so Apocalypse will think the bomb's still on its way to Bristol.'

'Right.'

'And I'll go and stop Naz from killing all those people,' I say.

'Right,' he says. 'Course you will.'

Even if I have to sit in his boat and blow him up.

9

Life is a Concrete Trampoline: No Ups Only Downs

'THE TRAIN'S STOPPING,' says Dave. 'You'll have to get out of the window and jump.'

Jump? I somehow hadn't figured on that bit.

'Yep, use that.' Dave points at the dotty mallet. 'Break the glass and jump. Wear this jacket.' He passes me his jacket. 'It's army issue and very tough.' He sees my look. 'Don't worry, I got a change of clothes.' He holds up a really flash sports top.

'Uh?'

'Picked it up in first class. That guy who was rude to you.'

That's kinda funny.

'Cool,' I say. I wasn't actually worrying about the jacket. I was thinking, *Jump? What about the vest?* But instead of saying so, I examine the mallet, test its point. Put on the jacket.

'Here's the phone, the earpiece. Bank card's in the pocket. Bit of cash. PIN's two-three-three-zero.'

I'll be OK in heaven then, if I want to buy a bottle of nectar.

'Now – high impact falls,' Dave says. 'Wait till the last possible moment. Wait till the train's as slow as you dare. Remember any speed at all and you'll kill yourself. Then let go, don't push off. Simply drop. If you can, run alongside the train, but it'll probably be going too fast so, after a few steps, draw your knees to your chest, curl up, and roll on to your shoulder or you'll break a leg.'

'What about the vest?' I say.

Dave dismisses that with a wave. 'C-Four explosive won't explode if it's hit by a truck. But watch out for those canisters winding you.'

The Unexploding Explosive Take on Life. LIFE IS DYNAMITE: BUT CANISTERS ARE WORSE.

'Right, shield your head by tucking your chin in. Lock your arms around your face while you make yourself into a ball. When you hit any surface think: *I am light. I am relaxed.* Try to hit feet-first and let them crumple upward. At all times try to protect your vital organs.'

'How do you know all that?' I ask, trying to take it in.

'Would you believe it?' he says. 'They get stunt men to train us.'

His voice is hoarse and a sad smile accompanies his words. I'm not sure I believe him.

I examine the window. It's quite big. Must have been designed as the last exit point on the train, in case of fire or something. There's a red dot at the top of it. All very logical.

'Won't they find the broken window when they search?' I'm really not keen on this jumping business.

'Don't worry. When I come out the toilet, I'll bust the lock. That will delay their search. Give you a head start.'

'All right then.' I've run out of excuses.

I've got to jump. I actually haven't got a choice. If I stay put the police will fire on me. Plus I'm going to blow up just the same if I get going or not. And this way, Dave may get through. He will tell the police about Oldbury. They may be able to evacuate all the people. I doubt that. But they may be able to get to the yacht club.

But how will they get through? All that traffic. Plus they don't know Naz's hidden mooring. I try to calculate how long a police speedboat would take from Bristol to Oldbury, with the river jammed full of eclipse tourists. Or a helicopter? Would there be enough space for it to land? Or would they phone the drafted-in, event-security police, all lining the access routes to the river bank?

And still none of them knows exactly where Naz moors his boat or when he's planning a trip up river.

Not like I do.

But how am I going to get through? I'm making this up as I go along. But I've got to try. The pale faces of the Moirai float for an instant in front of my eyes. Remind me.

You are the handmaiden. You are the firmament. You have been chosen.

Suddenly I catch my breath.

LIFE IS A JOURNEY OF HOPE: HOPEFULLY?

If I jump, at worst I'll only kill myself; at best I might reach Oldbury and save millions of people. The maths is very obvious.

OK. I smack on the glass with all the force I can. It jolts. It resists. It's surprisingly tough. I raise my arm a second time and, in a frenzy, smash the hammer down, again and again. I probably should have aimed better. Only one out of loads of tries actually hits the red dot.

Smashing glass is not all it's cracked up to be. Disappointingly. The shot that hits the dot works, though. The glass breaks, and I hear the pane literally give with the wind pressure. Fragments of glass go crack-crazy – all seem held together on a membrane, pulled by some scary kind of suction. I raise my arm again, but suddenly, with one sucking sound, the entire window is jerked out of its frame and spirals away down the track.

Dave leans out through the hole. A curious kind of howling starts. I hold my breath. The force of the slipstream whips my hair around.

I put the dotty mallet down on the loo seat. I look at the clean edges of the hole. I'm surprised at how well I did it. Maybe not so disappointing. I know why it's called a 'dotty' mallet now. That red dot is exactly the right spot to hit the glass.

The noise of air through the empty window sends a shiver down my spine. 'Get into position, but wait. We may be going at more than thirty,' says Dave, drawing his head back into the toilet cubicle.

'OK,' I say.

I climb on to the window ledge, duck my torso through the gap. I draw my knees up and squeeze through as best I can. I balance, clinging on to the upper frame – backwards, all of me outside, toes poised – looking in at Dave.

He tries to smile – lifts his arm, gives me the thumbs up.

'As soon as you can, tell the police? Tell them about Naz and Oldbury, be sure to mention the yacht club. If they can get through, they need to search the bank upriver

344

from there. There's an inlet before a mud flat.'

'I'll tell them everything I can, but I'm not taking time out over it. Nothing is going to get in the way of me getting to Somerset Street.' His chin is set. His eyes fixed. 'You've got your mission. They'll have theirs. I'm getting on with mine.' He really believes he can save me.

'OK, you save me, but save everybody else too. It's not just about me anymore. Tell the police. Keep these papers. Give them all the details.'

So slow now.

'Right,' says Dave. Kinda awkwardly.

I can see individual blades of grass. Barely moving. This is it. We're nearly stopped.

'Best of luck,' I say.

'We got this far,' says Dave.

Time to jump.

'I'm gonna do it,' I say, 'or die trying.'

Neither of us smile.

I want to say something else, like when all this is over, when we go for that drink with Marco and Bill . . . I want to say something about Holly. I want to say: *I think you're OK, I was wrong to dump you*. I want to say something kind of poetic and lovely that'll make me memorable, and make him feel like he used to, when we were kids, and he used to rush to my rescue – make him remember what it was like when we were together, when it was just the two of us – something that could be a Final Last Word – but I don't.

I don't know how the hell I'm going to make it. I suppose I'm not, really.

'Just live, Gen,' says Dave. 'Promise me.'

I look at him then. For the briefest of moments our eyes lock.

There's an awkward pause like he wants to say something poetic too, like he wants to promise something. And I hold my breath, waiting. But all he says is, 'Right?'

So here goes nothing.

And I let go.

10

Life is a Joke: Has to Be

As I DROP, I follow Dave's advice, try and run alongside the train. After that it just goes nuts. My feet seem whipped away. So I go for the shoulder roll. And then I'm dancing, and falling, and there's this terrible pain. Something's ripping at my side. My knuckles feel like they've been dragged across hot coals. Keep them tight over your head, I tell myself. Relax. Roll.

It's not so easy. I bash into something, hope I'm rolling the right way. A sharp pain radiates out from my knee. *Holy shit, I hope he's right about C-4.* I've snagged some kind of bush. The side of my leg hurts. Then I'm plummeting and somersaulting down a slope.

The bashing comes to an end. My face feels OK. Everything else feels like it's been dragged through the entire Amazon Rainforest backwards. I can hardly gasp, I can't draw breath. I lie still for a moment, predictably winded. Then open my eyes.

At first I can't see anything, just shrubs and a sort of filtering yellowish haze. And then I realize I'm looking up at a steep embankment towards the rail line. The train isn't anywhere in sight. OK – step one to me. *I did it.* I got off the train. Without detection. And I'm still in one piece. I slowly flex my arms, then legs. No bones broken either. The sky is clear. No police. Sun's still high, arcing a bit westward. The first tiny shadow of the moon has started to nibble at its edge.

I lie there for a moment, struggling to breathe, struck with the enormity, the beauty of it. If you look into the sky, you realize how small you are, how insignificant, how perfect the universe is and how much it doesn't need you. How the planets will keep on rotating, and the sun shining, long after you're gone. It helps, in a weird way. To know that everything passes and everything goes on.

And the moon will carry on too, eclipsing the sun. That encourages me as well. Today is a triumph for the small. Today, even the tiny moon can darken the huge sun.

A dark knot of smoke is wafting about down the track. Trains don't smoke, do they? Maybe it's a garden bonfire. The wind is whipping it round. It circles, twists.

If it blows this way I won't be able to see where I am.

I think of Dave, still on the train. When will he be able to call the police? I know he'll do it as soon as he can. I hope to God they'll listen to him and act fast. I hope to hell he can find Somerset Street as well. Not much point in hoping though. Just get up. Keep going.

I look up at the sun again. How long have I got till 4.44 p.m.? Maybe an hour? An hour to succeed when all the police in the UK may fail. An hour to stop Naz. What kind of a crazy hope is that? The only advantage I've got now is I'm already on the move and Naz doesn't know I'm coming. He's the hunted, and I'm the hunter.

I think of the kids on the train; all the others, picnicking out, watching the eclipse. All of them doomed. Strapped to their own little time bombs. Each waiting for their own detonation call, that letter from the hospital, that sudden, dizzy vomiting. And it will come. There is no escape. That is what it is to be human. You wake up one day and it's your last. You knew it would come, yet you hoped it wouldn't. Not today. You pleaded. Please, not today.

And I still can't really believe that the Naz I knew could want to do this. That anyone could. Even in the face of all the evidence. And I guess if there is any point to anything, it must be that in the end we'll be remembered for what we did in life. I'm just hoping that in some big book somewhere it will all be written down. So everyone will know.

I pull myself out of the briar patch. I must look terrible. My clothes weren't that good before. The flak jacket Dave gave me has taken most of the damage. I feel through the front pockets for the phone. And it's not there.

There's a huge tear right through the left side pocket. NO PHONE. NO EARPIECE. How will I know the time? How will I speak to Dave? If the Voice wants to speak to me, how will I know? I try to crawl back up the bank, but it's all bramble. The bloody phone could be anywhere. And the earpiece is so tiny, there's no hope of finding it. Do I stop and search? Do I carry on?

The black smoke swirls closer. The sun dims. My eyes water. And I can't even see to search. My heart sinks. I feel like lying here and giving up.

Instead I catch my breath; I pull off the jacket, take Dave's bank card and cash out of the top pocket (thank goodness that didn't rip), and throw the jacket away. I scrabble around in one desperate last attempt, looking, knowing it's hopeless. Then I clamber down the rest of the bank, across a patch of sandy ground. A road sign says: *Stoke Gifford*. And for the first time I realize I have no proper plan of how to get to Oldbury.

Just get somewhere, then. Keep going. Get on a bus. *You have been chosen.* That's all you can do.

LIFE IS A BUS: THOUGH IT KEEPS STOPPING, YOU HAVE TO KEEP GOING.

I walk fast to the corner of the road, and then I'm jogging, trying to run my hands through my hair and brush out bits of leaves. I yank on a twig. It comes free, hair strands still attached. Cars pass. A taxi comes round the corner. A taxi?

The Fates are with me! Obviously. Take a taxi to a town. Take a taxi all the way?

I hail the cab down.

The taxi slows. At first the driver looks at me as if I can't possibly be serious. I flail my arms up and down and screech 'TAXI!' at him. There. He can't mistake that.

He stops. A window slides down. 'Blimey,' says the driver. 'You all right? Look like you've been in the wars.'

'There's been an explosion,' I say. 'A train was nearly derailed. Just take me to the town centre.' Sometimes I wonder how I come out with all that stuff. S'pose I sort of take the truth and give it a shake.

He squints at me, screws up his face as if he's trying to work out the equation. Explosion + Train + Girl in a state + Town centre + Randomly on side of road + Me going into town centre anyway + Why not? Then he shrugs and says, 'It'll be a tenner.'

What a rip-off.

'OK,' I say.

I get in and we set off.

The town centre seems to be a row of shops on Ratcliffe Drive, two streets away. At least that's where the driver stops and demands his money. All of a one-minute ride.

There's a Tesco Express, a dentist's and a medical centre, a few more shops on one of the roads off it. I pay up, wondering if I shouldn't just ask him to take me all the way. I'm just about to when he says, 'This is as far as I go.'

'Please,' I say, 'couldn't you take me a bit further, like Oldbury?'

He laughs out loud. 'Are you nuts, lady?' he says. 'There's a three-hour queue on every road west of here.'

'How can I get there then?' I ask.

He raises his eyes like I must be totally bonkers. 'You can't,' he says. 'Not until after the eclipse.'

I'm not sure why I expected I could. So I just stand there on Stoke Gifford main street, thinking: *OK then, I need to head off somewhere pretty lonely, like a golf course*, when a shout goes up.

People come wailing out of Tesco. One woman is screaming and screaming. The taxi driver jumps out of the cab and yells, '*What's up?*'

'We're all doomed,' she yells.

11

Life is a Gamble:
Most of Us Lose

'A HUGE CRASH. THEN A BOOM.' The sound of the world ending. Everyone's running. Someone's shrieking, 'It's Nine-eleven all over.'

I freeze. I know what's happened. A shiver goes through me. I feel ill. I was right when I hoped I'd be so wrong. A man hurtles towards us, towing a kid. 'It's Armageddon,' he yells. 'NEW YORK'S BEEN HIT!'

A car draws up. Everyone gets out. Doors left wide open. 'Listen! Listen!' says the driver. He turns the radio on his loud speaker up to max. It booms out.

Massive explosion . . . terrorist attack . . . New York State, Indian Point Energy Centre . . . just south of Peekskill . . . a nuclear power plant station . . . east bank of the Hudson River . . . thirty-eight miles north of New York City . . .

millions of tourists watching the eclipse . . .'

A white van, going the other way, pulls up and yells out of his window, 'IT'S HAPPENED AGAIN!'

A biker swings his Kawasaki in front of the dentist's, pulls off his helmet, bungs it on the trunk, strips his jacket free, slings it over the seat, and races down the road. 'What's up?'

'TWO NUCLEAR POWER STATIONS BOMBED!'

A biker? Am I thinking what I'm thinking?

'We're next!'

'The train.'

'What?'

'They've bombed a train already, right near here,' yells the taxi driver, as if he suddenly gets what I told him earlier.

'Here?'

'THEY'RE COMING HERE!'

And then there's mayhem. Mums, babies, buggies, shoppers, kids, cars.

I watch the biker. I'm going to steal his bike. I don't know if I should feel bad about that or not. If you have less than an hour to live, does normal morality count? Like when does Last Request Time start? And could A Last Request include stealing someone's bike?

I watch the biker carefully. He questions the van

driver. He's all in shock with this latest horror. With a bit of luck, he's either left the key in the ignition or the spare in the trunk. As I get closer to the bike, I see I'm right: the keys are still in the engine, and the engine's still running.

I cross to the pavement, walking fast, down past the growing knot of shrieking people, straight up to his bike.

From way back down the street, someone's got a first-hand witness account blaring out of a boom-sound speaker.

'I heard a blast. That was a real blast – thought I'd be deafened by it. I hunkered down, but then everyone started running, so I did. Didn't know what I was running from. I wasn't able to see anything. So much dust. You couldn't open your mouth because of the dust. After a dozen steps I stumbled and fell over.

'The only sound was of people running. I couldn't breathe. One shoe slipped off . . .'

'It's the end of the world,' yells someone.

If it really *were* the End of the World, would that mean stealing bikes would be OK? Would personal ownership not count then? After all, you can't take it with you, can you?

The radio blares on . . .

'I heard a distant boom, like an earthquake or thunder, and it was just when the sky was at its darkest. I looked over the

water. *Stuff was whirling everywhere, like confetti. What On Earth, I thought and wondered if a recycle plant had caught on fire. It was so weird. When I saw stuff, chunks of building, I knew something terrible had happened . . .'*

Just like I figured, the key's in the ignition, the steering lock's off and his helmet's on the trunk. *Oh my God they really bombed New York.* I check the fuel's on, I switch down, check gears, pull up the kick stand and we're off.

Out, like a bat from hell.

There are lots of restrictions about riding a bike when you're a teenager, like you can't really ride anything above 50cc (which is basically everything worth riding). But that doesn't bother me now. Because I figure when you've stolen a bike and have the entire police force out looking for you, breaking a few more laws doesn't matter. Especially speeding ones.

So I don't check my speed going down the street, or out on to the dual carriageway. *They did it. The Brightness really did it.* A crosshatch of yellow lines zip under my wheels. *Why didn't I work it out before? We could have done something, told someone. If only I could have worked it out earlier. All those people in New York.*

You can only do what you can do, I tell myself. *You didn't know. Dave will call the police now and tell them about Oldbury.*

357

I check the wing mirror. I really need to hurry. The eclipse has already started. Just thirteen miles to Oldbury. Even if Dave has already called the police and they truly believe him, how will they get through? How will they disperse millions of people?

In less than an hour?

The Brightness are still set to do it all over again, and I may be the one person who can stop them.

I will stop them. *I am the firmament in the midst of the waters.*

I wonder what chances Dave will have of getting through to the hub. I never was very good at maths. My introduction to Probability was something to do with guestimating how many times a tossed coin would fall heads down.

LIFE IS A TOSS UP: YOU NEVER KNOW HOW THINGS WILL FALL OUT.

Except in this case I do.

Poor Dave. A painting by Van Gogh and the sound of train tracks was all it took. But what else could I do? Blow him up? There really wasn't any choice. And, after all, that flat might actually be the hub . . . And he had to try . . .

He must know there's practically no chance of him getting through, even if it is. He must have realized, especially when the train was actually stopping and the clock wasn't? I had to get rid of him somehow. I don't want him to die. I'm glad he's not here now. *Oh God, I miss you, Dave.*

I take the road easy, smooth like silk, as fast as I dare. Glance to my right. Roundabout intersection. A lorry coming. I beat him on to the roundabout. I belt it on a curve, shoot out on the second exit, straight across, through a little bit of a built-up area. Residential houses.

Oldbury-on-Severn. Half an hour in a car. Twenty-five minutes on a bike. Max. And that's sticking to speed limits. Maybe I can actually do it, actually stop Naz blowing up that power station.

For the first time since The Hut in The Woods, I feel hopeful. Not that I will survive. I sorted that out there, under those old beech trees – but that my death will count for something.

The bomb went off in New York. I was right. They are following the line of the eclipse. I'm right too about the yacht club and Oldbury Naite. Somehow it all comes down to me.

And now I've got to carry on without Dave.

Oh Dave, I wish you were here with me.

Up ahead is one of those hedge-trimming vehicles. Blue roof. Flashing red danger light. Driver in high-visibility yellow. Long orange arm, crooked up and trimming over the top of the hedge. Snipping. Bits of leaves swirling in the breeze. Twigs smacking the air around me. I bend out, pass by, hitting nearly eighty. Open country ahead. Speed. Love it. Freedom. And the wide blue sky.

I love bikes.

If it ends for me today – at least I got this last bike ride in.

LIFE IS A FAST BIKE: IT GOES SO QUICK, BEFORE YOU KNOW IT YOU'RE AT YOUR JOURNEY'S END.

I give the Kawasaki full throttle. The machine moves under me, pure velocity, like a plane on takeoff. I'm all that's left. Genesis One. I am the firmament. The world is the firmament. And I'm going to do my best to save my little bit of it.

I hit nearly ninety m.p.h.

Up ahead, a bus. Pink trim over the wheels, and a huge white sticker on the back. Darkened rear window. Keep things smooth. Don't slam the brakes. Get past the bus. Don't tear open the throttle. Keep the bike balanced. Another roundabout. And it's gone. Lampposts with flat lights over the road. Walkways on either side. Lush and green. Hedgerows and beech trees.

More yellow crosshatching on the road. A corner. Black and white chevrons. Dragging my knees, clipping apexes, thrown into the world around me. Beyond redbrick houses. Beyond that red van. Beyond and gone.

Not only strapped to a bomb.

But going like a bomb.

12

Life is Easy: Until It's Not

NAZ LIKED TO GO SPEEDBOATING. His favourite route was up past Oldbury, right on the edge of the Severn. Last time we were there he pointed out the nuclear power station to me. He must have been laughing all the time. He must have known he was going to strap a bomb to me. Boy, he was having a regular bubble bath. He must have been looking at the power station and looking at me and going *BOOM*.

A revelation strikes me. And I know how he's going to breach that spent fuel pool. He liked shooting. When we went out on the estuary, he'd shoot at birds with his air gun. We'd stay out long after dark, and he'd shoot them coming in to roost. Once he said, 'Even with this rubbish air gun, if you choose the exact angle you can kill a bird anywhere along the banks of this estuary.'

Once he shot a swan. I remembered how Dave loved

swans. I didn't often remember Dave when I was with Naz. But I did that evening. I remembered how Dave said swans mated for life. How when one died the other wasted away in sadness.

Naz was only worried about the £5,000 fine and the six months prison term.

I helped him tie stones around its black, webbed feet. Together we sank it midstream in the Severn.

Naz liked shooting.

So that's how he'll do it, I'll bet. He'll sail his speedboat upriver and shoot the bomb into the spent fuel pool. So simple. Forgotten old Oldbury. Decommissioned. Low security. Right on the banks of the Severn. Yet packed full of radioactive waste. So obvious. Why bother with checkpoints? Why bother with getting anyone on the inside? Why bother with flying a passenger plane into it? All you need is a speedboat, one man and a missile launcher. I remember him once quoting some stuff from a scientific bulletin.

HITTING THE SPENT FUEL POOL: RADIOLOGICAL TERRORISM

It would be possible for anti-tank missiles, in the hands of a terrorist, to breach a spent fuel pool. Modern missiles can pierce reinforced concrete up to a depth of three metres. They can be fired from the shoulder or launched from a boat or vehicle. They have a staggering two kilometre range.

I remember him laughing and saying how stupid, how arrogant the Government was. How vulnerable, how fragile their defences.

And how stupid *he* was to tell me. Because now I've guessed. Plus I know exactly where he keeps his boat as well. And I know the route he'll take. For a moment I blink. *Will he die of radiation poisoning too?* I push the thought away. *Do I still care?* He obviously doesn't.

I refocus myself on the bike. Open road. Nine miles to Oldbury. And I'm going the right way. To my left is scrubland that looks as if it was once meadows. Low hawthorn hedges, covered in weedy growth. Great blowing white flowers.

At one hundred miles an hour on a bike you go where you look. It's just how it works. With supernatural skill, you enter a corner, you turn your head, you look through the turn. You look out at the exit, give a little lean and you're there.

LIFE IS A CORNER THAT YOU TAKE STRAIGHT ON.

I'd just turned a corner in my life. I was almost perfectly

unhappy. *Why did you have to reappear, Dave? Just when death was at its most appealing? Damn you. Now I've got to die just when I want to live most. Just when all I want to see is your square face and your hazel eyes and your stupid haircut. Oh God.*

High hedges bear down on my left. At least it's a dual carriageway. I burn the tarmac. I glance up. Even through my visor the sky's very blue. Little wispy hazes of white working up from the right. The moon has moved. A dark crescent against a bright disc. From now on this is how it all will be: creeping, creeping darkness – no escape. I will never see the sun again.

Oh Dave, if not for you, I could almost have enjoyed dying. (In some warped, weird way.) Dying with Naz, I mean. My atoms irrevocably mixed with his. Yesterday it would have had its appeal. *Now, when they bury me, how will you know which is me and which him?*

I leave the dust of the tarmac smoking behind.

I want to live. Not just survive. But really live. Dave. You and me. Two swans reunited.

Away to my right a row of newish, urban houses and I'm past them. Road signs remind me it's a forty-mile-an-hour speed limit. I smile and give the Kawasaki more throttle.

A hundred m.p.h.

Today I can break every limit.

Ahead on the road, my bike-shadow races, like some strange mythical creature. Girl and machine, welded together. Not a car in sight. I speed past white-rendered houses, low concrete roofs. The next roundabout blooms up at me.

On my left are commercial buildings. Powder blue. Pistachio green. Single lanes in either direction and none too generous. I crouch lower over the handlebars and give my beauty full rein. Keep things in line, brake before I enter that curve.

Racing drivers preach the church of smoothness, and that means accelerating and decelerating in a straight line. Grabbing the brakes in the midst of a corner is seriously bad news. Slow in, fast out.

On my right, some kind of new elevation is going up and there's debris on the road. Not good. Sand too. Even worse. Avoid it. Stay away from the shoulder. Construction sites are bikers' graveyards.

Imagine that; racing towards death and afraid of graveyards.

LIFE IS A RACE: WHICH IN THE END YOU LOSE.

I'm over a bridge. The road narrows. Shadows cross it in a lattice of dark and light. The road stays a single carriageway. White lines down its side. Sun still there, the moon has bitten a third of it away. Turning in. Leaning down. Powering out. I get in the flow, cutting apex after apex.

Trees give way to stone walls, open banks, open fields. On my left are pylons. In the distance, white clouds with aeroplane vapour trails. I think of swans flying. Highways of the sky.

An exit pops up out of nowhere. I hit the brakes and shed some speed. Down the lane. Past sidings. Take centre-road and burn rubber.

How many more minutes? I wonder.

Twenty?

Past roadwork signs. Ahead, a hamlet and some low-lying buildings. Fields. Plated chrome gates and a motorbike come the other way. He kicks out his right foot to let me know when there's a big patch of gravel on a curve up ahead.

I downshift, chill a little. Leave the speed for my way out. Over the gravel, I keep it slow and smooth, no abrupt throttle, no brake inputs. Keep the bike as upright as possible. Lose traction at a fifty-degree angle and you'll go down.

T-junction. Cars. And a weird humming noise. I know that noise. I glance up. *Shit.* A helicopter.

Police. Me? Or has Dave told them?

Up ahead is a big white delivery van. It's going too slowly. The traffic starts here. I take a risk, pull out to overtake and see the line of cars stretching ahead. This is it then, the tail end of the eclipse rush hour.

I shoot past the van and a line of cars. I'm terrified someone will open a door. I glance up. The helicopter's still with me, swooping lower. The sky is definitely darker. The puffy white clouds have gone. I try to calculate what the time is. I must have about another fifteen minutes.

I let the throttle out. I zoom past the crawling queue, down towards the M5. The helicopter follows. Over the M5. Single carriageway. Cars still in a long line. I zip past. Must be me. I want to shout up: '*GET TO OLDBURY. THAT'S ALL THAT MATTERS.*'

How can I lose the 'copter?

Blur of wooden fencing, trimmed hedge. I'm doing eighty, overtaking on the wrong side of the road. And the 'copter's staying with me. Just let me reach the marina. If I lose the bike, I'll lose him.

Stained white walls, low bungalows, shoddily mown verges, flitting from built-up areas to country places. Thirty-mile-an-hour speed limit. People hurrying. The Masons Arms. Picnic parties already set up. Must be close now. Past a Church of England primary school. All the children out, sitting in the playground holding special darkened goggles to look through. I wonder if the radiation blast will reach them.

Streetlamps give way to hedges which give way to telegraph poles. The endless line of traffic stretches before me. I overtake saloon cars, white, black, silver, blue. And someone flicking his cigarette ash all over me.

Oldbury-on-Severn. The Anchor Inn. At last.

I slow down. Stop. Dump the bike. The helicopter circles in low. I run. In the distance I hear police sirens. I hope that means they've listened to Dave. Soon I am one moving figure amongst hundreds. People. Everywhere. All along the road to the marina. Sitting down on rugs, breaking open hard-boiled eggs, cracking cans of Coke, crunching crisps, sipping soda, chatting, laughing.

The police will never be able to evacuate them all in time.

The helicopter banks away. I catch my breath and heave a sigh. Lose the crowd. Get to the marina.

Just let me. Be. In. Time.

I run down the tarmac, past the boggy meadow. Up the road. But by the time I turn into the yacht club, I know I'm too late. The gentle swell of water slaps on a deserted concrete slipway. Down the bank. Find the inlet. Through the rushes. I know where he keeps his boat, but

I can see from here his secret mooring space is empty.

I'm too late. I'm too bloody late. I shield my eyes against the grey skies, see if I can catch a glimpse of white tail-water, heading up the Severn. *Oh Christ.* I bite my lip, clench my fists . . . *Oh Jesus Christ.* The river stretches, wide muddy brown, a strange tide on its surface. On the far shores the low Welsh horizon. *What to do? Steal a boat?* I'm not so sure I know how – and then I remember.

Naz won't have set out yet.

He has to pray.

13

Life is Not Fair: and Never Has Been

HE'LL STOP just up there on the crest of the creek. Up there by that knoll of long grass, where he can find the sun's directions. Where the wind will whip his words away.

The clouds race. A hurricane of air sweeps overhead. The riggings on the sail boats set up a manic tapping. The sun comes out from behind a cloud. What's left of it. A distant cheer goes up from the spectators on the tow path. It's only a crescent of gold. Half of its disc is obscured by the moon, casting the land into a strange dimness. The temperature drops. Chill night air in the middle of a sunny afternoon.

I flounder down the bank, through the mud, cursing it, blessing it. No eclipse tourist in their right mind will sit in mud. Soon I'm out of sight and alone. Long levels of sludge. I scan the river. Grey brown. Banks of rushes; sticky, stray shoots. Flattened grass. Driftwood. Barren. Bleak. No police motorboat. A bird sings, warbles, high notes; a few more join in. Over the estuary, low hills. Dark against the bright sky.

I pause. Only the tap tap of rigging against masts and the bitter breeze.

More birds. More warbling. Overhead a host of them flock and swoop. Calling and calling. The wind races. And I understand. It's coming. It's happening. It's getting darker. The birds think it's evening. The moment of totality will soon be here.

And I'm not too late. I know exactly what he'll do. He'll leave the boat moored up by the big boulder. And I can still stop him.

I jog. Run. Squelch through mud. My breath comes in ragged gasps. Even as I slop through the ooze, I see him climbing the knoll, up to the top. I struggle out across the mud flats, leaping over slime, pebbles, green weed.

How long is left?

Less than ten minutes?

He's got his back to me. There's something large dumped by his feet. He won't turn now. He'll use his shadow – align it with the stone – and start his salutations to the sun. He'll call out the prayer – *Bless This Mission. We are the greatest. We bear witness there is no greater god. We are the Sons of the Sun and God's chosen ones. Make haste to find us. We welcome you to greatness. Greater than any Greatness. There is no god but Our Bright God.*

He'll prostrate himself, intone himself into the mind zone where he can believe anything he wants. And I've got about two minutes until he's done.

I get to the jetty. Rickety. Wooden. With poles sunk into muddy water. There she is: *The Revelation.* Moored like I knew she would be, amongst the reeds. I take the jump. I kick off my shoes, run up the planks and fling myself into her. No muddy prints to betray me. After this I won't need shoes.

I pause as I wonder what to do. Start her up and leave Naz stranded? NO IGNITION KEY. Try to cast her loose from the mooring? She's chained to the jetty. NO PADLOCK KEY. Creep up on Naz and knock him out? NO HOPE. Stave her in and sink her? NO TIME. NO AXE. NO CHANCE.

I look down the long expanse of river. Boats bobbing on choppy waters. A launch speeding upriver towards the yacht club. Light flashing. TOO LATE. The helicopter circling over the mud flats. The distant sound of a police loudspeaker. YOU ARE LOOKING IN THE WRONG

PLACE. The wind muffles everything. NO WAY TO SHOUT FOR HELP. They won't find us here.

So I know what I'm going to have to do. Hide, and wait for 4.44 p.m. I get to the front of the boat where there's a covered hold. I open the hatch at the side and look in. It'll be a very tight squeeze. *The Revelation* is a Sea Sprite, compact, nippy, with no excess space. I pull a tarpaulin out, shift an empty petrol can around.

I glance up at the knoll. He's still praying. Praying for success. Praying to heaven to bless murder. I try to hurry, knock over the flare jar, right it. *Less haste, more speed.*

It's getting darker. The moon is already winning. I'm praying too. *What if Dave does get through? I won't be blown up.* I catch my breath. It's an unimaginably beautiful thought. I hold it like a bubble. Allow myself to think it only once.

I'll have to stop Naz all by myself then.

It would be useless to tackle him before he sets out, anyway. He could overpower me, throw me into the shallows, take off and deliver his missile straight into the Spent Fuel Pool. No, if Dave gets through I'll jump him in the middle of the estuary. Rock the boat. Push him overboard.

But if I surprise him? If I confront him in midstream, we could both end up in the river, and I can't swim. How will I fight against the current? I check inside the hatch and pull a life vest out. I put it on, on top of the explosive vest. How bizarre is that? I pull the straps tight.

I tuck the whistle close against my skin. It sticks there, glued by my sweat.

One vest to kill you. One vest to save you.

Same day. Different whistle.

14

Life is a Quote: It Makes You Think

I CLIMB INTO THE HATCH. A huge, padded creature. Heart pounding. Palms slippery with sweat. I wipe them on the life vest, but the waterproof nylon gives it straight back. I crouch down as far as I can. My chin is jammed against my knees. The first-aid kit digs into my back. The canisters on the explosive vest bruise my ribs. The tool box crunches against my shoulder. I pull the tarpaulin over me, and close the flap. I wait. I breathe hot and stuffy air. I can feel the last rays of the sun beating down on the hatch. The fibreglass above me is warm. My face is sticky, my hair clings to the back of my neck. I gnaw at my lip and wait.

Through a crack on the flap, I can still see the birds wheeling, hear the gentle slap of the water against the sides of *The Revelation*. The scratching of reeds against the hull. The dip and sway of the craft beneath me. And from the shore: a faint, solitary salutation. His last, haunting cry.

He'll be coming soon.

And then I hear him. The pound of trainers on wet earth. His tread on the echoing boards of the jetty. Hollow. Creaking. And now his breath, fast and raw. My heart goes crazy, beats irregularly – thumps that scare the hell out of me. I break into an even hotter flush. Rivulets of perspiration stream down the sides of my face. The vests are soaked and slippery. The whistle digs into my collar bone.

Dave? Where are you? I hope whatever happens you get them. Are you watching the clock and panicking? I wish I could tell you not to. That I'm quite calm. That nobody lives forever. That I am lucky to have had a chance to prepare. I wish I could explain how you can even come to terms with wearing a bomb. And that really it is no different. The wind still blows your hair about. You still bleed if you're scratched. The difference is just that the idea that life goes on forever, into a charmed old age, is gone. But you can let the idea pass. It was only an idea anyway. Nobody has a guaranteed ticket to old age. And even for the aged, there's still The Last Day of Your Life.

But I've had a chance to know mine. I've had a chance to get used to my Last Day. And the air actually smells sweeter somehow and each moment has a sharpness in it that almost hurts.

The craft lurches. He's loosening its mooring. I hear the padlock snap open. The sound of the chain dragging. I try to balance myself against the hatch floor. *Don't make a noise.* Don't clang against the cans. I push my head against the ceiling of the hatch, but as he jumps into the craft, I reel to one side. I can't help it.

I hear his breath, faster now. He thumps something heavy into the boat. He slams a petrol can down on to the top of the hatch, nearly on top of my head. I can hear the slosh of petrol. *Please God, don't let him open the hatch flap.*

It seems impossible that we are so close. Only centimetres apart. I hold my breath. *Surely he must know I'm here?* He must have a feeling, after all the closeness we shared? All the melting into each other, two pulses beating as one. Just a hatch flap and a tarpaulin away?

That must be a metaphor for something. Mum once said, when I accepted the place in drama school: *Geographical distance is nothing, Gen. It's emotional distance that really parts people.*

LIFE IS A MAP: ONE CENTIMETRE OF SEPARATION TO EVERY THOUSAND MILES.

Oh Mum. What will you do without your Genesis?

For a second I hold my breath.

There's a sudden pause, as if he's holding his, as if on some higher plane he senses me. It sounds as if he's stopped moving. Has he felt me near? In the sudden stillness, the boat balances itself. He must have. I hold my breath.

'Hello?' he calls. *'Hello?'*

His voice. I suddenly feel dizzy.

It really is him. And for one terrible second I think I'm discovered. I brace myself against the back of the hatch. Should I answer? With what words? Tell him to call his hub and stop the timer? Could I conjure him in the name of all the times we shared? *Then what?* What would move him to spare me?

There's no answer. Then he says, 'All set. Start countdown at zero hour.'

Perhaps he wasn't calling to me.

I hear him moving, wrestling with something, clanking it on to the deck. He jumps on top of the hatch, jumps down. I can hear him grunt over by the motor. Tightening up the clamp handles? Unlocking it. Is he nervous? He must have run through this a dozen times.

I hear a paddle or a pole hit wood. I feel us push off from the hidden jetty. The hull beneath me shakes as we

379

glide towards midstream, then tilts as Naz lowers the engine further into the water. I hear him fidget around, the slosh of petrol, the click of the fuel hose on to the tank. A pause as he adjusts the vents, clicks the fuel line to the engine, clicks the gears into neutral.

How often have I run through the routine with him, perched on the gunwales in sexy little shorts, throwing my arms around him, purposely getting in his way? Blowing him kisses.

He clicks the kill cord, pulls the choke, twists the throttle.

Then the whizz of the ignition pull. The engine coughs, splutters, dies. The whizz of the pull again. Naz swears. The engine catches. Revs. Dips. Then louder, like wheels over gravel. Louder still. Then it settles into a growl that blocks out all other sound.

The choke goes in. The engine stays on a fast idle. Naz balances the turnover. I unball my fists, stretch my hands out. The engine putters, throbs gently. I hear it hit deep water, hear that squeak of nylon as Naz slips the kill cord around his wrist. And I feel the hull move beneath me.

We've left the mooring. We've cleared the shallows.

This is it.

If he's on schedule, it's 4.39 p.m.

Five minutes left.

And I want so much to flap the hatch back and look at

him. I want to see his face, just see the broad angle of his chest. And I don't know why I want that – or *what* I even want. To punch him, maybe? To scream at him? Bite him with angry teeth and bitter words? To ask him why?

Why? Why? Why?

I wish for one very brief instant that we could wind back time, like hours were some kind of strange tape measure, coiling in upon themselves. *That once again we could go back to when we just lay in each other's arms beside this same river spouting stupid poetry and pretending to be Romeo and Juliet.*

And I tell myself to stop. STOP. The boy on this boat is not the Naz you knew. That Naz never existed. That Naz – the one I imagined – would not have wanted me to be crouched inside a hatch, inside a life vest inside a death vest, all scared and sweaty. He would have saved me.

But the boy with his hand on this tiller, just a few paces from me now, is not going to save me. He doesn't care. He's primed me, groomed me, set me up. I was just a cog in his wheel. His vision of how the world should end.

And for the first time, I actually wonder how did all my days lead on to this? How did I end up here? Did I do something wrong? Maybe many things wrong? How come I didn't see it coming? And I don't know. And that is more scary than even being here. *I just don't know.* Things can't be trusted. The people you love can't be trusted. Life itself is a lie.

The Revelation suddenly lurches into action. I'm thrown off balance. The empty fuel can crashes. I hope the noise of the engine is loud enough to cover it. I take a deep breath. The boat shoots forward.

LIFE IS A LIE: TRUST NOBODY. TRUST NOTHING.

And all of a sudden I see Dave's face. His straight eyebrows. That cropped hair. Is he not to be trusted either? And in the darkness under the tarpaulin, with the greenish light coming through the cracks round the hatch, I accept that truth too. Dave is not here with me. Though he swore he would be. And life itself is a lie.

And I just don't know anything any more.

And the wind, like great sheets of card flapping, slaps the side of the hatch. And the prow rises and smacks down on the water. And we race up the river. And I must accept that I just don't know anything. And soon we'll be opposite Oldbury Naite. And there's no figuring out the unknowable. And there's some kind of oxymoron in that that's more moron than anything else.

So I try calculating my time left, instead. The power station at New York went down over forty minutes ago. Must have. When I got in the hatch, the birds were singing their dusk chorus. The moon was more than halfway across. A total eclipse of the sun lasts between one and seven minutes. The one calculated for today is big. Maybe even the full seven minutes. Oldbury Power Station is only two minutes up river.

The whole show takes nearly an hour or so.

And the show has started.

The engine dips. The speed slows.

We're here. On schedule.

4.44 p.m. is coming very soon.

15

Life is Hard: and Then You Die

THERE'S NO POINT IN WORRYING about being heard any more. I stretch my cramped ankles. I try to bend my knees. It's a long time since I rode a bike, and never before at such total speed. My legs are a bit shaky. I feel the stab of cramp in my calf. I clench and unclench my hands. At what point should I appear, and how to do it? I realize I have no plan – if the bomb doesn't detonate.

Maybe the bomb hasn't detonated. Maybe Naz has chickened out? Maybe 4.44 p.m. is gone?

For a second I allow myself to think that. Allow myself a fleeting glimpse of an impossible future.

Dave might be in it. He might teach me to swim. We might just head back to Somerset and live by the coast . . .

Then I cut the crap.

I should rush Naz in midstream. Rush out and stop him. If he grabs me and tips me in, I'll try to drag him in

384

too. If I fail at that, I'll hold on to the sides of the boat and upset it.

It's not much of a plan.

I prepare myself. I can feel the wind whipping the sides of the craft. I can hear the splatter of spray bashing the prow at my back.

I don't know the time, so I'll just come out. Before he fires anything. Somehow it's all come down to that. This is where the whole day has been heading. At last the two of us – face to face, alone. And I'm glad. I'm glad that at last he'll have to speak to me.

I'll go for the weapon first, though. He must have some sort of missile on the boat. One of those anti-tank bazooka things. How else will he deliver the bomb? Maybe that was what was dumped beside him on the hill.

Then I'll say: 'It stops right here, Naz.'

And suddenly I realize that if I'm going to die, I don't want to go on into the next place with things left unsaid between us. I actually *want* to see Naz again. I want to speak to him. I want to understand. Because I don't understand any of it. I don't understand why he turned his back on me, on everything, and joined them. I don't understand how it even happened. I don't understand how being in the Brightness Brotherhood changed him. I don't understand why he stopped loving me.

And I want to.

And somehow, if I can, it will be all right and dying won't matter half so much.

Can't be much longer to go, anyway. Though suddenly I'm not sure. Time isn't behaving in the way it should. It's running far too fast. So I wait, heart pounding. I try not to hurry it; the seconds tick by. Then they go *sooo* slowly. Perhaps he won't stop the boat. Perhaps the missile launcher is one of those fire-and-forget things and can find its own target? Where are the police? By now they should be here. I cross my fingers and hope they are.

I'm just going to come out, then. No more hiding. I feel the cramp taking hold in my calf again. Sweat breaks out on my face. I take no notice. Tell my heart to shut the hell up. This is it. Nothing else matters. Even understanding doesn't matter. Only saving lives.

So I take one deep breath and rip the tarpaulin back. Kick the flap free. Wriggle out of the small hold and on to the deck. I lurch to my feet, slip dangerously on the wet boards. I sway and my eyes fall on the massive missile launcher cradled in a case by the aft flap.

Two paces away and Naz has his back to me. He's adjusting the engine. *He hasn't seen me.* Hasn't heard me, either, despite the clatter I made. And as I inch closer. I see why. He's got headphones on and he's talking to Them.

The wind whips down the gunwales. The roar of the engine drowns my steps. In a flash I take the scene in. Other boats out on the estuary. Masses of them. Tall sails, wide cruising waves in their wake. Small launches. Row boats. Dinghies. Pedalos. Even surf boards. There's no way the police can plough through all that, not without capsizing the tiny ones.

In the distance, the skeleton of Clifton Suspension Bridge. Muddy brown river. Howl of wind. There's the bulk of Oldbury Power Station. Right on the water's edge. Powder blue and white stripes run perpendicular on its two huge reactors.

Oldbury Power Station with its Spent Fuel Pool. Its Spent Fuel Dry Casks. Beige concrete. Pylons. Pipes. All of it safe behind two tiers of wire fencing. But not safe from the Brightness. Not safe from Naz and his missile launcher.

And the banks are lined with people. Crowds of them. Hundreds. Thousands. Millions. I search the coast for the police. I can't hear anything; only the wind. Then I see them. Sporadic blue light. There. On the road up to the power station. A convoy of bright flashes, trying to get through. And the helicopter, still swooping low, downstream, over the yacht club.

I am the firmament in the midst of the water. I will divide the waters from the waters. Even the gods cannot alter what is ordained.

Let alone the police.

And it's already nearly dark. Like late evening, after the sun has slipped below the hills.

I look up and see it. Magnificent. Awesome. The moon over the face of the sun. There's still a necklace of bright beads to go, as the last of the sunlight shines through the valleys of the moon. Already the bright ring, the corona, like a glowing halo around everything. Just a minute or two to totality. And then seven of total darkness.

If I can get to the missile launcher. If I can tip it into the estuary. How heavy can it be? If I can do it without him turning.

I stand for one moment, poised, and then I jump forward.

16

Life is a question: Isn't It?

I WANT TO RUSH IT, but one wrong move will spoil my advantage. I crouch down and balance myself on the deck. Underfoot is slick with varnish and the film of fine spray. He hasn't heard me. He hasn't turned. One more step.

I spring. I grab at the launcher. It's impossibly heavy. I slip. I crash into the gunwale. I forgot to take into account the boat speed, the velocity of the wind, the angle of the deck. And Naz wheels round. The boat skews slightly. His phone skids across the deck. I tumble forward.

'Gen?' Naz's face goes pale beneath his tan. His eyes widen. 'Gen?' he repeats, as if it can't possibly be me.

My eyes stay fixed on the missile launcher. 'Little old me, the girl you promised to love forever.' I can't help letting the bitterness creep into my voice.

And I can see his mind working fast: What do I do?

She should be on a train to Bristol Temple Meads. How come she's not? Why didn't they tell me? *What the hell do I do?* And I see his eyes flit from the missile launcher to the tiller to his phone. I try to read his mind: *Shall I swerve the craft and try to tip her overboard? Can I reach the missile launcher before her – or should I go for my phone and let the hub know?*

But all he says is, 'What're you doing here?' Like I've bumped into him in a supermarket.

A strange sensation comes over me. I look at him. And I know I'm not over him yet. It's just like nothing's happened. He's still the Naz I loved; I'm still his Genesis. And that's so crazy. But it's different too. I'm not going to give in to him like before. *Oh no. I will find the crack in you, Naz. And it won't be the one you think it is.* I'm not looking for love or reassurance or approval or attention any more. I'm not sobbing my heart out because you don't pick up my calls. I am beyond all that now. *I will open up a crack in you. I will become your Nemesis. I will follow you into the netherworld and make you curse yourself, for I am the one you loved. I am the one you betrayed.*

I am the unexploded bomb.

As if by osmosis, Naz seems to understand. He instinctively draws back, instinctively shudders.

I play for time. How ironic. When time is running out.

'Why?' I say. 'Just tell me WHY?'

And there we stand, at last, all pretences stripped away, facing each other – and the wind whips by and the engine falters.

17

Life is a Novel With the Last Page Ripped Out

HE LOOKS CONFUSED, tilts the tiller a little towards shore. There behind him rises the bulk of Oldbury Power Station. Ominous. Dark. Above him the shadow of the moon blocks out the sun. The temperature around us drops.

'Why what?' Naz says. His words lost against the roar of the wind. He's forced to raise his voice.

'Why what?'

Like he doesn't know.

His eyes flicker to the shoulder-launched missile, laid ready on the deck beside us.

'That.' I point at it.

He glances at the darkened face of the sun. A spasm contorts his face.

'Look at them!' I point at the crowds of people gathered around the power station, picnics spread, cool boxes, hampers, hopeful seagulls wheeling in the dark sky. Telescopes. Cameras. The sound of children, laughing over the wind, looking up in wonder.

And on the opposite bank, there in Wales, dimly visible, thousands more, just white and red and yellow and grey blobs in the shadow of the eclipse.

'You don't understand,' he says.

'Then tell me,' I say. Time. Keep him talking.

Naz reaches for the missile launcher.

'They'll die,' I say. 'You're condemning them to a horrible death.'

'We all have to die one day,' says Naz.

'No,' I say, 'we all have to live. Those kids haven't even started living yet, and you want to stop them.'

'Even the sun can be darkened,' he says, pointing at the sky. 'It demands a sacrifice. All of us must give up the things we love most.' He turns to me. 'You were the thing I loved most, Gen, in all the world. If I can give you up, then all of them mean nothing.'

My heart lurches. I look at him, bewildered. I don't get it.

'But you strapped me to a bomb?'

'It was the only way,' he says.

'But I loved you,' I say.

'You can't understand.' He shakes his head. 'I didn't want to lose you. When I knelt down beside you and zipped the jacket over the explosives, I smoothed your hair away. I didn't want you hurt. I turned your face, so you wouldn't choke.' He pauses.

'*You turned my face away?* Can you hear yourself? You were worried about me *choking* when you were strapping me to a *fricking bomb*?' I want to add, *How does that compute? How do you think turning my face away* in ANY WAY means ANYTHING – *when you were strapping me to a bomb*?

'So I should be *sorry* for you?' I say at last.

'You have to give up the thing you love,' he repeats, in a curious dead monotone.

'No. You don't.' I won't have it.

'You have to believe it,' he says. 'Give up all earthly things – that is what God wants you to do. And you get your reward in the next life.'

'Which is?' I say. I look at the missile. Can I throw myself at it? Can I tip the boat enough to drag it into the river?

'The reward was you, of course,' he says. '*Of course* it was you . . .' He seems horrified that I'd think there was any other thing he wanted as a reward. 'You are the thing

I love most. I love you *so totally* you don't understand. And you would be there, all reformed and born anew, purified by your martyrdom, and waiting for me. I don't need seventy-two virgins or God's right hand or any crap like that.' His voice breaks. He looks almost miserable.

Just grab the thing, sling it in the water, rock the boat, push him in.

'So . . .' I say, 'let me get this right. You blow me up, so I can wait for you in the afterlife and that's your reason?'

It's like he's gone brain-dead or something – or is under the influence of some psychotic drug. He doesn't seem to notice I'm still wearing the suicide vest at all. He doesn't seem to notice the darkened moon or the wide wash of water.

'If you understood,' he says, 'you would know that if you died a holy death, you would be fit to be with me there.'

I almost want to laugh.

'It was the only way I could sacrifice the thing I loved *and* keep you. Why wouldn't you convert, Gen? If you'd agreed to convert . . . all this . . .' He twists his face as if some huge sadness is hovering all around him and if he makes one slip it will overpower him.

Are all appeals to logic useless then? Has he gone so deep? And is he still thinking, right now, of a way to kill

395

me? So that I will be there, in his afterlife, waiting for him?

I don't know how to reach him any more. And suddenly my throat closes. All that time together, all those hours and days and weeks – I *should* have tried to reach him then.

It'll soon be 4.44 p.m. Just play for time I can still save those people. Blow us up together. Don't let him see the peril he's in. There, that's all. It's far too late now. Quite easy really.

'If you love me, Naz, what's wrong with this life? Couldn't we have made it here first? Couldn't you have shown your love for me here – on earth?'

'But this *is the way* I show my love for you,' says Naz.

18

Life Just Is

I POINT AT THE MISSILE LAUNCHER. 'Is this how you
show your love for them?' I point at the people on the
river banks.

Naz turns. He seems to switch into brainwashed mode.
His chin goes up and his hands form pointing fingers. 'I'm
going to be very brief and very direct, because it's all been
pointed out to you before – and by far more powerful
voices than mine. I can only reflect the words of former
martyrs . . .' Even the modulation of his voice is different.
'But it seems our speeches make no impression on you, so
you leave us no option but to speak to you in a tongue
that you respect.'

He bends down and my moment is gone. He picks up
the shoulder-launched missile.

'Our words are wasted until we give them immortality,'
he intones, his voice totally changed now. 'Your

government will always chose to vilify us with malign misinformation – and will conveniently try to put a slant on things to fit its own greedy capitalist agenda – it will try to intimidate the great majority into kowtowing to its supremacy and control . . .'

He's losing me. He's into rhetoric. He's quoting some source way beyond me. He lets the engine idle. 'The Brightness Brotherhood have been forced into abandoning everything to pursue their righteous ideology and expose your governments' misrepresentation and iniquity. Do you know the cost of that? To leave our families and the futures they had mapped out for us?'

'But you hated your stepdad,' I point out. 'And you felt your mum betrayed you when she married him.'

'Like you betrayed me,' he says.

'Me?'

'When I found another family, one who welcomed me just the way I was, you refused to acknowledge them. You refused to join them. You denied me and you must be punished.'

'No,' I say. 'No, you didn't. Look at you. They didn't *welcome* you the way you were, they changed you. Look at your hair, your tattoos. They took the Naz I knew and destroyed him.'

'I won't let you talk like that,' he says, advancing. 'I

gave myself to them. They took me. They embraced me. They don't take *everyone*, you know. I *chose* to dye my hair, *chose* to leave you. I did it to show them my love and loyalty. When you join the Brotherhood, you give them everything. They give you everything. You dedicate your life to them and they give your life meaning.'

'But Naz,' I say, my voice hoarse, 'you had everything – the school, your home, a future . . . me . . .'

'The motivating incentive of our calling doesn't come from the worldly possessions that this existence tries to manipulate us with,' Naz quotes in a lofty, almost hallowed tone. 'Or the empty love of one person.'

He swings, pointing the missile at my stomach.

'But you wanted me to embrace all those Brightness rules, agree with their beliefs, offer myself to them in their struggle,' I say. 'How was that anything to do with *us*? Can't you see?' Surely he *must* see.

'Our religion is everything. Our obedience to the one creed is all that matters. Our struggle to create an Empire true to our beliefs is paramount. Our fundamentalism will not be stopped . . .'

I want so much to shake him. None of this is an answer to anything. He sounds like some scripted pre-recording – programmed to voice THEIR views. I want to slap him, tell him *YOU DON'T BELIEVE ANY OF THIS, DO YOU?*

But it's no use. He can't meet my eyes.

'We will use all means, including force, to further our struggle. We have declared a campaign against all religions and all non-believers. We will build an Empire to the glory of the Sons of the Sun. The Brightness will shine when all the world are Luminaries.'

The moon slides ever on. Soon, very soon. The corona darkens – just keep him talking. *Oh God, let 4.44 p.m. come. Let it be over.*

'Your so-called egalitarian governments were voted into power by you – the great masses of Great Britain – and in your name they incessantly commit violence against us – that makes *you* complicit and a justifiable target, and that makes me answerable to my God for my actions – so I must take arms against you and take vengeance on you for those you have persecuted.'

I can't actually take much more of this. Something snaps. '*Take vengeance?*' I shout. 'Naz, do you have any idea of what you're spouting?'

'The Brightness glory in their martyrdom, and avenge their persecution,' he repeats.

Hopeless. Completely hopeless.

The moon is nearly there. Only the last fragment of the sun remains.

'Until we build our Empire, *you* will be our targets.'

He blinks once and intones: "Until you stop the terrorizing, killing and incarceration of our Luminaries; we will not stop this Bright war. We are in combat, you are the enemy and I am a Bright warrior.'

Terrorizing, killing and incarceration – is this what they've filled him up with?

'So prepare yourself to experience the truth.'

'Naz,' I say, 'it won't change anything. You'll only convince the authorities to clamp down harder. It's NOT OK, Naz. *Wake up.* Look at all the people over there.' *Please wake up.* 'What have they done to you? Kids, Naz? How can you want to kill kids?'

My words sound so lame. *NOT OK?* Can't I think of something better?

But Naz just intones, 'They who wage war in obedience to the Bright Command, or in conformity with Bright laws, have by no means transgressed against the commandment, "Thou shalt not kill" . . .'

I glance up. A slender ring of fire. All that is left of the sun.

And I'm thinking: *What next then? Get the launcher off him? Hit him over the head with something? Push him in?*

Smash him up. Push him down.

Am I not using the same logic?

Resorting to his same violence?

And I don't know whether to laugh or despair. Just let my vest go off, then – all the people will be saved. There may be a wash of water, but they are far enough away.

But if Dave gets through?

And that's where my logic ends. Should I hope he doesn't get through?

Such impossible choices.

Dave doesn't get through. The bomb goes off. It kills Naz. Saves people. I die.

Dave does get through. The bomb doesn't go off. Saves Naz. Kills people. I live.

Unless I do something.

Thinking is all very well, but it freezes you up. Whatever happens, it's time to act.

Like a crab, I inch sideways. I bend down. As quick as lightning I grab the launch oar. And I swing it at Naz.

He ducks, throws out a hand. The kill cord jerks. The engine cuts. The boat stalls. The tiller turns. The boat wheels. I lose my footing. The oar cracks against the gunwales.

Naz leaves the tiller and pounces on me. I fall back. I hit my head on the hatch. The sky spins. The darkened sun radiates out into a hundred spinning rings of fire. I taste blood.

Does he mean to tip me in? He tries to rip the life vest

off me. It's belted and buckled up too tight.

'No time. Shit,' he mutters, like I've spoiled everything. He looks up at the sun. 'OK,' he says to himself. He wrenches the kill cord off his wrist. 'If you move I swear I'll fire this missile right in your face, Gen,' he screams, 'because you don't understand anything.' He binds one end of the cord around my wrists, ties a knot. Tight. Painful. Then he stretches the coiled extension on the cord and ties its other end around my feet. I scream and try to fight, but my head's reeling. He grabs hold of my ankle and stamps on it, presses down and jerks the cord taut. I lie there, swallowing blood down the back of my throat.

Naz picks up the missile launcher again. He bends close to me. 'Goodbye, Genesis,' he says. His voice sad. His eyes empty.

And I want to say something that will change everything, but instead all I can do is swallow blood.

And I've failed.

Failed all those people.

19

Life Is Now

OVERHEAD THE SKY IS DARK. The wind falls as if the whole universe is waiting. Screams of excitement drift across the water. People crowd, point up at the sun. Somewhere, a police siren. Naz crouches down to steady himself, inches from me. I twist. I kick. I keep swallowing blood.

Oh God, let them have a marksman out there.

'The time is now,' he says and he squats back on his heels. He balances the missile on his shoulder, murmurs to it: 'Now, baby, now. Find your mark. Avenge the fallen. Punish the wicked.'

'*NO!*' I try to scream but instead blood and froth clog up my dry mouth. *All those people.*

He positions his phone in front of him, puts it on loudspeaker. Someone at the other end starts a countdown.

'TEN.'

'*STOP IT! STOP HIM!*' I try to scream, but all that comes out is a whisper.

He pauses, takes aim, freezes and locks himself on to target. I'm trembling. I try to kick out. I close my eyes. Put my head down. *Try again.*

'Stop.' *My voice so hoarse.*

'NINE.'

The face of the sun is totally dark. The sky is a dim, dull brown. Weird. Scary. My mouth tastes of blood, thick, awful. The boat creaks. I'm sweating. My armpits are sticky. My back is damp. Raising myself up, I try to think.

It's too dark now. A marksman wouldn't be able to see him.

'EIGHT.'

He starts a salutation to the sun.

'*We are the Sons of the Sun.*'

'SEVEN.'

I cry out, '*Please, Naz don't do it. Please!*'

'SIX.'

'*In His hour of Darkness, we send forth Brightness.*'

I writhe. Let me just get into a position where I can kick the missile. I don't care if my wrists break. I try to kick out yet again, but the cord slices into both ankles and wrists. And I lean back in agony.

It's no good. It's no good.

'FIVE.'

Think, Genesis. Think. Little kids. Happy families. Think.

'FOUR.'

'Accept our sacrifice. Punish the wicked. Avenge the fallen. Prepare us for the End of Days.'

Stand firm. Be the firmament. Be the fire. Be the bomb.

People shouting, far away. The wind howling in my ear. Blocking out all sound. I can't raise my hands. Something's tumbled from the life vest across my cheek. I twist. Something hard. The whistle.

'THREE.'

The bomb? The vest? The life vest. The death vest. The whistle.

The whistle!

I tilt my face. The whistle slides towards my mouth. I turn my cheek. Get my poor swollen lips around it.

'TWO.'

I remember it blasting my ear – the shock, the nausea. How I stumbled.

'GET READY.'

With a superhuman effort I raise myself, teeth gripped on the mouthpiece of the whistle. I'm right beside Naz. He's locked on aim.

'TAKE AIM.'

Surely it must be 4.44 p.m. already?

I lean forward. Even nearer. Stomach cramps. I don't care. I inhale sharply through my nose. Strands of his hair blow across my face. With every ounce of breath I possess, I blast out.

The whistle shrieks. Piercing. Shrill.

Naz jerks. The shoulder-launched missile loosens in his grip, it clicks off target, the aim is lost. I flop back. It swings free. It fires up, up into the air, straight at the darkened sun. And the launcher drops back against him, smashes his cheek, his shoulder, knocks him sideways. Sends a rush of burning air down the side of his face. Seems to knock him awake.

It misses the power station.

Naz screams, loses balance. The sound of the whistle reverberates into my ear. Naz falls on me. Hard. Hits his head. The boat lurches. The stern dips.

The sun's completely dark, only a rim of blurred gold. The shot going up like a lightning bolt, bright against the dark sun. Suddenly everything is obscured in brilliance.

Brightness, then heat; people run screaming from the banks. A hurricane from the skies hits down. The river rising up in strange, dancing spirals. The blast. *So loud.* One second. I lose my hearing. My head smacks on the gunwales. Just a ringing noise. And the river tumbling.

* * *

And I am back in the cavern and I'm below the surface of the water. And the Moirai floats towards me, dressed in a cloth of gauze.

And her face is pale as bleached bones. And she says: 'All hail Genesis. We are the Moirai.'

But she is not the same phantom as before.

She says, 'I am Atropos, last of the three. I cut the thread of life.' She tosses back her hair and it streams away from her pale face.

And on her finger is a ring.

She takes off the ring. She holds it out. I take it and rotate it in my fingers. It has engraved letters on it: E-V-I-L.

The choice was always between good and evil.

Even when they looked so similar.

'The truth you seek is: To live or not to live. That is the answer to the riddle of life.'

And Atropos holds out her shears. 'And now you must choose. Life or death. The time has come. You wanted to be with Naz till death did you part. Now you can be.'

Is this where my fate has being leading me?

Dimly, overhead, I see the ring of brightness spinning around the sun.

Spinning, like a ring of fire.

Atropos's ring spinning, spelling out E-V-I-L.

And I must choose.

But the eclipse will pass. The darkness will end. The sun will be back.

The air swirls, reverses the spin.

And I imagine the letters reversed. A new current, reversing all evil.

Spelling out a new word.

L-I-V-E.

The boat tips. The prow rises up. I slide across the deck. Naz rolls. A terrible gash has opened up the side of his head. One arm flops like his collar bone is broken. He grabs at me with the other, the boat smacks down.

And as I fall I still see the brightness against the dark eclipse.

Behind my eyes.

Blinded.

Dizzy.

And then everything changes. In a strange order. I remember what I was going to choose. The whole boat jumps beneath us – as if from some deep seismic shock. There's another searing flash.

We wait. Seconds crash. I realize I've bitten my lip so hard I can taste fresh blood. And we still wait. And we feel it, before we hear it. *The Revelation* rocks with the blast of the explosion. It seems to shake every bit of metal riveted together in its entire construction.

But the power station is safe. The people are safe.

Naz seems shocked awake. The fall, the blood, the blast of the missile seem to have roused him from some kind of trance.

'It's been so horrible, Gen, without you,' he says, blood racing from the gash across his head. 'But they made me give you up. They told me I had to. That I couldn't even speak to you. And once you join them, there's no way back. You must believe me about that. They scare me. And they have ways. They don't care. You have to do what they say. They do horrible things. I had to let them do horrible things. I wish I'd never joined them. I've prayed for a way out. I wanted to stop them, but I couldn't, and I'm scared all the time. And all I want is to be with you forever.'

And then he sees the explosive belt beneath the ripped orange of the life vest and his face spins. There's a new look of terror on it. And he reaches for his phone, as if he's about to call his hub and tell them to stop everything, but all he does is hold it up: 4.43 p.m.

'Gen,' he says. 'Oh God, I'm so sorry.' He looks at me and I see the old Naz at long last. '*Oh my God, I'm so, so sorry.*'

And whatever is about to happen next, I know I've

won him back, he's mine again. And I've saved the lives of all those people, and Holly did not die in vain.

I wish I could have said goodbye, though. Told all those I love how much I loved them. Told Dave how much I wanted to learn to swim, how I'd try again – if he'd teach me – how I could have swum with him, down there in Somerset.

Two swans swimming.

So what happens now?

Dave?

And I can almost hear him reply: 'Save you, Gen. That's what happens. That's what I'm good at. Saving people.'

So I hold out my tied hands to Naz. 'It's OK. I understand,' I whisper.

He crawls forward, grips my fingers, lays his wounded head on my lap.

'But we can't secure the future, any more than we can undo the past, Naz. There is no forever.'

And the countdown on his mobile hits 4.44 p.m.

LIFE IS A BOMB

Poem by Genesis Wainwright

And I am
strapped to this life,
and I have searched for its meaning, and I am
strapped to the bomb of existence.
For the bomb is life:
you cannot
undo its wires, lest you blow yourself into oblivion.
And you must carry it forever, knowing that it can
explode on you at any minute,
and wipe out all love
all laughter
all dreams.
And what is the meaning of life?
But to carry your burden into the unknowing future.
To show courage in the face of annihilation,
and to give life purpose.
The purpose of life
is to give life purpose.
The purpose of life
is to give life purpose.

Acknowledgements

The Internet for all its wisdom

Minty Barnor

Sakky Barnor

Jane Burnard

Claire Cartey

Nigel Baines

Joy Coombes

Matt Dickinson

Ruth Eastham

Jesus Fernandez

Naomi Greenwood

Sophie Hicks

Jane Howard

Caroline Johnson

Carla Spradbery

And all of Team Hodder for believing in Genesis

THANK YOU

Read on for an extract from SIEGE also by Sarah Mussi ...

9.22 a.m.
Friday, 18 September

The windows start rattling. They're small, thick things, made of cheap blast-proof plastic, suitable for our kind of school. They mask another sound, something like popcorn popping. I tilt my head, trying to make it out.

It's coming from the gym, from morning assembly. Must be some surprise show for Own Clothes Day. Something like a cheer goes up; people start screaming, chairs scraping, fireworks firing. They're having fun. I stare at the ceiling. If it hadn't been for stupid Connor I'd be in there enjoying myself.

I fix my gaze on the ceiling tiles. The rattling stops. I can still hear humming. That means Lock Down is still on. I stay tense. Miss Carter's going to pick on someone now. Rub it in. *See what you miss when you're late for school.* The rattling starts again. A sharper, crisper, popping noise. Another bout of screaming. Louder, or am I listening harder?

Then there's a crash, like a door slamming, the patter

of feet, like someone's sprinting. That don't sound right even to me.

Two benches away my mate Kady looks up.

I chew my lip. Miss Carter is still looking to pick on someone. She already sent Tariq to the Head's office. Could be anyone next. Although if she's sent him, she mightn't want to send another; might look like she can't cope. But sprinting in the corridors. Someone's gonna get it for sure.

Another crackling sound and definitely running. I cross my fingers under the bench. Miss Carter don't care if you ain't done nothing. She'll pick on you just the same. Please don't let it be me.

Miss Carter screws up her face, spins on her heel and marches towards the door. She snorts as she moves. She's going for the source. Good. I flex my ankles, breathe out slowly, uncross my fingers.

Before she makes it to the door some kids bust in. Two of them. No polite knock. No note. No uncertain hovering.

I half rise, alarmed. Now we're *all* going to get it. My head starts banging. That's so unfair. They're so stupid. They walk right up to Miss Carter. They crazy? She opens her mouth in a snarl. She ain't seen such rudeness since Psycho Sam.

There's something about the way they do it. With no fear. Even Psycho Sam picked his battles. Suddenly I'm on automatic. I ain't seen kids act like this before. Something's up. I start backing up towards the tech den door. I'm out my seat. Am I crazy too?

I can't help it. Something ain't right.

I crouch, ready for anything.

One of the kids pulls out something. He's smiling. My mouth drops slack. Looks like a gun. Can't be. It's realistic though. He's gone loop. Must have. He's *so* going to be on the Volunteers' Programme next week. It happens, you know. It's not just a rumour. The End of Your Education. You Are Now Officially Slave Labour. He shoves the gun at Miss Carter. Must be one of those copy weapons they sell everywhere.

It's not.

And then there's this noise and this hole appears in Miss Carter's forehead. A small, red, round hole. It's got delicate edges that unfold like rose petals. She's grunting like some kind of tribal pig. Then I see the blood and her eyes and her mouth starting to sag open, and it's all gone mad. And the kid is wheeling round with an impossible grin on his face, waving the gun at us. And somebody is screaming. They're all screaming. Except me.

For one mad second I think they've come to liberate

us. Do Away With Teachers. Do Away With Detentions. But I'm wrong. The boys' eyes tell me. I can't make out who they are. I'm so shocked I can't make out anything. They're out of school uniform; could be anyone. Don't stare at them, Leah. Don't make a sound. I'm too shocked to make a sound. School uniform makes you a school kid. Those two ain't school kids no more. They've bust loose. They don't care about students versus teachers. They've fricking bust loose. They don't care about nothing. They're just doing destruction. One of them is kicking over the teacher's stool. Aliesha's screaming, Kady's screaming, all the kids in detention are screaming.

I see Anton moving for the door to the tech den. I back up further. I forget about Kady and Aliesha and the screaming others. I'm going to follow Anton. Kady's a drama queen and Aliesha's a loser, but Anton's smart. I like him. He likes me. And what good will it do staying with Kady and Aliesha?

The first killer seems unsure whether to fire at me. Instead, he raises his gun. He points it at Aliesha. He swings it towards Kady. They're both screaming. He likes the screaming. He says, 'Eeny meeny miney mo. We are the Eternal Knights.' And then he shoots Aliesha. She falls. He carries on shooting.

I'm almost at the door to the tech den. Almost through

it. Anton is nearly there too. I look at Anton. I'm thinking: *Get out. Hide. Get out. Hide. Get out. Hide.*

Suddenly Anton is right beside me. 'Run,' he hisses.

I leap from the lab, burst through the tech door, don't bother with no one else; I'm into that tech den like a bullet. I pull at chairs and bins and leap the benches. Vials and shit crash to the floor. I tear through it, swerve shelves, rip through air like it's got a sell-by date.

Footsteps crash behind me. Them? Kady? Did she get out? Not her. Must be Anton. Clever Anton. He's in Year Ten, different, not really Challenge School material. It better fricking well be Anton.

I can hear ragged breath right at my back. Someone's bellowing. And getting closer. Up ahead is Lab Two. When I reach it, I see it's empty. Ten metres empty. I weave in between the lab benches, ducking, leaping, twisting. How good a shot can those kids be? The floor's covered with smooth plastic tiling. Treacherous. If I slip, I'll crash. A booming, popping, shrieking tears past me. Christ, they're shooting at me!

Holy shit! My only chance is to get across the lab. I topple a pile of books, kick over the apps systems. My lungs can't make it. I got one chance. On the other side of Lab Two is the Level A corridor, but down some stairs, round a corner, past office doors and toilets, the

Level B corridor leads to the Humanities wing and the side entrance.

One chance.

Get to the exit. Challenge Schools are built on the transparency system. It's going to be impossible. They call it the Nowhere To Hide build. But that's them. We call it the Know Where To Hide. But do I? And even if I know somewhere, they will too.

Just run.

Just pray.

Just make it to the side entrance.

Is Aliesha dead? If not, she needs help. She always needs help.

Is Kady dead?

Go back?

Out. Of. The. Question.

This is it then.

There's a deafening roar behind me. They're into Lab Two, only ten, fifteen metres behind me.

I run.

Just before the steps to Level B, I sprint, stopping at the turn of Level A; I take the stairs. I'm in the air. I scream, my arms outstretched in front of me. I hit the ground still running and tumble forward. Keep running.

I turn towards the toilets.